THE
QUIETING

Books by Suzanne Woods Fisher

Amish Peace: Simple Wisdom for a Complicated World

Amish Proverbs: Words of Wisdom from the Simple Life

*Amish Values for Your Family: What We Can Learn
from the Simple Life*

A Lancaster County Christmas

Christmas at Rose Hill Farm

Anna's Crossing

The Heart of the Amish

LANCASTER COUNTY SECRETS

The Choice

The Waiting

The Search

SEASONS OF STONEY RIDGE

The Keeper

The Haven

The Lesson

THE INN AT EAGLE HILL

The Letters

The Calling

The Revealing

THE BISHOP'S FAMILY

The Imposter

The Quieting

THE QUIETING

A Novel

SUZANNE WOODS FISHER

Revell

a division of Baker Publishing Group
Grand Rapids, Michigan

Published by Revell
a division of Baker Publishing Group
PO Box 6287, Grand Rapids, MI 49516-6287
www.revellbooks.com

Printed in the United States of America

Library of Congress Cataloging-in-Publication Data
Names: Fisher, Suzanne Woods, author.
Title: The quieting : a novel / Suzanne Woods Fisher.
Description: Grand Rapids, MI : Revell, a division of Baker Publishing Group,
    [2016] | Series: The bishop's family ; 2
Identifiers: LCCN 2016000104 | ISBN 9780800723217 (softcover)
Subjects: LCSH: Quieting | Amish—Fiction. | GSAFD: Christian fiction. | Love
    stories.
Classification: LCC PS3606.I78 Q54 2016 | DDC 813/.6—dc23
LC record available at http://lccn.loc.gov/2016000104

Most Scripture used in this book, whether quoted or paraphrased by the characters, is taken from the King James Version of the Bible.

Scripture quotations marked NIV are from the Holy Bible, New International Version®. NIV®. Copyright © 1973, 1978, 1984, 2011 by Biblica, Inc.™ Used by permission of Zondervan. All rights reserved worldwide. www.zondervan.com

Published in association with Joyce Hart of the Hartline Literary Agency, LLC.

16   17   18   19   20   21   22   7   6   5   4   3   2   1

To my dear friend Kathy Jenke,
who shares much of David Stoltzfus's wisdom, kindness,
and thoughtfulness in her leadership.
She's the best listener I know.

A "Quieting" is a rare occurrence among the Amish. It is a method of church discipline that revokes the ordination of a minister, deacon, or bishop. It is meant to act as a thunderclap to an individual who hears only what he wants to hear.

Cast of Characters

David Stoltzfus—in his early 40s, widowed minister, father to six children: Katrina, Jesse, Ruthie, Molly, Lydie, and Emily. Owner of the Bent N' Dent store in Stoney Ridge.

Abigail Stoltzfus—niece to David, visiting from Ohio.

Tillie Yoder Stoltzfus—62 years old, privately referred to as Mammi the Meddler, mother of David Stoltzfus, visiting as a long-term houseguest from Ohio.

Laura Stoltzfus—niece to David, sister to Abigail, visiting from Ohio.

Katrina Stoltzfus—19 years old, oldest daughter in the family. Lives at Moss Hill, where oil traps have been discovered.

Jesse Stoltzfus—16 years old, oldest son. Lives at Windmill Farm and works as a buggy repairman.

Ruthie Stoltzfus—14 years old, in the eighth grade, has a bit of an attitude.

Molly Stoltzfus—11 years old.

Lydie and Emily Stoltzfus—8-year-old twins.

Freeman Glick—in his 50s, bishop of Stoney Ridge.

Levi Glick—late 40s, minister of Stoney Ridge, brother of Freeman Flick.

Birdy Glick—32 years old, only sister to Freeman Glick. Lives at Moss Hill and teaches school.

Thelma Beiler—(touchy about her age), elderly widow of former bishop Elmo Beiler. Runs a farm called Moss Hill.

Andy Miller—20-something, farmhand for Thelma Beiler on Moss Hill.

Hank Lapp—60ish, uncle to Amos Lapp of Windmill Farm. Made his first appearance in *The Keeper*.

Fern Lapp—50ish, wife to Amos Lapp of Windmill Farm. Arrived in Stoney Ridge in *The Keeper*.

Luke Schrock—14 years old, in the eighth grade. If trouble or vandalism occurs in Stoney Ridge, most everyone looks to Luke as the cause.

Noah (Yardstick) Yoder—14 years old, in the eighth grade. Fastest boy in town.

Ruth Stoltzfus—David's sister, who left the Amish church behind to pursue higher education. Became a doctor and worked at the local hospital.

1

"Men, I believe I have just met my future bride!"

David Stoltzfus hurried out of his storeroom office to see who had just burst into the store to deliver such a bold announcement. Dane Glick stood at the open door with a delighted look on his face. The handful of graybeards, settled into rockers that circled the woodstove in the front of the Bent N' Dent store, turned from an endless discussion of the weather to consider Dane.

"BOY," Hank Lapp called out. "Matrimony is nothing you should rush into. Trust me on that. You know what my wife Edith has to say on the topic."

"What does Edith have to say?" one of the men asked.

"Wer heiert dutt gut; wer leddich bleibt, dutt so viel besser." *He who marrieth doth well, but he who marrieth not, better.*

"Hank," David said in the warning tone usually reserved for his children.

"It's high time I marry," Dane said. "I can't stand my own

cooking and my own company for one more day. I'm starting to talk to my buggy horse."

Dane had left the door open behind him, and cold air came into the store on a gust of wind. David walked around him to shut the door. "Lots of folks talk to their horses."

Dane turned to him with frustration. "Today she answered back."

"THEN, SON, YOU'VE COME TO THE RIGHT PLACE," Hank Lapp boomed. "Sit down and let's hear all about your future missus. Es is ken Heffel so grumm as net en Deckel druffbast." *No pot is so crooked that you can't find a lid for it.*

The graybeards all shuffled over to make room for Dane as he plunked down in the rocker next to Hank.

Community, David realized. He was all about building and strengthening community—and that was happening, right here, right now, in the Bent N' Dent store. A woodstove community, and it pleased him to his core.

Until this moment, watching the men surround Dane, David hadn't been convinced that his son Jesse's improvements to the store were all that beneficial—at least to the bottom line. Even more concerning was that Hank Lapp was a part of the improvement project. Hank Lapp and Jesse had started to sell premade sandwiches, made by his daughter Molly, who was just learning to cook. Happily, the graybeards weren't particularly fussy about the quality of the sandwiches, especially with the frequent-sandwich punch cards that Jesse had implemented.

Jesse and Hank also added rocking chairs by the woodstove in the store, and had plans for picnic benches out front, come springtime. The outcome was such that quite a few retired men gathered around the stove during the afternoons. In a good way, the store was filled with customers, and that was a change from a few months back. In a bad way, these particular customers rarely bought much other than Molly's dry sandwiches.

Hank Lapp was there every day. Newly married, his wife Edith shooed him out the door each morning, with orders not to return until sunset.

David shook his head. Never would he have thought he'd see the day when anyone would go to Hank Lapp for match-making advice. It was like asking an elephant to tie your shoe, but if Dane Glick wanted to put his fate in the hands of Hank Lapp and his cronies, then who was he to interfere? Besides, David had enough troubles on his plate. The church of Stoney Ridge, for one.

Maybe helping Dane find a wife would be a good thing. David did worry about the young man, fairly new to Stoney Ridge and all alone on that neglected hillside property. But who could handle a fellow like Dane Glick?

He thought of a news article he had just read this morning about the training of service dogs. Some dogs were dropped from the program because they were "too much dog." Too exuberant, too enthusiastic, too distractable, too much to handle.

That, David realized, described Dane Glick to a T: "Too much man."

Unpolished, rough around the edges, Dane was like a gust of wind blowing through an open window, somewhat oblivious to the effect he had on others. But, David thought, he had a kind heart and a way with animals. Maybe Hank was right. Es is en Deckel fer alle Haffe. *There's a lid for every pot.*

Suddenly, all of the graybeards' eyes turned toward him. "David's niece?" Hank said.

"My *niece*?"

Hank nodded. "That's who Dane has picked out for his future missus."

Dane slapped his palm against his forehead, knocking his hat off. "I forgot to mention, David. I dropped two of your nieces off at your house." He bent down to pick up his hat. "Not to worry. Ruthie was home to tend to them."

"Which nieces? What were their names?"

Dane's face went blank. "Come to think of it, I don't know. I was a little dazzled by their beauty and forgot to ask." He lit up and lifted a finger in the air. "Ohio! They said they were from Ohio."

That narrowed it down to all of David's nieces—sixteen at last count.

Well, as long as his daughter Ruthie was tending to the visiting nieces, he would wait to head home after he closed the store for the day. Without any actual paying customers in the store, David went back to his office to set his mind on this letter to Isaac Bender, a nearby bishop. He sat in his chair with the pen poised in his hands . . . stuck. How to put into words the dilemma facing the church?

His mind traveled to Dane's uncle, Freeman Glick, as it often did, and he said a prayer for the unrepentant, stubborn man. Freeman was—*is*—the bishop for Stoney Ridge.

But the church was facing an impossible, improbable, heartbreaking situation, a problem created by Freeman Glick. Switching the lots in the hymnals during the choosing of a minister or bishop was a serious sin, a sign of grave arrogance. Even more heinous was the knowledge that this lot switching had begun with former bishop Elmo Beiler, a man who was beloved. He had modeled the behavior to Freeman, who followed suit, doing what he thought was right.

So he said.

Freeman refused to believe he had done anything wrong. He was adamant that switching the lots was in the best interest of the church. David was still stunned by Freeman's response when he asked him why he had switched the lots. "I knew that God was calling me to be bishop."

But it wasn't up to an individual to determine whether God was calling him to the position. It was the voice of the church that constituted the call. Freeman *knew* that.

It weighed heavily on David's heart and conscience to help navigate the church through these troubled waters, and he knew that God alone could guide it safely through to the other side. It was a situation beyond his own limited supply of earthly wisdom. What was there to do when a good bishop goes bad?

Just as the dam broke and words started to flow, David heard the door to the store open and the voices around the woodstove quiet, like the hush before a storm.

"Oh no. No, no, no. This will never do. It all has to be changed."

Instantly, David recognized the high, loud, tinny voice and felt a shiver run down his spine, the way he used to feel when he was a boy and was found with his hand in the cookie jar.

"The layout is all wrong. The lighting is far too dim. The cooler should be in the back. And why is there a group of old men loitering by the stove? Have they no place to be? No, no, no . . . this simply will not do."

David took a deep breath, sent up a prayer for strength, and went to greet his mother.

❧

Abigail Stoltzfus was perplexed by the astonished look on her redheaded cousins' freckled faces as they opened the door. She expected them to be pleased, but they didn't seem at all happy to see them, especially Ruthie, who blocked the door as Molly, Lydie, and Emma peeked out around her. Abigail noticed they all had the same shade of light brown eyes that ran in the blood of this family—the color of brown eggshells.

Ruthie looked them up and down. "Gabby. Laura. What are you two doing here?"

"Mother sent us to fix your problems," Abigail said.

Laura stepped in front of her. "Mother told us about Katrina, poor dear, and about your father's . . . situation at church. We're here to lend moral support."

"I don't see why," Ruthie replied in a flat voice. "We don't need help."

That's exactly what Abigail had thought! "Excellent." It was unfortunate that the young man, who had happily offered a ride from town, had already left. Though, on second thought, she doubted she could tolerate a return bus ride all the way back to Ohio today. But after a good meal and a decent night's sleep, she would be fortified and ready to go. "We'll head home first thing in the morning."

Laura frowned at her. "No, we won't. We'll stay as long as we're wanted and needed." She smiled sweetly at Ruthie. "May we come in?"

"We're just coming in from school," Ruthie said. "Dad's

still at the store." But she did open the door wide to let them in.

Laura oohed and aahed at how tall the twins had grown, asked Molly about her cooking, and questioned Ruthie about how it felt to be in her last year of school. It was Laura's way with people, something Abigail admired but had trouble understanding how it worked. And it did work. "You catch more flies with honey than vinegar," Laura would often say. Abigail being more of the vinegar type, obviously.

Successfully thawed out, Ruthie offered to show them upstairs to the bedroom where they would be staying. Jesse's room, quite recently vacated, with a lingering scent of musty sneakers. Even the wrinkled bed was left unmade.

Abigail let Laura take care of unpacking their suitcases while she set out her manila file folders on the bureau top. For the last few years, she had worked alongside her father in his small side business of helping people map out their genealogies. Most of the research was easy work for her— she had developed stellar skills as a volunteer librarian in her county's bookmobile. Her father had been working on a client's genealogy when a bout of melancholia made it impossible for him to continue, and Abigail had felt it was her duty to finish what he had started. She picked up where he left off and started to correspond with the client, a young woman who lived in Stoney Ridge. Abigail was absolutely confident that finishing up the completion of this family tree would spur her father to return to his old self.

There was a tiny glitch in this plan. Abigail had posed as her father in the letters with the client. She hadn't intended to mislead the client. Her intention was only to honor her father by completing the genealogy. Plus, her father's hand-writing was atrocious.

But then she hit a brick wall that proved unpassable, insurmountable, a dead end. An entire piece of family history was missing! Amazing.

Despite the brick wall, letters kept passing between this client and Abigail, continuing with increased frequency and depth. They wandered off genealogy and on to other topics. Why was it easier to get to know a stranger, on paper, than it was the people Abigail knew her entire life? A conundrum.

Well, this unexpected mission to Stoney Ridge might have thrown her life into chaos, but it would provide an opportunity to right this wrong. She would find a way to break through the client's brick wall . . . and then admit that she had been posing as her father. She hoped the client was the forgiving type. From her letters, the woman seemed to be lighthearted and easygoing, with a good sense of humor.

Possibly, they might even become friends.

For some reason, Abigail had never had many friends, apart from her sister Laura. It turned out that she wasn't very good at making friends. Other girls didn't seem to like her. Laura thought the art of making friends was a weak muscle for Abigail and that she should keep practicing, try to work it and strengthen it. Abigail doubted she even had that particular muscle.

She had trouble understanding the subtleties of female friendship. Just last Sunday, a clump of young women were gathered together, questioning what it meant when Eddie Bender had winked at Sarah Hochstetler during church. Abigail had inched into their exclusive circle to offer the very logical possibility that Eddie Bender might have a facial tic, indicating the presence of a brain tumor. Or a serious illness. The girls gaped at her, exchanged looks with each other, and closed their ranks once again. Laura whispered that Abigail shouldn't take everything so seriously.

That seemed like poor advice. A brain tumor could be a very serious matter.

However, Eddie Bender's facial tic was not her top priority. She wondered what the hours of the Stoney Ridge library might be. She hoped hours extended into evening. Tonight, perhaps? It was possible that a Lancaster County library might have better resources at their disposal than the one in Ohio. After all, Lancaster County was the second original settlement of the Amish. Berks County was the first. In fact, a side trip to Berks County might be an even better option. Just as she was trying to calculate the distance to Berks County, she heard Laura gasp in horror.

"Gabby, come quick!" Laura was at the window, peering down with a look of astonishment on her face. Abigail hurried over to the window and saw a horse and buggy come to a stop by the front door. Her uncle David climbed out of the buggy. "Why, he looks to be in excellent health." Not sad or troubled or nearing a nervous breakdown, the way her mother painted him out to be.

"Gabby, you always overlook the obvious. Look more closely."

And then she saw someone else emerge out of the other side of the buggy. "Oh no."

"Yes."

Please, please, please, no. Not her.

But it *was* her. The most vexing woman on this earth.

Tillie Yoder Stoltzfus. Privately referred to by her children and grandchildren as Mammi die Nasiche. *Mammi the Meddler.* A woman who felt she knew best how to run everyone's life. Their grandmother.

All of Abigail's splendid plans to locate her client and spend hours completing the family genealogy in a quiet library together disappeared like the wisp of vapor from a teacup.

Jesse Stoltzfus heard his overeager puppy run to greet someone, but from where he was, lying underneath a buggy with a manual at his side, trying to figure out if he was working on an axle or a rod, he could only see four large black paws and a pair of women's shoes—feet that belonged to his landlady and chief hover-er, Fern Lapp.

Fern was the second wife of Amos Lapp, a gentle man who was born and raised on Windmill Farm and left Jesse, for the most part, alone to do his work. Not so with Fern. Her face, etched with lines of an undetermined age, rarely smiled, and her ears never missed a word that was said on Windmill Farm—whether or not the words were meant to be heard. But she came with the farm and took care of everybody and everything, Jesse included. That gave her the right—in her own mind, at least—to a great many opinions, none of which were left unspoken.

Jesse, whose own mother had passed, held Fern in a mixture of fear and reverence. He had been charmed by her immediately, although he was never quite sure whether the sentiment was returned. Probably not.

From underneath the buggy, he saw Fern's hands drop down to pat the puppy.

That *dog*. Mim Schrock had given him a black Labrador puppy for his birthday last week. She said he seemed lonely, especially now that he was no longer living with his family but in an apartment above the buggy shop at Windmill Farm, and she thought a canine companion would cheer him up. This was extremely awkward because, in truth, he was thoroughly content to be living alone—completely, deliriously, utterly happy!—and he did not want a dog. But Mim placed this young puppy into his arms without any suspicion that it might be the last thing in the world that Jesse wanted. It was a pity gift, Jesse was convinced, as Mim had jilted him in favor of Danny Riehl. The puppy was a consolation prize. One that chewed everything Jesse owned, relieved itself frequently and indiscriminately, and had a unique talent for selective deafness whenever he issued commands.

Jesse's cool indifference seemed to make the pup all the more passionate about him. Sometimes he thought he would never enjoy a moment alone for the rest of his life. Being alone was a slice of heaven! He came from a family of all girls; his sisters never stopped talking. For the first time in his life, he could complete a thought without being interrupted. Use the bathroom without first waiting in a long line. Take a shower without fear of running out of hot water. Sheer bliss. Until this puppy arrived. It woke as Fern's annoying rooster gave its first loud crow, and it made sure Jesse was up too by licking his face. An odious way to start the day.

Worst of all, the puppy served as a continual reminder of Mim, to whom many of Jesse's thoughts kept returning, like birds roosting in trees at nightfall. All in all, he would much rather spend time thinking of ways to woo her back than manage this unmanageable dog, which he had named C.P., short for Consolation Prize.

"Your father called from the store and left a phone message for you."

Jesse pushed himself out from underneath the buggy to answer Fern and immediately blocked his face from a tackle by the puppy. "Anything important?"

Fern pursed her lips in that disapproving way she had. "Only if you consider a visit from your grandmother and cousins to be important."

"Which grandmother?" He hoped it would be his mother's mother, who was sweet and kind and not at all nosy. His father's mother . . . well, there was something about Tillie Yoder Stoltzfus that made nearly everyone stand up straight and throw their shoulders back. "And which cousins? I have dozens." Girls, all girls. Family gatherings were a sore trial to Jesse.

"No idea. The message is that you are due home for dinner." Fern was watching him, wearing her I-know-what-you're-thinking look. "Tonight."

That was rather disconcerting news to Jesse. As much as he enjoyed his family, he tried to circumvent any visit home during mealtimes. His sister Molly's cooking was *that* bad. And Fern's cooking was *that* good. He had only lived at Windmill Farm for a short time, but he was feeling very settled in. The puzzle of buggy repairs held a certain intellectual complexity that appealed to his restless mind. And the customers of Stoney Ridge, which included each and every family, were overjoyed at Jesse's generally speedy completion of repairs. His predecessor, Hank Lapp, did not concern himself with matters of timeliness.

Another plus was that buggy repair work allowed Jesse time to pursue other interests, such as helping his father's store, the Bent N' Dent, attain new levels of customer service and satisfaction. The All-in-One Bent N' Dent, he envisioned. His father had been remarkably open (perhaps nonresistant was a more apt description) to improvements, though Jesse suspected that was only because he was thoroughly distracted with the church ruckus. And, of course, there was also the Birdy diversion.

Strange, Jesse thought, to think of his father with a girl-friend. Fortunately, Jesse was fond of Birdy. Everyone was. It was regrettable that she happened to be the sister of Freeman Glick, but you couldn't help the family you were born into.

Fern sighed, pulling Jesse out of his musings and into the present. An uncomfortable vision suddenly shot across his mind. His grandmother . . . encountering his sister Katrina in her . . . condition. A ripple of dread blew over him.

He'd better get home, fast. First, though, he should fortify himself at Fern's supper table.

2

David's house was filled to the brim with well-meaning, overly helpful relatives.

He had forgotten to stop by the phone shanty to pick up messages for the last few days, and apparently, there had been quite a few important ones waiting for him. Like the one yesterday from his sister-in-law, informing him that Gabby and Laura were on their way to save the day, and to please fetch them at the bus stop. And another one from his mother, who said she had heard of his travails and was heading to Stoney Ridge. And probably a few others that he would rather not even know about.

How had the news traveled through the Amish grapevine so quickly? News of the earthquake in the Stoney Ridge church had spread to at least two states in scarcely a week's time.

Tonight's dinner did not go well. Molly had tried a new chili recipe. She couldn't find the chili powder, so she improvised with ground cayenne pepper. The chili was so spicy that it left everyone's taste buds numb. Laura bravely soldiered through, Gabby pushed it away, and his mother gave Molly a step-by-step critique of what she had done wrong. The meal was strained, stressed, and by the end, Molly was fighting tears. David's stomach felt as if a pilot light had been lit from the inside out.

As soon as supper was over, his mother took the children upstairs to bed while Gabby and Laura washed and dried dishes. Normally, Ruthie never went to bed this early, but she was delighted to be excused from dishwashing. Molly had a habit of using every utensil and pot as she cooked, using them hard. David's nightly chore was to scrub the pots. No one else could get them clean; each evening, there was usually a thickly burned and unrecognizable glob on the bottom.

He picked up the chili pot to scrape it out, knowing it would be a fearsome task. He had to use a wire brush to loosen the burnt beans on the bottom of the pot. He had barely made a dent in it when his mother returned from upstairs and walked into the kitchen. Laura and Gabby picked up their pace considerably, finishing the rest of the dishes in record time before slipping out of the kitchen like barn cats.

"So, David, what are you going to do about Freeman Glick?" his mother asked.

His stomach felt as if someone was turning up the burner. "I'm not sure yet." That was the truth.

"Well, I'm sure I know. When he switched those lots, it was as if he was playing God. You need to silence him."

"I'd like to avoid that torturous inquiry." The process was rare, but David had observed a Quieting in his former church when he was a teen. He remembered the sorrow that covered the church like a heavy blanket. "My hope is that

Freeman will repent on his own. Truth discovered is better than truth told."

"Was waahr is, darf mer saage." *Truth bears telling.* "If you don't take care of this now, your church will be wounded."

He lifted his eyes to look at his mother. "It already is."

At that, he heard a clopping of hooves and the jingle of a harness. Minutes later, his son, Jesse, burst through the kitchen door, and it seemed as if the temperature in the house rose from bone-chilling cold to toasty warm. Funny, David thought, how one person could completely change an atmosphere. Jesse had always been able to do that—instantly warm up a room.

"Oh, no! Did I miss Molly's dinner?" Jesse tried to look disappointed, but David wasn't fooled for a second. "Mammi! What a wonderful surprise!" The conversation abruptly switched from the quagmire with Freeman Glick to Jesse's new career as a buggy repairman. When David's mother left the room for a moment, Jesse jabbed him in the ribs. "Dad," he whispered, "Katrina didn't come by?"

"No. I left a message, but she must not have gotten it. I'll tell her about Mammi's visit tomorrow."

"Warn her, you mean."

Yes. Yes, that might be a more fitting description.

After Jesse left and everyone was settled in for the night, David stayed downstairs to sit by the fire with a book. His favorite time of day. He stretched out his legs and opened *Life Together* by Dietrich Bonhoeffer. It was said that Bonhoeffer wrote the book in one month's time, a fact that David marveled at.

Just as he was feeling the pressures of the day melt away, he heard light footsteps descend the stairs.

Ruthie. She had a blanket wrapped around her and didn't look happy. He closed the book. "Can't sleep?"

"Mammi is snoring so loudly that the windows are rattling."

"I know. I can hear her from downstairs."

"Dad, do you think they're going to stay a long time?"

"I asked Mammi how long she planned to be here. She said, 'As long as it takes.'"

"What did that mean?"

"Honey, I wish I knew." But judging by the quantity of luggage David hauled up the stairs, he figured they were settling in for a long winter's stay.

Ruthie ventured a little farther into the room. "Gabby's as annoying as having fire ants in your drawers."

"Ruthie, don't be unkind. Gabby just has her own way of interpreting people. And events."

"And everything else. She's . . . snooty."

David frowned. "I think you're misinterpreting Gabby's intentions. Everything is black and white to her, not gray. She doesn't complicate situations with feelings." Frankly, he thought everyone could use a little bit of Gabby's logical outlook. Her literal interpretations were something that David had always found rather appealing. In fact, she had always been his favorite niece.

"Gabby said that our kitchen is in utter chaos and that she will show me how to organize it. She said that a kitchen should have departments."

"Organizing is Gabby's area of strength. Maybe we could learn a few things." He reached out and patted the chair next to him, then waited until she sat down. She curled up her legs under her the way she had done as a little girl. "Ruthie, let me teach you a trick I've learned. If you can accept a frustrating quality about a person, understand that you can't change it, and then look past that behavior to see many other fine qualities, I think you'll be pleasantly surprised. Take Gabby, for example."

He could tell that Ruthie was listening, but just barely.

"Let's say her bluntness is what bothers you. Set that aside and you'll start to see other things, like how committed she is. If she says she's going to do something, she'll do it. And she's very loyal." Gabby was the one who had been a faithful caregiver to her father, a gentle man prone to severe depression. His wife, David's sister-in-law, had lost patience with her husband's fragility years ago, and David didn't fault her. It couldn't be easy to raise a brood with a husband who was often unable or unwilling to get out of bed.

Ruthie sighed. "Gabby said they're all here to fix us."

"Me. Not you. You and your sisters and brother are doing just fine."

"Not Katrina."

"She's doing very well, all things considered. Moss Hill has proven to be a blessing in all sorts of ways."

"Do you think Andy Miller is going to marry her?"

"Marry? That's getting a little ahead of things. They've only known each other a few months. Besides, Katrina seems a little gun-shy."

"Mammi asked me to make a list of every suitable bachelor in Stoney Ridge between the ages of twenty-five and forty-five." She uncurled her legs and leaned forward. "So here's my theory. I think Mammi might be here to try to find a husband for Katrina."

David laughed. "It couldn't have been a long list of bachelors."

"No. I could only think of six names. And only three could be reasonable possibilities." She considered this for a while with her head tipped slightly to one side, reminding David of a brooding sparrow. "Was Mammi always the way she is now?"

"She's had to be strong, if that's what you mean. My father was killed in an accident before I was born. She raised the six of us on her own. It couldn't have been easy to . . ." He left the thought dangling as he studied his daughter quizzically.

Ruthie was barely listening; she was caught on something he had said. "Wait. There's *six* of you? I thought there were just five."

"I have a sister who left the Amish. She loved to learn. She went on to college, then medical school. She's a doctor. And I'm sure she's a good one. She was always very capable." He thought he had told his children about this sister, but from the shocked look on Ruthie's face, he realized he must not have. For that, he felt ashamed.

"Dad! You mean to say that we might have more cousins?"

"No. She never married."

"And no one ever sees her? Or talks to her? Just because she left the Amish!" She had a disapproving look on her face. "I don't get the whole shunning thing. Luke says it's extremely hypocritical and—"

"Luke . . . as in Luke Schrock? Luke from the Inn at Eagle Hill?"

"Yes. He says the Meidung is completely ironic and—"

"Wait a minute. You have always described Luke Schrock as subhuman." Ruthie disliked Luke intensely. And now she was quoting him?

She looked down at her toes. "He's not so bad . . ." Her voice drizzled off.

Deep breath. This happened, he knew. "What happened to Yardstick Yoder?" He had thought there was something brewing between Noah Yoder, also known as Yardstick, the fastest boy in town, and his Ruthie.

"Nothing. He just . . . spends a lot of time running."

"Oh no. Don't tell me Jesse's still sponsoring him to run in races." David had hoped that his son's fondness for gambling was a thing of the past.

"No. Yardstick just likes to run." She frowned. "The point is that shunning is the one thing that would stop me from getting baptized."

"You don't have to decide that now. You're only fourteen."

She rolled her eyes. "Nearly fifteen."

What? Could that be? He did a quick mental calculation. She was right. Her birthday was in January. How could time be passing so quickly?

"I would never turn my back on Jesse or Katrina or Molly or Lydie or Emily, not the way you turned your back on this mystery aunt."

"I've never turned my back on my sister, Ruthie. She's the one who chooses to stay away. My door is always open to her." He looked straight at her. "Always."

"It seems like we could do more than just leave a door open." Ruthie rose to her feet and took a couple of steps, then pivoted around. "What's the name of this mystery aunt, anyway?"

David looked up at her. "Ruth. Her name is Ruth. You were named for her."

30

Abigail got up at half past six the next morning, dressed, and went downstairs to work so that she could slip past her grandmother's watchful eye—only to discover that the house was already stirring with activity. Her cousin Molly was in the kitchen, furiously pounding a lump of bread dough on the countertop. Ruthie was down in the basement wrestling with the laundry. Uncle David had books covering his desk in the living room and seemed completely absorbed in scribbling down notes. She didn't dare go back upstairs and risk waking Mammi. Heaven forefend. But there was no place to *be* here. Every corner of the house was filled. And she was on the brink of a breakthrough! She could feel it in her bones.

She simply must find a library and get to work to break through the brick wall for her Stoney Ridge client. Though it was still dark outside, she decided that if she could just get on the road, sooner or later, some buggy would pass by and give her a lift to town. Yesterday afternoon, she had noticed The Sweet Tooth Bakery on Main Street. She could wait there until the library opened.

Her hand was on the doorknob, turning it ever so cautiously, when she heard The Voice. Shrill and loud and domineering.

"Gabby! Where in heaven's name do you think you're going at this hour?"

Abigail turned slowly to face her grandmother. "I have an errand to do in town."

"Nonsense!" She stood watching Abigail, blinking her eyes behind those round wire spectacles. She had a piercing look, one that made a person's hair stand up on end. "A young woman shouldn't be going to town at this hour. And it's going to rain. Come with me. We need to have a chat."

She followed her grandmother into the living room and exchanged a look with her uncle, who quickly gathered up his books from his desktop and left the room without being asked.

Mammi crossed the thread-worn rug to the woodstove, pointing to a chair. "Sit."

Abigail sat.

"What was so important that you were leaving the house before the sun rose?"

"I'm working on a project. Genealogy. Tracing people's family trees. Finding their ancestors. I'm trying to complete a case for Dad."

Mammi adjusted her glasses and nodded. "I know all about your father's work."

"We have a client in Stoney Ridge. Dad has given me the responsibility of working on this woman's family tree. That's why I want to get to the library as soon as it opens."

Molly appeared at the open door with the ball of dough, now tinged a light shade of gray, in her hands. "Stoney Ridge's library is closed. It has a leaky roof and the books got ruined in the last big storm. They're trying to fix it this winter."

What?! This was extremely disconcerting news.

"But you could go into Lancaster," Molly said. "That's a thirty-minute bus ride."

Abigail slapped her hands to her cheeks. "How will I get my work done?"

Her grandmother turned to her, raised an eyebrow, peering down over her glasses. "May I remind you that you are not here to work on your futile pursuits?"

"Futile . . . ?" Brick walls were definitely frustrating but not futile. "Family history is important."

"Your family is right here. Under your nose."

"Not my family's history, actually. Our client's. Our paying client." Well, that might be stretching things a bit. The client, a woman named Francis, hadn't paid Abigail anything yet because she hadn't completed the family tree. Her father had a strict policy: they only billed clients after they had finished the work.

Her grandmother paced in front of her. "Gabby, first and foremost, you and your sister are here to bring comfort and solace and—" she ran her finger along a tabletop and lifted it up to reveal a very dusty fingertip—"practical help to your extended family."

"There seems to be a mistaken perception. Everything seems to be shipshape." Perhaps that was an overstatement. Uncle David's household could certainly use some improvements in efficiency and organization. But it wasn't in quite the disastrous condition that her mother had described it to be.

It still astounded Abigail to think that, only two days ago, her life was carrying on in its predictable course. Each morning, she devoted a few hours to help her father on genealogy projects. He was at his best in the morning. Three afternoons a week, she volunteered as a librarian in the county's bookmobile. Out of the clear blue sky, her mother banished her to Stoney Ridge to help Uncle David and his household of redheaded children. It was extremely frustrating.

"I would go myself," her mother had said, as she hugged Abigail and Laura goodbye at the bus stop. "But someone needs to look after your father."

Abigail presented an alternative solution. "Mother, you go to Stoney Ridge. Let me tend to Dad." After all, that's how they'd been managing for the last year or so.

Her mother waved Abigail's outstanding idea off with a flick of her wrist. "Gabby, consider yourself freed of all responsibilities. You shouldn't give us a second thought." As an afterthought, she added, "Besides, I like to sleep in my own bed at night."

And Abigail was the one so often accused of being too inflexible!

She suddenly realized her grandmother was still talking. ". . . And the second reason you're here is to find a suitable husband."

"For whom?" But as soon as Abigail said the words, she knew for whom: her cousin Katrina. It was a reasonable quest, given the circumstances. "Katrina?"

"No." Her grandmother polished her spectacles with her apron, then put them back on and blinked. "For you."

Abigail stared, not liking the direction this conversation was taking.

"How old are you now?"

"Twenty-one."

"Nearly twenty-two," Laura said.

Abigail whipped her head around to find her sister standing by the doorjamb.

Her grandmother sighed. "You cannot keep hiding away behind old papers and books, thinking yourself immune to God's great plan."

This was exactly the reason she took great pains to avoid her grandmother. Mammi the Meddler felt she had a mission in life: to make sure her eligible granddaughters were doing their part in God's great plan. Marriage and motherhood, in that order.

For the last few years, each time she visited Abigail's

family—which was quite often because she only lived a few hours away—Mammi had been determined to find a fellow for Abigail. However, the relationships she had with these young men had never lasted long.

The Black Raspberry Incident was a good example.

Mammi had come for a visit on a warm summer day and brought along her friend's grandson, a highly intelligent carpenter named Ben Miller. At Mammi's meddlesome urging, Ben and Abigail headed out for a picnic at a pond near the Stoltzfuses' home. The outing proceeded very smoothly, thanks largely to Ben's interest in reading. They had a very stimulating conversation about the value of bookmobile libraries in rural locations. For once, Mammi had found someone who was interesting to Abigail. She could already envision the possibility of a relationship developing.

Just before they reached the pond, Ben stopped to buy fresh blackberries from a farm stand. Abigail determined that the blackberries were not blackberries at all, but black raspberries. She said as much to the salesgirl.

"Same thing," the salesgirl said. "Three baskets for five dollars."

Abigail couldn't believe it. "They're completely different," she said. "Blackberries are one thing, raspberries are another, and black raspberries are a whole other kind of berry." She explained the differences in some detail. The easiest way to tell the difference between the two was by the core, where the stem attached to the berry. Blackberries always have a white core, whereas black raspberries are hollow in the center, just like raspberries.

Abigail assumed that anyone who was in the business of selling fresh produce would appreciate the opportunity to be educated about her products. But from the look on the salesgirl's face, she did not appear at all grateful. By the time Abigail finished sharing her wealth of knowledge about the differences between the two berries—that black raspberries were less sour than blackberries, which made them better for eating fresh (excellent material for a sales pitch, she pointed out), whereas blackberries, which weren't even ripe yet, were the best choice for desserts—the salesgirl had started to cry.

Ben Miller suggested that Abigail wait for him in the buggy. He spent quite some time trying to comfort the upset salesgirl. Quite a long time.

In retrospect, Laura said that Abigail should have recognized that gap of time as a warning sign. When Ben did return, he brought with him a large flat of black raspberries. He had bought out the entire supply. And then he said he felt a headache coming on and needed to cancel the picnic.

A few weeks later, she saw Ben Miller and that very same salesgirl holding hands underneath the table during a hymn singing at a youth gathering.

Mammi released a long-suffering sigh. There had been quite a long lull since either of them had spoken, and Abigail realized it must be her turn. "I am not closed to the topic, Mammi, but I have not found anyone of interest."

"I can tell you that if you put off things for too long, you might miss the boat altogether. Mind you, you're not getting any younger." Mammi raised a sparse eyebrow hiding behind her wire-framed glasses. "It's time for you to get your head out of your books and papers and libraries and consider your opportunities."

Opportunities?

"You're in Pennsylvania now, Gabby," Laura said. "Surely,

you could be open-minded to meeting potential suitors in a new state."

Mammi smiled at her. "You see? We have only your best interests in mind."

We? So . . . Mammi and Laura had become a team, which probably meant her mother was in on it too. Abigail opened her mouth to respond, but words failed her.

Mammi took two steps toward Abigail and put a hand on her shoulder. "It's time to turn your thoughts seriously toward the future. Find a good husband and end up with a houseful of children." She patted Abigail like she was a child. "That's our winter goal."

It's not that Abigail was impervious to the thought of romance, but she had never run her life in order to find it. She had never assumed love could arrive on demand, just because a certain grandmother thought it was high time.

When Abigail didn't respond, Mammi returned to the kitchen in a businesslike fashion to supervise Molly and her bread-dough kneading. Abigail settled back into the sofa to mull over this development.

Laura walked tentatively toward her. "I'm sorry. I know I should have warned you."

"That would have been preferable to a Mammi ambush." A complete betrayal. "Why have you joined the Meddling Conspiracy?"

"Well, because . . ." She took a few steps closer. "Well, the truth is that Tim wants to get married and I refuse to set a date until you get married. Or at least . . . until you have a boyfriend."

Tenacious Tim would not be Abigail's choice for a mate. While she admired his persistence to win her sister's adoration, obviously successful, he had a pair of caterpillar eyebrows that hinted to be a frightful sight in his old age. What if they had a daughter who inherited Tenacious Tim's wooly eyebrows? "No one is stopping you from getting married. Certainly not me."

"I can't do it. I would worry about you too much." Laura plopped down in the chair across from her. "I can't leave you alone. Mom would turn you into Dad's permanent nurse and you'd let her."

Why would that be considered a problem? Their mother was a very unenthusiastic caregiver. Someone had to take care of their father. Why not her?

Laura read her mind. "We don't want you to miss opportunities to have a life of your own."

Opportunities. There was that word again. What opportunities was she missing? Men did not consider Abigail as marriage material. As soon as a man started a conversation with her, he rapidly lost interest. Laura said it was because Abigail made small talk a challenge. In fact, she often reminded her, the nickname Gabby (which Abigail loathed) was given to her in school as a joke.

"Do you think, Laura, it matters so much to say the right things and act the right way?"

"What do you mean?"

"I mean . . . what if . . . why do I have to pretend to be someone that I'm not? What if I end up fooling someone into thinking I'm someone different than he wants? And then, one day, he wakes up and realizes I'm not at all the person he hoped I was."

"Maybe . . . you can change. Become the person he wants you to be."

That kind of future left Abigail feeling like an animal trapped in a too-small cage. "Or maybe I'm just not the type to marry. There are plenty of maiden aunts and bachelor uncles in our family tree. Perhaps I'm one of those."

"Most of those are rather eccentric. Think of old Aunt Louise, who refuses to wear her choppers because she says they pinch. She looks like a dried apple doll. Or Uncle Simon, who won't leave his house." Laura stood and put a hand on Abigail's shoulder. "Of course you should get married. You're not like those batty old aunts and uncles."

But that was just it. She was.

"Gabby . . . be open to Mammi's ideas while we're here," Laura said, a pleading tone in her voice. "That's all we're asking."

This conversation with Laura left Abigail even more frustrated. There were serious matters at stake. Her client needed help to break through her brick wall. Her father needed an incentive to get well.

But her sister wanted to get married and Abigail stood in the way, despite the illogic of that assumption. Laura was her sister, and her only friend, so she had no choice.

Abigail supposed she could try to be open-minded, as long as it didn't interfere with the brick wall. She reflected on the kind of men her grandmother would find suitable, the type she would introduce her to, in hopes of marrying her off. It was a truly terrible thought.

She frantically searched her mind and came up with a sudden stroke of genius. She hurried to the kitchen. "Mammi, what about Katrina?"

Mammi stopped mixing dough in a bowl to look at her. "What about her?"

Abigail noticed Molly standing in the corner. A bowl with her gray dough was on the counter, set aside. Clearly, Mammi had demoted Molly from being chief bread baker. "I would think Katrina's situation . . . her unfortunate circumstance . . . time being of the essence . . . I would think she might require all of your attention."

Mammi gave Abigail a satisfied smile and reached over to cover her hand with her own floury one. "And so she shall have it. I'm here to help you both embrace God's great plan."

3

Rain began to fall during breakfast, starting with a drizzle before it turned into a steady downpour, so David offered to drive his daughters to school in the buggy. To his surprise, Gabby quickly volunteered. "Really?" he said to her. "Then maybe I'll have you drop me at the store on the way."

"I don't mind at all," Gabby said. "That's why we're here. To help."

His mother was pleased by Gabby's offer. "Precisely. We are here to bring blessings." She glanced out the window. "Showers of blessings."

David wasn't as confident that the outcome of his mother's long-term visit would be quite so beneficial, if history was any indication. The last time she stayed with the family for a period of time was after the accident that took the life of his wife, Anna, and left his daughter Katrina hospitalized with severe injuries. The entire family was in shock, barely able to go through the motions of living. His mother made everything worse. During the preparation of the house for the funeral, she packed up Anna's clothing and personal belongings and gave away the boxes. David wasn't aware of what she had done until the night after the funeral. He went to put away his shirt in the closet and found half of it empty. Cleaned out. The sight of it had made him double over, as if someone had hit him, hard, in the abdomen.

But that was then and this was now. David wanted to be optimistic, to be grateful, and believe that his mother had come to Stoney Ridge with the best of intentions. Still, a niggling part of his brain sensed impending doom on the horizon.

As for this rainy morning, he could find things to be grateful for: Gabby's offer to drive the girls to school, for one. Time alone in the store to work on Sunday's sermon before the old codgers arrived to play checkers, for another.

Not thirty minutes later, in his office, David opened his Bible and pulled out a fresh piece of paper from his desk drawer. Then, as he began to concentrate on Noah building an ark because God had warned him of the flood, he thought of Abraham, leaving his home and relatives because God had promised him a new home, a new posterity. He thought of Moses leading the Israelites to the Promised Land. In all those cases, a word of God came first.

A word of God came first.

He paused and ran a hand over his chin. Wouldn't it be wonderful to have that kind of confirmation before one acted? Such specific, clear directions. And yet David knew, that while God may not normally address his loved ones with direct speech, he did continue to speak through Scripture.

A word of God came first.

He bowed his head. *Speak, Lord. Speak to me, first.*

David's eyes flickered over to a piece of paper on the corner of his desk. He picked up the letter he'd been hemming and hawing over. He had started only one line to Isaac Bender, a nearby bishop whom he highly regarded.

> *Dear Isaac,*
>   *Mer wees nimmi wu naus.* I am at a loss to know what to do.

David Stoltzfus picked up his pen and tried, yet again, to write this letter, but all he could think was that he had no idea how to proceed. He'd postponed the unpleasant duty for weeks, hoping there might be a reason to avoid it, but the situation was only getting worse. How in the world could he succinctly put into words the crisis that faced the little church of Stoney Ridge? No words fell from his pen.

He sighed. He knew what he had to do: state the facts and ask for help.

Just as the next few sentences started to come together in his mind, he heard someone tap on the store's front door. It was only a little after eight thirty; Bethany Schrock wasn't due in to work until ten, so he left his chair and went to answer the knock.

Katrina waved to him from the window. "Dad! Thelma and I need to talk to you."

David hurried to hold the door open as Katrina helped Thelma Beiler over the threshold, into the store, and settled her gently into a rocking chair by the warm woodstove. David set her cane beside her, within easy reach. Thelma used a cane but insisted it was only temporary. She'd never been a sturdy woman, even when young, but the years had worn her down until she wasn't much more than a wisp, a dandelion puff, held together by frail bones. There was nothing wrong with her mind, though. Thelma was as sharp as a tack. "Good morning, ladies. Can I get you some coffee?"

"No coffee for me," Katrina said.

"I'll drink hers," Thelma said, warming her wrinkled hands by the hot stove. "With cream and three teaspoons of sugar."

"One teaspoon for her," Katrina corrected. "The doctor said she has to cut down on sugar."

David poured a cup of coffee for Thelma, stirred in cream and two teaspoons of sugar—a compromise—and handed it to her. He poured himself a mug and sat across from them in Hank Lapp's oak rocking chair. "So . . . what did you need to see me about?"

As he watched them exchange an excited look, he marveled at how God had brought these two together. Thelma, a widow in her late seventies, without any heirs, chose to amend her will and leave the land to Katrina, an unmarried nineteen-year-old, soon to be a mother, come spring. David's first grandchild. A great blessing, he believed, though the circumstances weren't exactly what he had expected for his daughter. Nevertheless, God was always in the business of redemption, and he was clearly at work in Katrina's life. And in the life of this little one.

"Dad, Thelma and I have talked about it, studied the subject from every angle, listened to Andy's descriptions of pros and cons, and we want to go ahead and lease the land to the oil company."

David leaned back in his chair but forgot it was a rocker. He lurched forward to catch himself, spilling his coffee all over his tan pants. Good grief, he was getting as accident-prone as Birdy!

"We want your blessing."

"We do," Thelma echoed. "We won't proceed without it."

"Tell me more."

Katrina's heels tapped on the floorboards, a hint of her excitement. "Well, you know that the oil company interpreted the seismic data that Andy had gathered and determined that Thelma's property does have a large oil trap."

"Our property," Thelma corrected. "Hers *and* mine."

David nodded. Andy Miller, Thelma's farmhand, had spent months determining if the hillside had an oil trap and where it might be located. He'd had experience with doodle-bugging, an old-fashioned method of finding oil traps by collecting crude seismic data, taught to him by his grandfather. He used his grandfather's generations-old equipment, and somehow, someway that was beyond David's comprehension, it did the job. Over the course of a few months, all over Moss Hill, Andy dug holes twenty feet deep, shot a bullet or threw down a lighted half-stick of dynamite, and recorded the seismic data on a geophone. He took that crude seismic data to another company to be interpreted, and then to a land agent who acted as a broker for independent oil companies.

"We're satisfied that the oil pumps won't pollute any water source or contaminate the ground. The oil company wants a five-year lease." Katrina handed David a file of papers, with a check paper-clipped to the front of the file. "They gave us this check as an up-front bonus. And then they'll pay us 17½ percent royalties on the oil, once they drill the wells and start pumping."

He looked at the amount on the check and had to do a

double take. Fifteen thousand dollars! A sizable figure. "Have you signed anything?"

"No. Not yet. We wanted to talk to you first." She leaned forward. "Dad, Thelma and I want to donate this bonus to our church. And a goodly portion of future royalties."

David looked up sharply. "That could end up being quite a bit of money."

"We know, we know," Thelma said, eyes sparkling. "We think it could be God's answer to help our church's situation."

Maybe. "I'd like to look over the paperwork. And I'd like to have a conversation with Andy." He knew Andy would be able to explain the fine print of terms and conditions.

Thelma was barely listening. "We've decided that we want you to disperse the money as you see fit."

"No," David said. "Not me. The entire church can make decisions about this money together. If we've learned nothing else from this . . . this . . . lot-switching debacle . . . it's that we are a community." He opened the file and scanned the first page. "Why is it a five-year lease?"

"The broker explained it's typical to have a five-year lease," Katrina said. "Then they'll have options to continue to lease the land. They'll pass us a yearly rental fee for the acreage."

It amazed David to hear this new knowledge, this bold confidence, coming out of his oldest daughter's mouth. Katrina had always been flighty, scatterbrained, dreamy, and distracted. Was this the same girl? It amazed him to see how God was working in her life to bring all things—all things!—together for good.

"So what do you think?" she asked.

David flipped through a few pages of the lease. "Well,

I'll be honest with you. My first thought is I'd rather have a three-year lease so we can evaluate how this venture is affecting our community. There might be negative results."

Katrina's face was utter astonishment. "Dad, how could money ever be considered negative? It's the very thing Freeman Glick was desperate for! It's the reason he wanted to be bishop. He saw the writing on the wall for Stoney Ridge. He knew we were going to be in trouble soon. The church is half the size it used to be. Everyone's leaving to find cheaper land for their children."

"And think of the bills we're facing," Thelma said. "Think of Ephraim Yoder's enormous hospital bills. And the plight of his widow. And poor Noah. That boy is working two jobs after school."

David's eyes went straight to another folder on his desktop, fat with hospital bills. Ephraim Yoder was a young father who'd been fatally injured in a farming accident just a month ago. The bills were sailing in, horrifying his widow, and David was working through them, trying to discern which could be discounted if cash were paid immediately and which could be delayed. He was still waiting to hear back from the Amish Aid Society about how much assistance could be provided. "I'll talk to Abraham and see what he has to say. But my leaning is toward a three-year lease, despite the drawbacks. We need to evaluate how this venture affects the church."

Thelma leaned forward in her rocker. "David, this money is God's answer."

But money, David knew, was not an answer. It was only a tool. "Ich will erscht driwwer schlofe." *I want to sleep over it.*

As the two women got up to leave, David reached out to

take Katrina's hand. "Hold on a moment, honey. We have some visitors. Your cousins Gabby and Laura are here."

"All the way from Ohio?"

"Mammi arrived too."

Katrina pulled her hand from his and pressed it against her belly, a small mound. "She knows, doesn't she?"

David gave a quick nod.

Katrina paled. "How long is she staying?"

"A long, long time, it seems."

"Oh Dad, do I have to see her?"

"I'm afraid so. In fact, it might be best if you find her before she finds you. Why don't you plan to come for dinner tonight?" He watched Katrina sink back down into her chair. "Mammi will be cooking instead of Molly, if that's any consolation."

"I'd rather just hide until she leaves town."

Thelma smiled and reached out to pat Katrina's arm. "Your father is right. Best to face these things head-on."

"You're welcome for dinner too," David said as he handed Thelma her cane.

She smiled sweetly at him. "Not a chance."

⁓

Jesse wiggled under Eli Smucker's old buggy, partly to try to figure out how to take off the wheels like Eli wanted him to, and partly to keep out of the rain. "Tell me again why you want these wheels off."

Eli reached into the back of the buggy and pulled out handmade wooden sled attachments. "So that you can put these on them." He leaned the skis upright against the buggy. "It's the only way to travel, come winter."

Talk about outdated. That notion was as old as Eli's buggy. "Eli, those won't help you on snowplowed roads."

"*Farmer's Almanac* said it's going to be a doozy of a winter." He stroked his long, wiry beard. "So when will it be ready?"

Jesse looked at the old bolts that held the wheels in place. "I'm not sure, Eli."

Eli leaned down to shake a finger at him. "Well, you'd better hop to it. Weather will change any day now."

Jesse looked over at Eli, who was upside down to him, beard covering his face, and tried not to laugh. C.P., Jesse's nothing-but-sheer-nuisance puppy, had crawled under the buggy and wiggled right up to him. Then the puppy froze, pricked his ears, and let out a low growl. Jesse stopped. Something didn't feel right.

What followed was a silence, an eerie, deafening silence. Jesse reached into his pocket for a screwdriver when an explosion—*BOOM!*—shook the buggy. C.P. whimpered, Jesse jumped out of his skin, banging his forehead on the axle of the buggy. Eli's knees buckled and he fell to the ground. "I've been shot!"

Jesse rolled out from under the buggy to help Eli, who hadn't been at all shot and was only startled. He helped Eli to his feet as Amos Lapp burst out of the barn. Fern appeared from somewhere. They all met up at the crest of the driveway to peer down toward the road, not even aware of the pelting rain. There was a splintered post left where the mailbox used to be, and metal pieces of mailbox were scattered all over the driveway. Somebody had blown Windmill Farm's mailbox to smithereens.

Fern crossed her arms against her chest. "Luke Schrock,"

she said, like that explained everything. "That boy has nothing but vinegar in his veins."

⁓

As soon as Katrina and Thelma left, David tried to get his mind back to the letter he had started to Isaac Bender, but he couldn't concentrate. Instead, he picked up the phone to call Abraham, his deacon, and leave a message that he wanted to talk to him. He sat back in his chair and rubbed his forehead, thinking back to the last conversation he'd had with him.

Just a few days ago, David had gone to the Big House to talk with Freeman. Abraham went with him.

Freeman opened the door of the Big House but didn't welcome them in. He was a big man, taller than most, with piercing eyes that pinned people up against the wall. "What do you want?"

David took the lead. "We want you to make things right with the church."

Freeman scowled. "I have only had the church's best interests in mind."

"I believe you. I really do." And David did. It was the way Freeman went about it that was wrong.

Freeman jabbed a finger at David's chest. "I've gotten more done for our church than anyone else."

"Getting things done is something the world is very good at. But that's not what the church is about. A man can't just go off in a corner and do his own thing."

Freeman jeered at him. "Do my own 'thing'?"

"That's exactly what you were doing when you switched the lots."

"Hold on. You're wrong there. 'The lot is cast into the

lap; but the whole disposing thereof is of the LORD.' The final choice is made by God alone."

David couldn't believe his ears. That very Bible verse was written on the slip of paper inside the hymnal that indicated which man had been chosen. Was Freeman using Scripture to justify his deception? It was such a sacred and important event in their church, the choosing of lots. It might be the most important event of all. A lifetime commitment. The impact of leadership, good and bad, could last for decades. Did he truly believe he was doing God's work by determining the outcome? Acting as if God had asked him to?

On the day in which the Stoney Ridge church had selected a new bishop, there were only two candidates chosen from the current ministers: David and Freeman. As a minister, Freeman had gone to another room to prepare the hymnals, and David hadn't thought twice about it. He was the longest serving minister. What he hadn't realized was that Freeman had put a slip of paper into each hymnal, knowing that as the eldest nominee, he would pick first.

David remembered the moment vividly. Freeman rose, put his hand on one hymnal, let it hover for a long, suspenseful moment—church members leaned forward on their benches—then he reached for the other hymnal. David didn't consider that to be unusual. No one did. He had even heard some stories of men who tried to pick up a particular hymnal, but felt some kind of invisible pressure to hold back. Slowly, Freeman slid the rubber band off his chosen hymnal and opened it. *There* was the slip of paper. His wife burst into tears. That, also, was not unusual. Because of the solemn procedure and great responsibility involved in being an ordained leader, when the chosen man's name is announced, often many shed tears for him and his family. Everyone is encouraged to pray for him, for he has been selected to serve from among them. The Amish believe the hand of God is involved in the selection process. David affirmed the selection of Freeman. He didn't even bother to pick up the remaining hymnal. God had spoken.

But . . . it turned out that as Freeman had prepared the hymnals and had placed lots in both of them, he hadn't realized that someone was observing his actions. His sister, Birdy.

Freeman was watching him now, as if he could read the thought process running through his mind. "David, do you honestly think *you* should have received the lot for bishop? Someone new to our community? Someone who can't manage his own family?"

David ignored the insult. "No, not at all. But we can't pick and choose our way. Whoever is given the task to lead our church must do it in a way that's appropriate to following Jesus. Our following must be consistent with his leading."

"And you think I haven't done that?"

"I think, by switching the lots, you discarded Jesus's way and adopted the world's way. You took a shortcut."

Freeman's eyes narrowed. "And *I* think you are positioning yourself to become bishop."

David exhaled a puff of air. This wasn't going well. "Freeman, Abraham and I came to ask you to make things right with the church. To repent."

"Or?"

David exchanged a glance with Abraham. "Or you will have to be put under the bann."

"You are forgetting, David, that I am the bishop and you are the minister."

"Of course I haven't forgotten. But wrong is wrong, whomever you are."

Freeman closed the door on them.

"Well," David said, turning to Abraham, "that didn't go as well as I had hoped." The two men walked down the steps to the buggy. "I've only been in Stoney Ridge for a little more than a year. Was he always like this?"

"No, not at all," Abraham said. "When I first became deacon, I held him in the highest regard. He was a very dedicated minister. He was always available, always the first one to arrive in a crisis—middle of the night, hospital visits, funerals—anytime, he'd be there." He adjusted a harness buckle so it wouldn't irritate the horse's thigh. "A while back, I started to notice some peculiar behavior. Peculiar for Freeman, anyway."

"How so?"

"He lost his temper quite a bit. He made decisions without talking to anyone, even Elmo. I thought maybe he was working too hard, getting exhausted. I felt, I don't know, protective of him. So I tried to help him out. I took on more responsibilities."

David had experienced that cycle of weariness. Pastoring required the fortitude to take what comes: Your schedule was jam packed, the hour might be late, your family was waiting for you, but if a problem arose, you had to do what was necessary. Ministers were supposed to be tougher, steadier, better able to handle pressure than most, but David knew that wasn't at all true. Ministers were as human, as vulnerable to sin and weaknesses and failures and mistakes as anyone else. Maybe even more so. David had just read the warnings of the apostle James to those who became ordained leaders:

"My brethren, be not many masters, knowing that we shall receive greater condemnation." Not only would leaders be held responsible by God for what they taught, but they would be prime targets for the devil's mischief.

"At one point or another, a few of us—Amos Lapp, me—each acting on our own, took Freeman aside. We'd ask how he was doing, tell him that we had concerns. But I'll be honest, David, we just . . . dithered around the topic."

"Did Freeman listen to any of you?"

"Yes, sure, he listened to what we had to say. He nodded and admitted that he felt overworked, at times overwhelmed. He assured us that he would make changes. The thing was, not all the problems were obvious. Or consistent. We were like a family that didn't want to admit Grandpa was getting senile. Our intention was good, but the result wasn't. So in the end, nothing changed." He rubbed his forehead. "There was just no easy way to help."

David understood their confusion. Even when a problem was obvious, like the lot switching, he and Abraham found themselves unable to do anything decisive.

Abraham folded his arms against his chest and leaned against the buggy. "I've been thinking something through."

"I'm open to anything that might help to bring about a peaceful resolution to this."

"I'm a cousin to Freeman. I didn't know about the lot switching when I received the lot to be deacon, but now that I do know, I'm guilty too."

David lifted a hand to interrupt, but Abraham wouldn't let him. "This Sunday, I want to tell the church that I no longer consider the deacon lot to have come from the hand of God, nor did it come from the blessing of the community.

I want the church members to start all over again and draw a new lot."

David considered that idea for a moment. Abraham was a fine deacon. It would be a great loss to not have him by David's side in ministry. "Do you think such an action might influence Freeman and Levi to do the same?"

"That's my hope."

"All right," David said, but with disappointment. "Maybe you're right. Maybe it could help solve this problem before it gets any bigger."

Abraham opened the door of the buggy. "Heaven help us."

That conversation had taken place on Monday. Wednesday brought the unexpected arrival of David's mother and his two nieces. That meant that his mother, who was never shy to share her opinion, would be here for Sunday church. A crimping pain began in David's abdomen.

4

Rain. Normally a nuisance, the rain this morning made Abigail extraordinarily grateful. It presented an excellent opportunity for her to start work on breaking through the brick wall. After dropping Uncle David at the store and the redheaded cousins at the schoolhouse, Abigail planned to go straight to the post office. She hadn't traveled to town on her own before. Fortunately, navigation was straightforward because all roads in Stoney Ridge led toward Main Street, like the hub of a wheel. She felt this road system really should be made mandatory in all towns.

She parked the horse and buggy in front of the post office. The sign on the door stated it didn't open for another fifteen minutes, so she drove around for a while to keep the horse warm, then returned to the front of the post office as soon as the town bell chimed nine strokes. She waited by the door for the post office worker to open the door. Five minutes late! And then he acted irritated that he had a customer.

She followed right behind him and waited at the counter. "I'd like to know the street address for whomever is renting post office box 247."

The postal worker barely glanced at her. He had a long, droopy mustache that curled at each end, so wild and wooly it completely covered his upper lip. "I can't tell you. That would be a violation of federal law."

"But I know whose box it belongs to. I only want to know her home address."

"No can do." He pulled out a drawer of stamps and took out his ink pad.

"Could you tell me what times of day she comes in to get her mail?"

"Absolutely not. It's a breach of privacy." Droopy Mustache put his hands on his hips. "I thought you Plain People were supposed to be honest and upright." He wagged a finger at her, like a teacher scolding a child. "You ought to be ashamed of yourself."

Abigail was very sensitive to matters of morality. She did not think this particular request hinted of anything immoral or illegal, certainly not shame worthy. Besides, wasn't it the job of a postal worker to try to deliver information? Wasn't he employed to provide customer service? She outlined her argument, but the postal worker showed no reaction. He went about his work behind the counter as if she were invisible. Astonishing! She was thoroughly frustrated by the unreasonableness of the situation.

And then the door opened and a gust of wind blew in. "Well, hello there!"

Abigail spun around to face the young man who had driven her and Laura to their uncle's house yesterday. He gazed at her with unrestrained delight, as if he had just seen a sunrise for the first time in his life.

She looked at him curiously.

"Dane. That's my name." He jerked his head toward the door. "Easy to remember. It rhymes with rain."

It was an odd comment. "What makes you think I need memory aids?"

"I guess . . . because you look like you have no idea who I am."

"But we only met yesterday. And it wasn't raining."

Dane like Rain held himself completely still, his hat in his hand.

As they stared at each other, she tried to review the things she had noted about Dane like Rain on yesterday's buggy ride. He had a face that wasn't unpleasant. No, not at all unpleasant. No feature was too big or too small, and the resulting mixture was one that her sister Laura might call distinctive or handsome. He was tall and broad and appeared strong, like a farmer. He had dark brown eyes, framed by thick, straight brows that looked as if he spent quite a bit of time in thought. He was dressed in a heavy black coat with brown pants that were faded at the knees—same pants as yesterday. And he was wearing the same blue shirt. It was quite rumpled, as if it had never been ironed. His curly dark hair also looked rumpled.

She stepped around Dane like Rain and went outside to stand under the awning to consider her options. Option one: she could write to her client to inform her that her father had sent her to Stoney Ridge to complete the work. It wasn't entirely the truth, nor was it a lie. Abigail had been sent to Stoney Ridge and she did intend to complete her father's work.

Option two: she could wait for a few hours and see if any woman came in to get mail from that specific post office box. But . . . Mammi was baking bread this morning and wanted the buggy back to deliver it to the Bent N' Dent before lunchtime. This morning, Mammi had caught the twins as they dropped Molly's cookies from their second-story bedroom window. The cookies never broke, never even chipped or cracked. After that discovery, Mammi decided that Molly's bread might cause someone illness.

Abigail suddenly noticed that Dane like Rain had come outside to stand beside her.

"Apparently, I didn't do a very good job of dropping a hint to ask what your name was."

She watched a streak of red travel up his cheeks. "I told you yesterday."

"Not that I recall. Not you or your sister's name. I wouldn't have forgotten. You just said you were David Stoltzfus's nieces."

Abigail was confident she had given Dane like Rain her name yesterday. Coming on top of the suggestion for a memory aid, she was beginning to think that this young man wasn't the sharpest pencil in the box. But she knew that her sister would recommend that she allow a margin of grace. "My name is Abigail. My sister is named Laura."

In one hand, he held a thick stack of mail bundled by a rubber band. He lifted it up. "I only come in once or twice a week to get my mail. It piles up."

Oh no. She hadn't considered that as a possible scenario. "Is that typical?"

"It is for me."

"Why would anyone do such a thing?" Mail was vitally important. At home, Abigail often waited at the mailbox around the time when the mail truck was due. Nearly each day, the mail brought something of interest: circle letters from her sisters, replies to her requests for genealogical information, magazines and newsletters, including her very favorite, *GeneaMusing*.

Dane like Rain shrugged. "If folks have a farm, they have to wait. Not easy to get into town when you have livestock that needs attention." He looked past her. "I see you brought Thistle." He walked out in the rain to greet Uncle David's horse. The horse lifted her head in a big nod and pushed her nose against him.

"The horse—" she caught herself, because she was catching on that names were important to Dane like Rain—"Thistle seems to recognize you."

"Horses have excellent memories." He stroked the horse between her eyes and she practically purred. "I sold Thistle to your uncle when he first moved here. She's the first horse I ever trained on my own. Had to work hard to get her to trust me. She used to balk at anything and everything. I called her Thistle because she was so prickly. Beautiful too. Just like a thistle. But we made friends, and she worked out what was bothering her."

"What *was* bothering her?"

"She'd had a harsh master and had been put under too much stress at too young an age. She coped by shutting down. Balking, bolting, retreating."

Interesting. "How did you help her?"

"I had to think the way she thought."

"How many horses do you have?"

"For now, just one." He lifted a hand toward a chestnut Thoroughbred harnessed to a gray-topped buggy. "My buggy horse."

"One? So, Thistle is the only horse you've trained? I thought you said you were a horse trainer."

Dane looked down at the tips of his boots. "Eventually. That's the plan, down the road. I had to sell Thistle so I could afford some ewe lambs for a starter flock. There's a good market for sheep and I have just the land for it. Gotta pay the bills, you know? Someday, though, I want to be a full-time horse trainer. I sold Thistle to David, knowing she'd be well cared for."

Abigail looked at Thistle, standing patiently in the drizzling rain. She was very well cared for. "Ewe lambs?"

"Yes. Sheep. Do you know much about sheep?"

"Yes, actually, I do." Quite a bit, in fact. Her father had tried to raise a small flock. It was a disaster. "They can be far more challenging to raise than most people realize. Very accident-prone, quite nearsighted—"

Dane took a step toward her. "Abigail," he said in a low, soft voice.

"Right. Stay on task." She nodded. "I've been told I have a tendency to get mired in detail."

"No, no. I'm interested in what you have to say." A streak of red started to travel up Dane's cheeks. "Maybe we could get together sometime and talk about it."

"What specifically do you need to know?" She had read quite a few books on the subject of sheep raising and might be able to suggest a few for him to read.

"Well," he said, starting to look as if his collar was too tight. "I thought we could just talk generally . . . get to know each other a bit."

That sounded unnecessary. "I'll make a list of books and give it to my cousin Jesse. He'll find a way to get it to you."

"Well, that wasn't exactly what I was asking." Now his face had gone flush. A bead of sweat popped out on his brow.

She was about to ask what exactly he was trying to ask when she spotted something of interest. Next to the post office was the drugstore. A poster on the glass door read "Missionary Aid Society's Bible Drive." She walked up to read it. A local church was collecting extra Bibles to be shipped to churches overseas.

She had not even finished reading the fine print of the poster when a light went on in her head—not literally, of course. Bibles! Such an obvious solution.

"Abigail?" Dane was standing right behind her. "What would you think about going on a hike on Sunday? After church. It's supposed to be an unusually mild weekend for November. Won't be long before winter hits."

"It's not possible," she said, focused on the poster. She was going to need all available time for the Bible plan. "My schedule is full."

The town bell rang and she knew she'd better get back to her uncle's house or her grandmother would be fussing at her all day. She lifted one foot onto the buggy step, then stopped. She dashed up to Thistle's big head, gave her a gentle stroke on her neck, then jumped into the buggy and flicked the reins. She was halfway down Main Street when she realized she hadn't said goodbye to Dane like Rain. She looked in the rearview mirror and saw him standing in the rain where she'd left him.

How ridiculous! He was getting soaked.

In the afternoon, David set aside some time to carefully read the contracts to lease the minerals on Moss Hill. The digging of the wells—only two wells—would take roughly fifteen days, weather permitting. The wells would be shallow, the contract said, about four thousand feet deep. Two pump jacks would be installed, along with five holding tanks. Because there was no electricity on the hill, they would use a very low-tech engine, run by a portable generator. A truck would arrive daily or weekly to collect the oil in the holding tanks. One tank would hold the salt water that came up the pump with the oil. All water deep in the earth was salt water—a leftover residual from when ocean waters covered the earth.

He sat back in his chair for a moment, pondering that thought. It filled him with awe to think of the acts of creation. He reached for his Bible and flipped it open to the first few pages of Genesis. "And God said, 'Let there be a firmament in the midst of the waters, and let it divide the waters from the waters.' And God made the firmament, and divided the waters which were under the firmament from the waters which were above the firmament: and it was so."

And it was so.

The greatness of God, setting blessings into the earth for generation upon generation. It enlarged and expanded David's faith to dwell on these mysteries.

He picked up his pencil and did a little math. If the oil trap brought in one hundred barrels a day—a very low estimate—and oil was sold for around $100/barrel, that meant that Thelma and Katrina would be making about seventeen hundred dollars a day. Over $50,000 a month! Over $600,000 a year. David felt his heart start to race. No wonder Katrina

and Thelma were excited. Perhaps . . . this *was* the miracle
the little church needed to get back on track.

$\backsim$

"Hey, buggy man!"

Jesse looked up to see Dane Glick standing in the shop's
doorway, completely drenched. His Labrador puppy bounded
toward Dane. He dropped down and scooped him up in his
arms.

"You shouldn't pick up that puppy. You'll spoil him. He's
already hopelessly spoiled."

Dane ignored Jesse's instruction about the puppy and
actually let him lick the raindrops off his face. Disgusting.

Buggy man. Is that who Jesse had become? A buggy man.
It wasn't the worst thing, he supposed. He had never thought
of himself as particularly mechanical, but he didn't mind the
fix-it work quite as much as he thought he would. Frankly,
buggies weren't all that complicated. He didn't know why
Hank Lapp had such a slow turnaround time, but he was
careful to not let others know how easy the work really was.
It gave him plenty of time for other pursuits. He had some
new ideas percolating—

"By the way, Jesse, didn't there used to be a mailbox by
the road?"

"Yes. But it's been relieved of its duties."

"Luke Schrock?"

"What makes you say that?"

"Folks say he's been blowing up mailboxes all over town.
Throws a cherry bomb in them and runs off."

"Why doesn't someone stop him?"

"No one has ever actually seen him do it." Dane shrugged.

"From what I've heard, it's usually early in the morning. Probably as he's on the way to school."

Unbelievable! Even worse, how had Jesse missed out on that vital piece of town gossip?

"Anyway, Jesse, I've got news. I've found her."

"Found whom?"

"The woman I want to spend the rest of my life with."

Jesse put down the sidebar he was working on. Matters of the heart were definitely worth stopping work for, especially when Fern Lapp, his landlady, who felt the need to be a vigilant supervisor over his activities, was not at home. "Well, this is big news. Tell me more. Who is she?" He brushed off his hands and put the hot water kettle on top of the woodstove.

"She's your cousin. I dropped her off at your house last night. And just now, I saw her in town."

Ah. Poor, hopeful Dane. He was smitten with his fair cousin, like so many men before him. Jesse got out two mugs, put a tea bag in each one, and turned to Dane while he waited for the water to heat up. "What makes you think she's the one for you?"

"I just knew it, the minute I saw her. No. Before that. The minute I heard her voice."

"Dane, are you feeling all right?" Maybe he'd been alone too long up on that hill. Maybe this was what happened when someone lived alone too long. Jesse had been living on his own in the apartment above the buggy shop for only a few weeks, but he took most of his meals in the Lapp kitchen, and Fern was constantly in and out of his buggy shop, giving him a to-do list and checking up on his work, so he didn't feel at all alone. Not at all.

"The sound of a voice tells you a lot. That's how I get

horses to trust me. My sheep too. They know the sound of my voice. They like my voice. Well, I like your cousin's voice. It's low and soft. The second I heard it, I knew *that* was the voice I'd been waiting for all my life."

Jesse had never heard anything quite so preposterous, but he suspected Dane had limited experience in the pursuit of women. "I can't deny you've got fine taste. She's a lovely lass. But don't you think you should give it a little time? Make sure you know more about her before you profess your love?"

Dane shook his head and water spattered off. "Nope. I was struck by Cupid's arrow. Nothing can change my mind."

Nothing except the fact that Laura had a serious boyfriend. But who was Jesse to counsel others in matters of the heart? After all, look at his own rather blank love life. His devoted companion was a fifteen-pound puppy with paws the size of dinner plates. The teakettle whistled and Jesse filled each mug with hot water.

Dane set the puppy gently on the floor and took the mug from Jesse's outstretched hand. "You won't tell her, right?" The puppy went right to work chewing Dane's shoelaces.

Jesse made an X on his chest. "Your secret is safe with me."

Relief passed through Dane's eyes. "Thank you, Jesse." He blew on the tea and took a sip. "The old men at the Bent N' Dent said you're the go-to fellow on girls since Jimmy Fisher left for Colorado."

That was cheering news. Jesse was not immune to admiration. Mim Schrock seemed resistant to his charms, which was very disappointing. Still, there were other girls to consider in Stoney Ridge, many of whom would appreciate his dry wit and carefree approach to life—two things Mim had complained about. His spirits started to lift and he found he was glad Dane stopped by for a chat.

Jesse sat down on a nail keg. "Mind if I ask you something? What do you think Freeman is planning to do?"

"My uncle Freeman? You mean, about the lot switch?" He shrugged his shoulders. "Nothing, is my guess. Just let it blow over."

"So you're not hearing any rumbles that Freeman will repent?"

Dane shook his head. "The only thing I've heard rumbles about is Freeman blaming Elmo Beiler for starting the whole lot switching in the first place. Most of the finger-pointing among my relatives is aimed at Elmo." The old bishop had believed there was a dearth of leadership and thought it would be best for the church to put trusted, reliable relatives in those positions.

"That amazes me. Elmo wasn't shrewd. Not like Freeman." Jesse glanced up. "No offense."

"None taken." Dane leaned against the workbench. "So any idea of the kinds of things your cousin likes to do? I tried asking her out on a date but she blew me off."

"She won't go and never will."

Dane's face fell. "Is there someone else?"

"Yes. Always."

Dane dropped his chin to his chest.

"Don't look so sad. Laura goes through guys pretty quickly. Maybe you can catch her in between boyfriends." Why not? Dane Glick had his good points. His sisters thought so. Molly called him dreamy, but then, she was a little head-in-the-clouds herself. Ruthie said that Dane had been a chief topic of conversation among the girls since his arrival last year—mostly out of annoyance because he showed no interest in any of them. Clueless, Ruthie called him.

"Laura?" Dane's head jerked up. "I'm not interested in Laura. Abigail's the one for me."

Jesse spit out his tea. "Gabby? You like Gabby?"

Dane nodded solemnly.

Imagine that! Why, there was no end to the twists and turns of life. And Dane? Of all the men in Stoney Ridge. He was as boisterous and animated and filled with emotions as Gabby was deliberate and contained and logical.

And then there was that uncomfortable Glick connection. Did Dane realize how tenuous the relations were between the two families, Glick and Stoltzfus?

"Don't tell me Abigail has a serious boyfriend too."

"No. Definitely not." Of that, Jesse was certain. "Have you had an actual conversation with her?" To Jesse, a conversation with Gabby was something to avoid unless it was absolutely necessary. Either you'd get a one-word answer, or she would spend an hour explaining something in great detail. If you made a joke, her face would take on a blank look and there would be an awkward silence, while the joke fell flat.

"Sure, we've talked."

"And she conversed back to you?"

"Yes, of course." Dane brightened. "Would you do a little sniffing around for me? Try to convince her to go out with me? A word from you—" he snapped his fingers "—would do the trick."

Jesse leaned his elbows on the workbench. How did this kind of thing always happen to him? "I can save myself the trouble. Gabby won't go out with you. She's too busy with her project."

"What's her project?"

"No idea. She has a bunch of manila folders and books and scribbles things down on papers."

"Sounds important." Dane swirled the dregs of tea in his mug. "Here's an idea: How about if you think up a way we can go out together? Maybe a double date?"

"Dane . . . I'm not really the matchmaker type."

"Sure you are. You've got a reputation for gambling. Isn't that a form of matchmaking?"

Jesse scratched his head. He couldn't deny there was a certain logic to that argument. "Let me think this through." It wouldn't be a problem to get Gabby to say yes—all he had to do was to bring it up in front of Mammi. Ruthie said she heard that Mammi was on a husband-hunting mission for Gabby and Katrina.

It was finding a date for himself that was the problem. Mim Schrock was the only girl he wanted to date in Stoney Ridge, and she refused to go out with him.

Then his eyes caught sight of C.P., curled up, sleeping in the corner. On *top* of his coat! He grabbed the coat out from under the puppy, who scrambled to get off it. The coat was full of holes and chewed corners. His brand-new birthday coat, given to him by his sisters. Blast that puppy! Blast Mim Schrock.

Dane had the puppy back in his arms. "So what do you think?"

"I don't know, Dane. Let me give it some thought." He held the coat up, disgusted.

"Would you . . . just ask her?" Dane looked forlorn.

This whole go-between business seemed like a lost cause, and Jesse was ready to get back to work, which hardly ever happened. "I'll think about it."

Dane looked like he'd just been handed the moon. "Jesse, you are the best friend a fellow could ever hope for."

Jesse frowned. "No promises! No guarantees."

"Of course. None assumed."

"And don't rush me. I need to proceed carefully. If I come on too strong, Gabby will be scared off."

"Take all the time you need." Dane scratched the puppy's ears. "I'll check back later today."

5

David might feel ambivalent about his mother's visit, but he was looking forward to a dinner cooked by her. She was a stellar cook. It was a bit of a disappointment when he was confronted by the unexpected arrival of Marvin King, a bishop in a neighboring church, just as he was thinking about leaving the store a little early for the day.

Marvin King was in his late sixties. Considerably smaller and rounder than David, with short arms and narrow shoulders, he had a crooked mouth that turned any attempt at a smile into a sneer. He was head of the local committee for the Amish Aid Society, and David assumed he had come because of the request he had sent him for donations to cover Ephraim Yoder's hospital bills. But covering bills didn't seem to be on the top of Marvin's mind today.

"I'm more than a little concerned," Marvin said, easing himself into David's chair, "about the rumors and stories that are trickling out of Stoney Ridge."

David's spirits sank. This conversation did not seem to

71

be one that would end quickly. "Marvin, I can't be held responsible for gossip."

"The situation seems to have gotten rather out of hand." As Marvin spoke, he tapped his fingers on the desktop as if to emphasize his point.

"Well, I agree with you on that. I'm hopeful that this Sunday will bring a positive resolution to our troubling circumstance." He explained what Abraham planned to do, and said that he hoped Freeman would do the same.

Marvin pretended to reflect on what David had said, but it was obvious from his relentlessly tapping fingers that he shared another view. "David, I fear you're in danger of failing to see the whole picture. Sometimes a minister needs to step back and take a more objective view. A wider view. There's a great deal at stake in this situation. Perhaps you're getting bogged down in the detail."

David bristled. He was well aware of the dangers between the detail and the wider picture. He decided to redirect the conversation. "So, Marvin, about the bills for Ephraim Yoder."

"Yes, yes. Unfortunately, our reserve is quite low right now. Did you hear about those barn fires in Mifflin? Struck by lightning, all three."

"Yes, I did hear, but—"

"Of course, you can understand the need to get those barns rebuilt before winter arrives in full fury. Perhaps there might be some other way to raise funds for Ephraim Yoder. An auction? A pancake breakfast?"

A pancake breakfast? Was Marvin serious? It would take years of pancake breakfasts to raise the kind of money that was required to pay off Ephraim's hospital bills. David's mind wandered to the lease for oil wells on Moss Hill. Perhaps

Thelma was right—this lease might be God's provision for their little church. A just-in-time windfall.

Marvin leaned forward. "I have also heard a rumor—"

David put a hand in the air to stop him before he began to pontificate. He had expected this. "I can guess what it is."

"I trust there is no substance to it."

"If you're referring to my daughter Katrina, there is no possibility of her marrying the father of her baby. He is already planning to marry someone else."

Marvin's bushy eyebrows lifted. "I hadn't heard anything about your daughter . . ."

What? David winced. He had just stepped into a trap of his own making.

"Well, you certainly have a cup of troubles running over." Marvin laced his fingers together. "I was speaking about your . . . friendship with Birdy Glick. No doubt, David, you're eager to remarry."

Was nothing private? David resented being lectured to in this manner, by a man he hardly knew. "Well, it's something I hope for, eventually, but it's not quite as simple as it might sound."

"Nothing is simple in this world, David, but the life of a minister is a good deal easier if he's got himself a wife. I'd be lost without my Florence. However . . . and I'm speaking to you as a friend here, not as a bishop . . . perhaps it would be wise to set your sights on someone other than Freeman Glick's only sister." He pushed himself out of the chair and walked to the door. "I'm glad we had this little chat, David."

Alone in the storeroom, David found himself extremely agitated by the bishop's generous dose of uninvited advice. He felt a sharp pain in his abdomen and rubbed his sore stomach. Was Molly's spicy chili still lingering, still causing aftereffects?

He needed relief from the constant onslaught of problems. He needed a different perspective. Someone who felt like a breath of fresh air.

He needed Birdy.

⁓

As soon as the clock reached four o'clock, David told Bethany Schrock that he was leaving for the day and to lock up at 5:00 p.m. He tipped his hat to the old codgers who sat around the potbellied stove as he walked past them.

"Quitting time already?" Hank Lapp called out, barely looking up from his game of checkers.

"Just have something to do," David said.

"Like . . . maybe a little Bird-y watching?" Hank elbowed the man sitting next to him and they started to cackle like old hens.

David sighed. It seemed that nothing he did could ever be private, and that everyone must know and comment on his business. He wrapped the collar of his coat around his neck and started walking toward the schoolhouse. It had started to sprinkle again, and from the heavy set of the clouds, it would turn to a hard rain before long, but he hadn't had a chance to see Birdy all week and he missed her. Just as he turned the corner to the road that led to the schoolhouse, he saw her up the road. She walked everywhere—school, town, store, library, post office, church. As he watched her, he thought that her long, purposeful stride reflected a sense of optimism, as if anything were possible.

"Birdy! Wait up!"

She spun around when she heard his voice. By the time he reached her, she was smiling. Something about her expression lifted his spirits too. Then he started to smile. He stood there like an awkward schoolboy, grinning from ear to ear. "Mind if I tag along?"

A flame of red went up Birdy's cheeks, a girlish feature he found endearing. "I'd be delighted."

They started up the road. "Where are you headed?"

"Over to the Big House."

David stopped. "You're going to see Freeman?" That would surprise him, if that's where she was headed. She had been living in a small house on the property of the Big House, her childhood home, but when she confessed to the church that she had seen her brother switch the lots, Freeman insisted that she leave home. Thelma Beiler offered a room in her house over at Moss Hill, so that's where she'd been staying the last few weeks.

Birdy slowed and turned, waiting for him to catch up with her. "Goodness no. I'm going nowhere near the house. Just a jaunt up into the hills."

"In this rain?"

She looked up at the sky. "Barely a spitting rain. Do you have time to come along?"

"I wish I could, but it turns out I have some unexpected houseguests." He explained the arrival of his mother and nieces. "They've heard about the . . . problem . . . at the church and have come to help." Interference might be a more apt word.

"Well, if you can't come with me now," Birdy said, "perhaps you could plan to meet soon for a hike. There's something I want to show you." She grinned. "But it will require you to join me on a hike at a frightfully early hour."

"An unusual bird?" David said.

"Yes!" She practically brimmed with happiness. "It's a great blue heron. Absolutely stunning. It's built a stick nest in a dead white oak tree near the far edge of the property. It's really quite a sight."

"Tomorrow morning, then."

They walked companionably along the road, chatting about their day. Now and then, Birdy would point out birds that flew overhead. David had never really noticed birds before, though many in his church were dedicated bird-watchers. None as skilled as Birdy, though.

She could peer up into the sky and identify any bird in flight. She said it was simple if you knew four basic things: size and shape, color pattern, behavior, habitat. Field marks, she called them. Each time they took a walk, like now, she did her best to try to teach him field marks of a bird's distinguishing characteristics. A large black crow hopped along ahead of them on the road, looking for worms.

"Look at that crow," she said. "See its bill? Long, with a slight hook. You know it eats carrion because that kind of a bird's bill is designed to tear flesh."

He cringed and she laughed.

"Don't look so squeamish, David. Crows are quite intelligent. They're thought to be as intelligent as apes."

Crows were nothing but a nuisance to him. Pests! They raided gardens, stole eggs from other birds' nests. There was good reason a gang of crows was called a murder. Only Birdy could find something noble about a crow. "You're kidding me."

"It's true. They can remember all kinds of things, including faces. I heard a story once about an Amish family that raised a crow named Charlie . . ."

David watched her as she spoke, half listening, half admiring. Unlike most Amish men, he preferred being indoors. His ideal day was a rainy one, like today, sitting by the fireplace with a pile of books at his side. Birdy wasn't much of a reader, but her book was the great outdoors. And he was discovering the outdoors through her eyes. She said that nature had spiritual treasures, just waiting to be mined. Through her eyes, he felt as if he was waking up to the majesty and mystery of the created world. Birdy loved everything about nature—insects, birds, animals, the play of light on the leaves. She studied the world of nature with the same ferocity that David studied Scripture. Nature was God's first book, she often said, and he had to agree.

The constant tension that had been dogging him all day started to dissipate. This, *this* was what he needed. A reminder to rest in God's sovereignty. Birdy always helped bring him back to that important truth.

Then the rain turned hard and Birdy had the only umbrella. When she put her arm through his, so that they could share it, and she squeezed up against him, it felt like the most natural thing in the world. "So let's plan to meet at the schoolhouse at five."

"That *is* frightfully early."

Birdy laughed. "But David, everyone needs a daily serving of nature as well as bread."

Bread. Bread! Katrina would be arriving for dinner soon, encountering David's mother, without any reinforcements. He'd better get home before she arrived. It occurred to him that he should probably invite Birdy to meet his mother, but somehow the idea never made it past his thought process.

Soon.

Ruthie's annoyance was obvious. Abigail couldn't fathom why she was so irritated. The kitchen had been completely improved. Mammi had stressed, numerous times, that she and Laura were here in Stoney Ridge to help their cousins. So, today, while the girl cousins were at school, Abigail reorganized the kitchen from its state of complete and utter chaos to a new system with specific departments. The pantry, in particular, had a high level of organization: Each shelf contained similar products. Bottom shelf: flour, sugar, brown sugar, powdered sugar, molasses, honey. Eye-level shelf: spices, herbs. (She briefly considered hiding the ground cayenne pepper so that Molly couldn't find it. She seemed to have a fondness for that particular spice, which deadened a person's taste buds.) Abigail carried similar organizational strategies throughout each drawer and cupboard. She had also made carefully written labels for the contents of each drawer, because she assumed the cousins would revert to their sloppy ways after she returned to Ohio.

When the girls came home from school, Ruthie sniffed around the entire kitchen, opening drawers and cupboards, banging them shut, muttering, sighing. "I see no reason," she said. "No reason in the world."

That was when it dawned on Abigail that Ruthie was not happy with the newly implemented Kitchen Department Program.

Molly was, though. As she followed behind Ruthie, opening and closing drawers, she exclaimed with delight, "Why, it makes perfect sense to put all the measuring cups together in one place. Why hadn't I thought of that? I spend most of my time looking for things."

"Precisely the purpose of an organized system," Abigail said. "Everything has a place." She listed the major advantages of the Kitchen Department Program:

1. No time was lost wondering where ingredients or tools were situated.
2. Almost no waste. Ingredients were shelved face out. Labels were easy to read.
3. Less time spent cleaning up and wondering where to return ingredients and tools.

The last one, in particular, was Abigail's favorite advantage. She loathed washing dishes. Even Mammi, who had been the first to use the new system because she made an enormous beef and cheese noodle casserole this afternoon for tonight's supper, expressed pleasure with Abigail's use of time. "This is just what I hoped for, Gabby. We are spreading blessings all around us."

Excellent. Abigail had thought this through. By displaying early on that she was taking her grandmother's mandate to help very seriously, she felt confident Mammi would turn her officious attentions toward someone else. Ruthie's poor attitude, for example.

"Gabby thinks we're stupid," Ruthie whispered to Molly, pointing to the labels on each drawer.

"I don't think you're stupid, Ruthie," Abigail said. She had excellent hearing. "Organization is something that is taught, not intrinsic." To be fair, she did have a natural talent for it. Most people didn't.

"You're going to have to use simpler words," Ruthie said, speaking in a tone that seemed more appropriate to instructing children. "I can't understand more than two syllables strung together at a time."

Abigail reviewed the previous sentence she had said. "Intrinsic? That's a word that means innate. Natural. Inborn. I have a dictionary upstairs if you'd like to see for yourself."

Ruthie's eyes closed to a pair of dangerous slits. Abigail wondered if she might be feeling unwell. Molly's taste-bud-killing chili had taken a toll on her own stomach too. She watched Ruthie carefully in case she was about to faint.

But suddenly Ruthie flounced out of the room.

"She lost the staring match!" Molly said.

The twins, Emily and Lydie, looked at each other in shock. "She never loses."

"Don't be offended, Gabby," Mammi said as she swept past, though Abigail wasn't at all offended. "Ruthie's reached the troublesome age. It's always worse with girls."

In the kitchen, Mammi started pulling out ingredients for a coleslaw salad: cabbage, carrots, onions. She set to work chopping the cabbage, grating carrots, dicing onions as if she was in a race to the finish. Then she started to whip together the dressing: large spoonfuls of mayonnaise, Dijon mustard, apple cider vinegar, salt, and pepper.

Her grandmother had a way of moving about the kitchen with a certain purposeful motion that let everyone around her know she had everything under control. Molly offered to help, but Mammi assigned her nothing more than the table to set. Emily was between pages of a book, Lydie scooted her chair flush with Abigail's at the kitchen table, helping to fold napkins, Molly remained in the background, at the edge of the kitchen, neither in nor out of it.

Abigail heard a horse whinny and Thistle answer back from her stall in the barn, then looked out the window to see a buggy climb the driveway. Behind it, Uncle David was running at full speed. Behind him, striding along at a much less frantic pace, walked cousin Jesse and Dane like Rain, with the black Labrador puppy zigzagging around their legs. Mammi was already on her way to the door.

Cousin Katrina had arrived.

A disaster was in the making.

6

David felt relieved when he saw that Jesse had brought Dane Glick home for dinner—he assumed his mother would keep some topics off-limits with a guest at the table. That assumption was his first mistake. The moment he lifted his head after offering a silent prayer, his mother peppered Katrina with pointed questions. "Why aren't you living at home? . . . How are you going to manage on your own? . . . What will people think? . . . How can you let a child grow up without a father?"

As David straightened in the chair, a faint cramp caught him low across the stomach. He felt as if he were a boy again, living in his mother's home and sitting around the family dinner table. His mother used the evening meals to grill each child. It bothered him then and it bothered him now. Shouldn't time around a dinner table be as nourishing to the soul as it was to the stomach?

Just as Mammi started to circle in on the big question that she was going to land on—"Why don't you give the child up for adoption?"—David opened his mouth to head her off, but Jesse beat him to it. His son stepped in and aimed the spotlight right on his friend Dane. "Gabby, did you know that Dane raises sheep?"

Dane grinned.

Gabby kept her eyes on her plate of food. "Yes."

Jesse said, "Gabby loves sheep."

Dane beamed.

Gabby looked up, startled. "Not really. I like sheep. I don't love them. Not all of them. I've been fond of one or two, perhaps. But not all."

Encouraged, Jesse kept going. "Mammi, did you know that Dane is considered to be one of Stoney Ridge's most eligible bachelors?"

Now it was Dane's turn to look puzzled. He cleared his throat, raised a loose fist to his mouth, and half coughed into it. "Truth to tell, I might be the only eligible bachelor under thirty, since Jimmy Fisher and Peter Stoltzfus left town for greener pastures."

His mother promptly lost interest in Katrina and turned her total attention on Dane. David saw Katrina mouth a "thank you" to Jesse.

Katrina was off the hot seat but at the expense of poor Dane. "How old are you?" his mother said.

"Twenty-five."

She seemed pleased by that fact. "Really. You have a boyish-looking face. I assumed you were fifteen, like our Jesse."

"Actually, I'm sailing on a fast wind toward seventeen, Mammi," Jesse said.

David swallowed a grin. Jesse just had his sixteenth birthday.

His mother leaned across the table. "So you raise sheep?"

"Yes. At least, that's what I'm trying to do. Start a flock."

"There's more money in dairy cows."

David winced. Since when did his mother know much about farm animals? She had worked her entire life in a store.

"The land I have isn't suited for dairy." Dane lifted a shoulder in a shrug. "It's a pretty small patch of land, and hilly too. Turned out raising sheep was the most practical choice. For now, anyway."

"For market?" David asked. "Or wool?"

"Both, I hope."

"Young man, you need to give up this sheep nonsense and find something that will be profitable."

"Mother . . ."

"Think of Simon's sheep venture, David." She slapped the table with her palms. "That was catastrophic."

Gabby intervened. "Catastrophic might be a dramatic description. It was definitely a disaster, but it wasn't catastrophic."

His mother turned to Gabby. "What's the difference?"

"Why?" Dane's fork was suspended in midair. "What happened?"

"Long story," Laura said quickly. "Have more bread." She pushed the basket of bread toward him.

Dane finished his bite, swallowed, and gently laid his fork down on the plate and patted his lips with his napkin. "I'd like to know more. I'm new at sheep raising. I'm trying to learn all I can."

Gabby piped up. "Two words. Poison ivy."

"They ate poison ivy?" Dane leaned back in his chair. "They must have eaten a lot of it for the toxins to hurt them."

"They did," Gabby said in a matter-of-fact tone.

"Catastrophic," David's mother said.

Molly stretched a hand across the table to grab a roll from the bread basket, but his mother reached it first and snatched it out of her reach. Molly's face flooded red with embarrassment.

"Disastrous." Gabby buttered a piece of bread. "Poison ivy can kill goats too."

"That's very helpful to know. I need to make sure I've cleared it all." Dane asked Gabby a few questions about Simon's disastrous sheep venture, which was odd because David knew Dane was quite knowledgeable about sheep raising. Extremely knowledgeable.

David was impressed with the care and attention Dane gave to his woolies. David's brother, Simon, was not nearly as conscientious with his flock. He remembered a conversation in which Dane explained that sheep were prey animals, so their first response was always to flee, to panic. The shepherd needed to form a partnership with his sheep, Dane had told him. It was a balance of leadership, love, and clear communication.

It's like a minister's role should be, David just now realized. *A balance of leadership, love, and clear communication. Yes, exactly that.*

"One day," Dane said, "I want to work full-time with horses. Soon, I hope."

His mother approved. "Now that's a far more profitable venture. Buggy horse training. There will always be a need for a well-trained buggy horse."

"Well, not just train them," Dane said. "Mend them."

"They're broken?" His mother leaned over and rapped

Molly's knuckles with the handle of her spoon as the girl reached for a second serving of the beef and cheese noodle casserole. David watched Molly rub her stinging knuckles. He reached over and gently touched her arm, trying to give her some sympathy.

"Yes. I work with broken horses." Dane got a shy look on his face. "I just adopted another rescue horse. Bella. It means—"

"Beautiful," Gabby said. "In Italian."

Dane beamed, positively beamed.

David's mother wasn't finished. "You break horses?"

Dane looked increasingly flustered by the relentless grilling. "No, they're already broken when I adopt them from a rescue shelter. I heal them. And then I train them."

His mother was baffled, a rare occurrence. "You're a healer? A horse healer?"

David tucked his chin to hide a smile.

"That's it!" Jesse said, delighted. "Mammi, you nailed it! Dane's a horse healer."

"Isn't there a veterinarian in Stoney Ridge?"

"Not *that* kind of healing." Dane pointed to his forehead. "This kind. They're damaged and need rehabilitation."

"Like Thistle," Molly said.

"That's our buggy horse, Mammi," Jesse added. "Dane fixed her and sold her to us."

"Fixed her? What was wrong with her?"

"Thistle had been overly stressed when she was young," Dane said. "She shut down."

"Luke says it can happen to people too," Ruthie said. "He thinks that's what happened to his father. His grandmother badgered his father so much, he started to shut down." She cast a cautious glance in Mammi's direction, who didn't miss its meaning.

An awkward silence fell over the table, over everyone. David's mind was spinning so fast he didn't know how to react. His brother Simon, Gabby and Laura's father, had always assumed the burden of responsibility for others. Fifteen years ago, at the urging of his wife, Simon went on his first vacation, and curiously, it was on the vacation when he experienced a nervous breakdown. His first episode of clinical depression, laid flat on his back. David never understood the timing . . . until this moment. Simon had been like a spring under tight tension, and on the vacation—without constant pressure—the spring let loose. His brother had never been the same since. Depression was always lingering on his shoulders, like a late-in-the-day shadow.

How interesting! And unusually insightful of Ruthie, though he felt a stab of rising concern to hear her quote Luke Schrock as if he were the town sage. Yet the awkward silence still needed to be addressed. David could see the look of bewilderment on his mother's face as she tried to process this information. On top of that, she wasn't accustomed to being challenged, and it was clear she didn't like it. "Dane found Thistle at a rescue center and rehabilitated her," David said in his most conciliatory voice. "She's been a fine horse for us."

Dane put down his fork and rumpled the napkin to wipe his face. "I could tell she had wonderful potential." He grinned. "My first sale was to David. My only sale." He reached out for his water glass. "I use a training method called Parelli."

Gabby made a little squeaking sound. "Pat Parelli?"

"Yes. Yes! Pat Parelli." Dane's smile was all amazement

and wide eyes. "Well, imagine that. Hardly anyone knows of Parelli."

"Parelli is another horse?" Mammi was grasping for straws, trying to make sense of this conversation.

Gabby jumped up to fill water glasses with the water pitcher.

Dane's eyes followed Gabby, bright with excitement. "Parelli is a man. Pat Parelli. He developed a method of natural training for horses. It's based on a relationship of trust with the horse and its owner."

When David bought Thistle, Dane had insisted that he work with him to continue training in the Parelli method. Thistle was turning into a fine buggy horse, nearly spook-proof, possibly the calmest horse in traffic he'd ever owned.

"Most horse trainers use dominance and force to make their horses obey. The Parelli method has success without force. The trainer and the horse have a partnership. It's a balance of leadership, love, and clear communication. The trainer reads the horse's body for cues to manage behavior."

David noticed that the entire time Dane talked, he had his eyes on Gabby. Really, he was *staring* at her. Why was that? Suddenly he remembered Dane's announcement at the store yesterday that he had found his future missus. Gabby? He had meant *Gabby*? What a curious development! He wondered what Gabby thought about Dane. She seemed more interested in her water glass.

His mother had gone silent. Then she suddenly leaned forward, pinning Dane to his chair. "What was your name again?"

"Dane."

"Who are your people?"

"My people? I don't have any employees. Someday I hope to. But, for now, I'm just starting out."

"She wants to know your last name," Jesse whispered.

"Oh. It's Glick."

Gabby whipped her head up to look at Dane. "Are there many Glicks in Stoney Ridge?"

"Yes," Dane said. "Quite a lot." He lifted his hand and bent each finger as he spoke. "Zook, Fisher, Stoltzfus, King, Smucker, and Glick. Those are the Lancaster Amish. The first settlers from the Old World. All are very proud of that legacy." He rolled his eyes. "Very proud."

Gabby seemed disappointed. "But how many Glicks are there, exactly? Females, in particular?"

Dane looked confused. "I don't know. It's not just Stoney Ridge. They live everywhere in Lancaster County."

Gabby put her hands on her cheeks in exasperation and groaned.

Under the table, Laura kicked David's shin and he winced. "I'm sorry!" she whispered. "That was meant for Gabby."

His mother's face puckered as if she'd found a mouse in her soup. "Glick . . . as in Freeman Glick?"

"Why, yes."

In a cold voice, she repeated the question. "You're related to Freeman Glick?"

"Yes. My father is his youngest brother. He's my uncle."

An awkward silence fell over the table, but for the occasional clink of a fork on a plate. Poor Dane seemed bewildered by the unmasked hostility of David's mother, a look on her face as if she had just chewed cactus, then he "got it." He dropped his eyes and picked up his fork to stab at his pickled beets, but he wasn't really eating.

David should say something, but what? He looked around the table, hoping one of his daughters would say something, but all eyes, even Katrina's—and she hadn't uttered one word since the focus shifted to Dane, though she of all people knew exactly how the poor boy must be feeling—were glued to their dinner plates. All but Jesse's, which should have been a red flag of warning.

"Mammi," Jesse said, all wide-eyed and innocent, "did you know that Dad has a sweetheart?"

⸻

Glick, Glick, Glick. The sheer number of Glicks in Lancaster County was appalling. Abigail combed through a directory she had found in Uncle David's bookshelves and didn't even know where to begin. This brick wall was consuming an enormous amount of time with zero outcome. At the earliest opportunity, she decided she would ask Uncle David about the Glicks and see if he might have any leads.

That moment came before daybreak. Abigail set her alarm clock for half past four in the morning because she knew Mammi didn't rise until half past five. She lit the kerosene lamp and sat at the kitchen table, spreading out her manila folders. She pulled out another book she had found among her uncle's books—a history of Lancaster County, Pennsylvania, with reminiscences by early immigrants, published back in 1937. She was startled when Uncle David walked into the kitchen, fully dressed, and went straight to the coffeepot.

"Did I wake you?"

"No," he said, opening and shutting cupboards.

"Coffee mugs are in the mug department."

"Huh?"

"Above the coffeepot." It seemed so logical.

He opened the cupboard, grabbed a mug, and lifted it in her direction with a grin.

"I need a little help with my genealogy project," she said. "I hoped I could ask you a few questions."

He filled his mug with coffee and sat across from her at the table. The only sound came from the hissing kerosene lamp above their heads. "Ask away, Gabby."

"Abigail, actually. I prefer Abigail over Gabby."

"Yes. Sorry. It's hard to make the switch."

That made no sense to Abigail because she never wanted nor encouraged a nickname. She made a point to always introduce herself as Abigail. "If someone has a post office box in Stoney Ridge, does that mean they live in the town limits?"

"Not necessarily. The post office is centrally located for some of the towns in the area. It's the way the topography of the land is set up. I know a number of people in Gap and Leola who have Stoney Ridge PO boxes."

That was discouraging news.

"Tell me about your project. I know your dad always loved history."

"Well, it's fascinating, actually. Genealogies tell a story. And I do think we shouldn't forget those who have gone before us."

Her uncle smiled. "I agree with you there. So tell me more. How do you go about tracing a pedigree?"

"Usually, the last few generations go fairly smoothly. There's all kinds of official records that help. Birth certificates, land deeds, death records, census. But go back a hundred years, and it's quite a challenge."

"Why is that?"

"There was usually a war or two that ground record keeping to a halt." She tucked a stray lock of hair behind her ear. "Go back a few hundred years and it's nearly impossible."

"More wars?"

"Partly that. The Amish of Europe didn't keep formal records, for a variety of reasons."

He blew on his coffee, then took a sip. "Why not?"

"Because they were persecuted. It would have been dangerous to keep records. That's how the government could find them."

"So how are you able to trace anyone back to Europe?"

"Passenger lists on ships, for one. Old Bibles are a wealth of information. They usually have births and deaths recorded."

He took a sip of coffee and swallowed. "Interesting stuff, Gab—uh, Abigail."

"There's one case, now, that should be easy but it's proving to be quite difficult. I have hit an insurmountable brick wall. Perhaps you can help me track down the client."

"Who's that?"

"I'm tracing the family tree of a young woman named Glick."

He grimaced. "There are a lot of Glicks. Quite a lot."

"A woman named Francis Glick. She's in her midtwenties. Not married."

"There's Dottie Glick, but she's in her seventies. Leah and Lonnie, they're sisters, but they must be in their fifties. Oh, then there is a family of Glick girls—Dorothy, Danielle, Dee, Diane . . . and I think twin baby girls . . . but I can't remember their names. They all start with *D*, though. I don't recall a Francis. Could you have mistaken her surname?"

"No. I'm quite sure I've got my details correct."

He took a big swallow of coffee. "Do you know her parents' names?"

Abigail riffled through some papers and found the family tree she had started for Francis. "John Glick and his wife, Ella."

Uncle David shook his head. "I don't know any Glicks named John and Ella. What's Francis's address?"

"That's my dilemma. I only have a PO box."

"Could you write to her and ask for her street address?"

"Yes. That might be the best option." The only option.

Uncle David snapped his fingers. "Too bad we didn't ask Jesse's friend."

"Who?"

"Dane Glick."

Ah. Dane like Rain.

Uncle David swirled his coffee in the mug. "He's quite a guy, that Dane."

"You must be relieved that Jesse is making better choices for friends."

"Yes, but—"

"I seem to remember hearing something about Jesse being involved recently in a gambling scandal."

"Well, he might have made a few poor choices—"

"And last summer, didn't Aunt Nancy have to take to her bed after his visit?"

Her uncle frowned. "I didn't hear that she took to her bed . . ."

"And then—"

Uncle David cut her off. "I only meant to say that Dane Glick is a fine young man. That's all. Church is on Sunday. I'll ask around during the fellowship lunch and see if she's there. It's possible I've overlooked someone."

"This Sunday?" Two days from today? That information was unexpected. "Thanks, but don't trouble yourself. I'm sure I'll be able to find her."

"It's no trouble at all." The grandfather clock in the hall chimed out five bells and Uncle David gulped down his coffee. "There's someone I'm supposed to meet and I'm already late." A rooster started to crow, as if to hurry him along.

A timely conclusion to their conversation. Problem solving required time. But time was proving to be rather limited.

Abigail would need to act quickly. For multiple reasons, she would prefer to find Francis Glick before her uncle did.

⌒〜⌒

David had to trot to keep up with Birdy. She was tall, taller than he was, and her legs had a striding gait. He had woken extra early to be right on time to meet her for the hike to see this great blue heron, but his niece had slowed him down with her questions about tracing genealogies. By the time he had arrived at the schoolhouse, Birdy looked chilled to the bone in the brisk morning air.

She gave him a big smile as he approached. "We'll have to hurry if we want to see the great blue heron before he heads out for breakfast." He barely caught his breath before she launched off, crossing the road to cut through a field.

David padded behind her. "So tell me more about this bird's nest. Did you just stumble across it?"

"Earlier this week, I was walking to Thelma's after school and noticed the bird as it flew overhead. I followed it to its nest."

"Seems like the time of year when the bird should be heading south."

"Yes, you're right. But sometimes they don't fly south. It all depends on the kind of winter that's in store for us. I believe the one I've seen is a male heron." Her eyes sparkled as she turned to him. "Wouldn't it be wonderful if it's the start of a colony?"

"Don't they need . . . space?"

"Not really. Great blue herons aren't particularly territorial if there's an abundance of food to hunt."

"Ah! Now I understand. The Big House property backs up to Blue Lake Pond."

"Yes, exactly. Opportunity for ample fishing."

As they made their way through the woods, the sun was just starting to rise, and light filtered through the trees. She stopped abruptly and he nearly walked right into her. "Look. Up there. There he is."

Utter stillness. Nothing but the sound of the bird's wings, slowly flapping, as it soared overhead. He could see why Birdy was captivated by this large, graceful bird. Its wingspan must've been five to six feet wide, and it flew through the air as if it was gliding. They watched in awe.

In a reverent voice, she said, "Sometimes I feel like this is what it must have been like on the first morning of creation. This is the first day. And this is the first time the sun has come up. Those shadows coming up—it's the first time they'd ever appeared." She sighed a happy sigh. "It's amazing how a single moment can last forever."

A tonic. These hikes with Birdy always had the same effect on David, like a shot-in-the-arm of vitality. He could leave behind the routine of daily work, along with his fatigue, his weariness, his worries. Soon the beauty of creation would begin to penetrate his senses, then his interest, and his eyes and heart opened up to what he had been missing.

After the large bird disappeared from their view, Birdy started walking again. Marching. He jogged to catch up. "If the weather turns, couldn't it freeze to death?" He was surprised to find he felt a little worried about this majestic bird.

"Herons can tolerate cold temperatures. Those feathers provide wonderful insulation. And as long as the lake doesn't freeze over, there's plenty of food. But usually the birds do go southward to warmer temperatures and return to breeding grounds by March." They came to an opening of a field and Birdy pointed to the dead white oak. A local legend surrounded this tree, though David considered it more myth than fact. It was known in Stoney Ridge as The Hanging Tree.

The nest, though, was no myth. Just as Birdy promised, it was quite a sight. The nest was huge, filled with sticks, and sat at the top of the branches, about fifty feet high. To her delight, as they watched, the great blue heron returned to the nest with a fish in its talons.

"My guess," Birdy said, peering at the bird through her binoculars, "is this is a young male. Maybe a year."

"What's the life expectancy of a great blue heron?"

"Five years or so. But the oldest known one lived to be twenty-three."

"Think he's lonely?"

"I don't know."

"What about you, Birdy? Are you ever lonely?" He worried about her. The conversation he'd had with Gabby this morning had got him thinking about how many Glicks there were in Stoney Ridge, and how clannish they could be. Would the Glicks exclude her from family gatherings? From being one of them?

But she turned toward him with a peaceful look on her face. "Why, David, I might be alone, but in the presence of everything around me, I'm never truly alone." She lifted up her binoculars to watch the great blue heron.

Birdy's eyes, David realized, weren't on the sky, weren't really even on the great blue heron, but fixed on God's great heavens.

There was something about a new day that spoke to David's heart. In the warm barn, he fed Thistle and filled her water bucket, then led their one cow, Moomoo—named by the twins—to the stanchion and set a forkful of hay in the trough. Ruthie would be in soon to milk Moomoo; the twins' job was to feed the chickens and the bellicose rooster. Ever since Molly had taken on the job of family cook, she was excused from morning barn chores. He supposed he would have to rethink that division of labor, now that his mother had taken over the kitchen.

As David waited for Ruthie, he swept up the hay he had dropped and thanked God for the gift of this day, for the time with Birdy to watch the sun rise before hurrying back to their busy lives. He listened to the crunching of hay by the satisfied animals, the sound of the swallows as they fluttered around the rafters, and breathed in deeply the earthy smells of the barn. Through the small windows, he could see the sun cresting the treetops.

As he swept, his mind was filled with Bible verses that he liked to meditate on in the morning, to chew them over the way the horse and cow chewed their hay. "It is of the Lord's mercies that we are not consumed, because his compassions fail not. They are new every morning: great is thy faithfulness."

David wondered which dire circumstances the prophet Jeremiah faced as he penned those words. Far worse than any he'd ever encountered, no doubt. He had read somewhere that Jeremiah was only seventeen when he was called by God to deliver words of warning to the idolatrous tribe of Judah, and was forbidden to marry or have children. How lonely, how alone Jeremiah must have been. No family to speak of, and friends who turned their backs on him. No wonder he was called the Weeping Prophet. God alone brought comfort to Jeremiah. And what a beautiful illustration of God's reassuring presence in that verse: "His compassions fail not. They are new every morning."

Thousands of years later, David thought, those words continued to bring comfort and assurance to those who sought the Lord. The church had its origin in God's plan, and after the end of time the church will coexist with God through eternity.

David was suddenly overwhelmed by an extraordinary feeling—not of satisfaction but of absolute, bone-deep joy. Peace filled him, as it always did when he focused his mind on the sovereignty of God.

The little church of Stoney Ridge would never be consumed because it belonged to God. While certainty of what to do about Freeman Glick eluded him, he knew God would answer his prayers for discernment at the right time. His mercies were new every morning.

The rusty hinge of the barn door squeaked and he turned, expecting Ruthie, but there was his mother, arms akimbo.

He straightened his back, reminding himself of the peace he had just been given.

"There you are," she said, in a tone as if he were a child who needed scolding. "What is it about men and barns? They disappear into them and never return."

"I was waiting for Ruthie to come milk the cow."

"She's on her way. I have to keep after those girls, every minute." She walked toward him and stopped, standing too close, as usual. It was a strategy, he thought, to hold the upper hand in a confrontation. Tillie Yoder Stoltzfus loved all confrontation, great and small. "There's not enough discipline in your household, David. I can see that straightaway."

That was not a new complaint about David's parenting. Calmly, he stepped back to move to a comfortable speaking distance. "Well, it was a late night with Katrina and Jesse and Dane over for supper."

"My point exactly. And that brings us to Katrina. I didn't sleep well last night. I'm terribly worried about her. Aren't you?"

"No, I'm not. She might be young but she's stronger than you might think. I've seen her grow leaps and bounds in the last few months. I'm not at all worried." He didn't dare mention a word about Andy Miller. The relationship between Andy and Katrina was progressing quite nicely, as far as David was concerned. Andy was proving himself to Katrina, and she was slowly learning to trust again. If his mother got involved with them, applying pressure where it wasn't needed, forcing something to bloom before its time, he was confident that it would end badly.

"Those oil traps she mentioned sound very risky. I don't like risk, David."

"The company is leasing the land from her to drill for oil. Katrina won't be at risk."

"She's facing all kinds of risk, David. She's in quite a predicament. She's always been such a flighty girl."

"Yes, true, but that's changing. She's maturing."

"I don't see that you're doing anything about it."

"Because I'm not worried about her?"

"Exactly."

He sighed, suddenly impatient with his mother's stiff ways. "I believe that God is working in Katrina's life, in all sorts of ways. I don't deny that having a baby out of wedlock is not ideal. But I also know that God is faithful, even when we are not. In the last few months, I've observed Katrina to be depending on God in a way she never has before. And isn't that what we should want for our children, more than anything else?"

His mother didn't answer. "So Jesse said you are spending time with a young lady."

Ah. Now he realized why she was really here: Her conversation about Katrina was a warm-up pretext to question him about Birdy. He set the broom against the wall. "I suppose you could say that."

"Will I ever meet her?" she asked.

"Yes. Of course." But not for a while, if he could help it.

"Are you in love with her?"

David felt himself flush a little. He pretended that he hadn't heard the question as he picked up the broom again and swept some stray hay into an empty stall.

"Shall I take your silence as assent?"

"It's a rather new relationship. Too early for those kinds of declarations."

"That means you are."

"In love? I don't know. But I think I feel most like my best self when I am with her."

"So are you planning to marry her?"

David hesitated. He imagined himself sitting at his kitchen table with Birdy. She looked so *right* there. He could even picture a small child, a son perhaps, standing in the doorway, asking him if he'd help mend his kite. It was a lovely thought. He would like to have more children.

"Are you going to answer my question?"

He felt his mother's eyes on his back and turned to face her. "No. I'm not going to answer your question. Mother, I appreciate the help you are providing my family. But just as I said about Katrina, I think it's best to leave matters of the heart in God's hands." He looked straight at her. "That means you are not to interfere."

"Did I say such a thing?"

You didn't have to, David thought. A cloud covered the sun and the faint light in the barn grew even more dim. A perfect picture, he realized, of the effect his mother had on him.

"David, you must do something about Freeman Glick. Now. I don't know what you're waiting for. Not acting on the information you have about him means that nothing is happening. Time is of the essence. If you don't act soon, it will be brushed under the rug and people will move on with their lives. Freeman will keep on being bishop."

Would that be so wrong? David wasn't concerned about whether he remained as bishop or not; he only wanted re-pentance in Freeman's heart. *We are a Gemeide, a redemptive community. Isn't that what church is meant to be?* "And then what?"

101

"And then you will take your place as bishop, as it was meant to be."

David winced. His mother had a distorted view that becoming a bishop was a position of status. A prize. David knew it wasn't. It was a lifelong position of immense responsibility. "This is a man's life we're talking about. I'm not going to treat the matter like a cat waiting to pounce on a bird. I'm waiting to hear from God. When the circumstances are ready, when others are in the right place, when my heart is prepared, then God will let me know what to do."

She frowned at him. "Waiting is a substitute for passivity."

"Waiting, yes, but waiting in prayer means refusing to act on the situation before God acts."

His mother slowly turned her head and looked at him as if she wondered where he'd sprung from. Then Ruthie slid open the barn door to come milk the cow, and the day got under way.

7

Abigail's mother would say she was getting obsessive. She could hear her mother's voice as if she were standing in front of her, fists planted on her hips, exasperation written on her face: "Why must you always be looking backward? Look at your sisters. They only look forward." Abigail was used to the inevitable comparisons between her and her sisters. The comparisons didn't really bother her. Quite frankly, she agreed with them.

Besides, Abigail couldn't help what drove her. She was gripped by the past. The stories and struggles of olden days worked their way from the pages of old books and records into her mind and soul. It felt as if she was figuring out a gigantic jigsaw puzzle.

It was her father who understood. He would teach her how to collect references and track down leads. He tacked a large world map to the wall in the basement, and they would plot out origins of family histories on it, sticking little pins into Europe.

Her father never failed to point out the good qualities she did have. "You're as smart as they come, you are," he'd say with a hug. Or, "In your own unique way, you can find a solution to any problem."

However, a solution seemed unlikely in this particular circumstance.

Early Saturday morning, she arrived at the post office to coerce that recalcitrant clerk into revealing to whom Box 247 belonged. She brought with her a loaf of her grandmother's cinnamon raisin bread, still warm from the oven—guaranteed to make anyone sing like a canary. She hoped.

Naturally, this particular droopy-mustached postal worker was immune to delectable baked goods, the one canary who wouldn't sing. He glared at her, even when she waved the loaf of bread under his nose. Finally, as a line was forming behind her and Droopy Mustache threatened to fetch the police if she didn't leave, she turned to go. In the outer room, where the boxes lined the walls, there was Dane Glick, turning the key to close his postal box.

He smiled brightly when he saw her, then his smile faded. "Why are you staring at me?" He swiped his mouth with the back of his hand. "Is there something on my face?"

"Why are *you* getting Francis's mail?"

"Because . . . that'd be me."

"That's impossible!" She pulled a letter out of the stack in his hands. "Look." It was a bill addressed to Francis D. Glick, Box 247, Stoney Ridge, Pennsylvania.

"Yup. That's my official name."

A fog started to obscure his words in Abigail's mind. "But you can't be."

One of those thick black brows of his rose. "But I am."

"But you're not . . ." Anything like Francis Glick. "You just can't be."

"I go by Dane but my full name is Francis Dana Glick."

She was stunned. Nearly speechless. Francis was a he, not a she. "But . . . why? Why would you do such a thing?"

"Me? It wasn't *my* idea. My mother always wanted a girl and kept having boys. I think she just gave up and used the names she'd been saving for a girl on me. I hate my name. Can't stand it. All through school, I insisted that everyone called me Dane. But for anything written, I use Francis."

Abigail was remembering all the correspondence that had passed between Francis Glick and herself. And all of those times she had imagined her—him—to be a woman much like herself.

As they had discovered how much they had in common, their letters started to drift from family trees and genealogies, and on to hopes and dreams. Oh, the things Abigail had confided in her. No, not her. Him! How she had always felt as if she were on the outside of the circle. As if she was peering into windows but never invited inside. How studying genealogies made her feel as if, for once, she was inside the circle.

That odd shiver she felt last night when Dane had talked about Pat Parelli's horse management at dinner—that was a precognition. She had ignored the foreboding, convinced herself it was just a coincidence, but somewhere deep inside, it triggered a tiny doubt.

It had always struck her as odd to think of Francis, a woman, as a horse trainer. But she had dismissed those thoughts as she grew to know Francis in her letters, realizing she was more open-minded than most women she knew. A little odd. And yet Abigail liked odd people.

But Francis wasn't an unusual and bold female horse trainer. She was a man.

She felt her palms get sweaty and her heart start to pound. She wanted to respond rationally but her mind was spinning. Her emotions were out of control.

Dane was posing as Francis Dana Glick. She had been posing as her father. She felt queasy. This was bad news. This man knew too much about her. This was a disaster.

"Abigail, are you all right? You look like you've just taken a bite of some bad fish."

She looked up, into those dark, trusting eyes. "I have to go."

Abigail had no direction in mind as she left Dane. She just knew she had to go someplace to clear her thoughts. She came across a path that led through the woods and veered onto it, picking up speed, breaking into a run, then running hard until she was hot and panting. She stopped at the base of an old dead oak tree and fell on the ground beside it, gasping for breath. When she opened her eyes, there was Dane, walking up the hill toward her.

He must have run to keep up with her, but he wasn't out of breath like she was.

"Why did you—" she gulped in some air—"follow me?"

"I was worried about you." Dane sat down on the ground beside her and leaned on his elbows. "Horses run when they're frightened. Sheep do it even when they're not frightened."

"I'm not—" she said, still panting—"a horse. Or a sheep."

"No, but you do seem frightened."

She was. She waited until she caught her breath, extremely

agitated. She didn't want to have to explain anything to him. Where would she even begin?

But Dane didn't seem to expect anything from her. He didn't say anything else. He just sat beside her, legs stretched out, one ankle crossed over the other boot, his eyes on the clouds above as if he hadn't a care in the world. "This property, as far as you can see, once belonged to my grandfather." He pointed toward a distant hill. "You can see the top of my horse barn from here, if you squint."

She looked in the direction that he pointed, and she could see the peaked metal roof of a barn. She was conscious of her heart starting to return to a normal pace.

Dane seemed unaware of the inner quandary she was experiencing. He was gazing up in the tree. "Interesting that this is the spot you chose to stop running. The Hanging Tree."

"The hanging tree?"

"Legend has it that the sheriff chose it to hang outlaws on because it was the tallest, oldest tree in Stoney Ridge."

She craned her neck to look up at the dead branches. A chill went down her spine. "Think there's truth in it? The hanging part?"

He glanced over at her and smiled. "No idea. What I do know is that whenever we could come to visit my grandparents, I would try to disappear at the earliest opportunity. I used to climb up this old tree to hide. My grandfather, he was scary. A lot like Freeman."

"Like Tillie Yoder Stoltzfus," she said flatly.

"Your grandmother? Oh, not so much. She's got a bigger bark than her bite. It's all about intention."

"How so?"

"Your grandmother only wants the best for her family. She just doesn't go about it in the right way."

"Exactly right." She was startled by Dane's insight. Then she realized that the letters he had written, when she thought he was a she, showed great sensitivity and insight. She was still trying to get her mind around the fact that Francis, whom she had pictured as a petite young woman, very much like herself, and in whom she had hoped she would find a true friend, was in fact, Dane, a rather manly man.

And right between them was a stack of mail that Dane had brought, with the letter she had written to him and mailed yesterday, asking to meet, sitting on top like a hot potato. She looked at the toes of her shoes.

She would have to confess, partially, at least. "My father . . . he helps people with genealogies."

Dane Glick's brows furrowed together. "Abigail, what are you talking about?"

She closed her mouth with a frown and then tried again. "My father helps people trace their family tree." She pointed to the stack of mail.

He picked up the letter. "Father? Simon Stoltzfus is your father?"

She hoped he wasn't noticing the local postmark. "Yes. He's . . . been a little under the weather lately and asked me to help finish up your case." She looked down at her hands. "He was explaining all that in the letter you're holding. He was . . . introducing me. I had no idea you were the client . . . not until I saw you opening up Box 247. I thought . . . that is, my father assumed . . . he thought you were a woman."

Dane grimaced. "Because of my horrible name."

She nodded. A truly awful name for a manly man.

He looked at her for a long time, then he put the letter down without opening it, lifted his head, and grinned at her. "Well, maybe I can help. We can figure it out together." He winked at her. "It'll give me an excuse to see more of you."

It occurred to her that Dane did not have any suspicion that she was posing in the letters as her father. With any sort of luck it might never become known that it was Abigail with whom he had corresponded. But she never had any luck. Besides, she didn't believe in luck. Her deception was safe, though that seemed like an oxymoron.

She felt a sense of shame—and at the same time, over-whelming relief. The two emotions went to battle inside her.

Jesse tried to rub the grease off his hands with an old rag. "Hank, wake up."

Hank Lapp had stopped by the buggy shop to offer his wisdom and advice, he said, which meant that he was look-ing for a place to catch a nap. He had lain down in the front bench of Eli Smucker's old buggy, with his stocking feet hanging out the window.

"Mer schloft net wimmer, wammer die Aage zu hot," Hank mumbled. *Closing one's eyes is not always a sign of sleeping.*

"Perhaps it's not a sign for a preacher, but it is for you." Jesse tossed the rag on the workbench. "Have you been bor-rowing some of my tools without asking?"

Hank popped his head up. "MY TOOLS, you mean. Don't forget you are my apprentice."

"*Was* your apprentice. You retired." Jesse stared at his pegboard. His good Stanley hammer and expensive cat's claw nail puller were gone from their spot. His tools had specific spots. It was something he was very particular about since he had moved into his own apartment. There was a place for everything and everything in its place. He had never cared about things before, but he certainly did now.

Hank crossed his arms on the window opening, bent forward, and propped his chin on a wrist. Ever since he married Edith, he'd been trying to grow a beard, but he had only enough chin whiskers to make him look prickly. "They don't make buggies like this anymore. Benches stuffed with sheep's wool—softer than a goose down pillow." He patted the outside of the buggy. "I'd be in no hurry to fix this one up."

Hank was in no hurry to do anything.

"Eli is breathing down my neck. He wants the wheels switched out and runners replaced on it before the first snowfall." Jesse pointed to the old wooden sled attachments that Eli had brought over, lined against the wall.

"He'll be stuck at home if we don't get much snow this year."

"On the other hand, if we do get a lot of snow, he'll be the one who's laughing while the rest of us are snowbound, stuck at home 'til the snowplows come through." Jesse searched his workbench for the missing tools. "You're sure you don't know where my tools are? I use that hammer all the time." C.P. whined to go out, and Jesse stared at him, wondering if the puppy was the guilty one. But the hammer would have been too heavy for his little mouth to drag out. Besides, how could he have jumped up on the workbench to reach the pegboard?

"No idea. But I do know one thing."

"What's that?"

"En schlechder Schitz as net immer ee Laaf gelaad hot." *It's a poor hunter who does not always have one barrel loaded.*

Jesse turned to look at him. "Meaning?"

"Besser scheel as blind." *Better blind in one eye than both.*

"Try again?"

"Jesse, ol' boy, you gotta get up to speed. There's always another way to get the job done." He thumped his black hat on top of his wiry white hair and left the shop to go beg a cup of coffee off Fern, C.P. trailing behind him with his tail wagging in a circle.

Abigail looked out the window to see Ruthie hanging laundry. She rushed downstairs, grabbed a shawl off the wall peg, and hurried out to help. "You want to hang pants the other way."

Ruthie spoke around a laundry pin pinched between her lips. "This is the way my mother used to do it."

"Perhaps, but it isn't the correct way." She reached out to unclip a clothespin as Ruthie grabbed her hand.

Ruthie took the pin out of her mouth to speak clearly and distinctly. "Gabby, it doesn't really matter."

Abigail was frankly astonished. "Doesn't really matter? Of course it matters! Details have enormous consequences. The way you hang clothes on a clothesline makes a huge difference to reducing wrinkles and drying more quickly." She licked her finger and held it up in the air. "When you hang your clothes on a clothesline, make a note of which way the wind is blowing and hang your clothes so that the smaller items are in the front. That way the wind can pass through to dry the large things at the back. If you put the large things in front, they block the wind from getting to the smaller items behind them."

"I knew that."

"If you were aware of that fact, then why have you hung the clothes in the opposite way?" She reached out for a pair of pants that were hung incorrectly. "Always hang pants by the legs. Then the water will wick down to the waistband, which is the heaviest part. The weight of that water and the waistband combined will pull on the pant legs, drawing out the wrinkles." She pulled out all the pockets. "In cold weather, the pockets won't dry unless they're exposed."

"Our pockets have always dried just fine."

"Next," Abigail said, "hang shirts upside down by the side seams. Just like with the pants, this puts the heaviest part of the garment at the bottom so that the water wicks out. Additionally, you won't get the puckers from the clothespins that you'll get if you hang shirts by the shoulders." She smoothed out the last shirt, then started to redo the socks. "What day do you do sheets?"

"Day?"

"Yes. What day of the week do you wash sheets?"

"They have to be washed once a week?"

Abigail gasped. Her hands flew to her throat. "Never mind. Never mind." She took a deep breath. "We can plan out a schedule."

Ruthie scowled at her. "I didn't ask for any help."

"It's no bother at all," Abigail said. "I'm an excellent problem solver."

"But who said we had a problem?"

"Socks must always be hung by the toes. I usually hang two socks together to save time and clothespins." One by one, Abigail redid each of the socks on the line. It was distressing to find that there were many socks without partners. "Ruthie, how could this be? Where would the missing socks have gone?"

"There's a lot of socks in this house! I can't keep track of everything."

Abigail stood back to examine her fine work, satisfied. "Next, we can work on ironing skills. There's a right way to iron and a wrong way to iron. I find most everyone irons the wrong way. I will teach you the right way. I've noticed that your sisters have a severe rumpled appearance."

In the distance, Abigail heard a door slam. She looked around but Ruthie was gone.

Well, well. It was abundantly clear that Ruthie took after their grandmother. She was always quite certain she was right.

8

If there was one thing David had learned in the years since he had drawn the lot and become ordained as a minister, it was that he never knew what was coming next. He had just experienced the strangest Sunday service he'd ever seen as a minister, ever even as a church member.

It was a brisk, bright mid-November morning. David and Abraham shook hands with the men and women as they strode into the Smucker farmhouse where church would be held. The kitchen had been cleared of table and chairs to make space for the benches; every room was lined with benches, and every bench was lined with people. Because church members entered by gender and age in the same order each Sunday, absences were easily noted. Women and girls entered first, in descending age, and sat on the women's side. Then the ministers and older laymen entered, followed by the other men and boys in descending age. The ordained men all sat together. Such seating symbolized the importance of the church community, even above family ties.

But on this morning, Freeman and Levi Glick had yet to appear.

The morning's service officially began as the Vorsinger drew out the first note of the mournful hymn, a long, sustained, piercing note. Time slowed and slowed, and slowed even more. Eyes closed, minds focused, hearts softened in anticipation of worship. The rest of the men's voices, low and deep and rumbly, rolled out, and soon the women's voices, high and sweet and warbly, spun out to join the men. The walls of the humble farmhouse practically swelled with the voices, young and old, male and female. This sound, David always sensed, deep in his heart, pleased the Lord. Many voices, one note. A beautiful illustration of unity, of oneness.

And still no Freeman and Levi in sight.

As the long hymn got under way—over twenty verses— David and Abraham went upstairs to a bedroom for *Abrot*, a time for counsel and prayer, as was their custom. They barely knelt to pray when into the room came Freeman, with his typical tall-in-the-saddle confidence. Behind him came Levi. And behind both of them was Marvin King, the bishop from a neighboring church who had visited David at the store a few days back. David and Abraham looked up in surprise, silent and curious, waiting to see what they had to say. It was not unusual to include visiting ordained leaders into *Abrot*. Marvin knelt to pray. Freeman and Levi did the same, keeping their eyes averted and their heads down.

David wanted to take their late arrival as a good sign, that they might have come today with soft, penitent hearts, ready to confess their sins, to ask for forgiveness. He decided to give them the benefit of the doubt.

And that was his first mistake.

A little later downstairs, when the time came to deliver the sermon, Freeman stood quickly, rather than wait until David and Levi deferred to him, as they normally would have. He preached the way they sang their hymns, in a slow, singsong rhythm. His dark eyes flashed with the passion of his words. He mentioned, twice, that his own ancestors had come over in 1748, all the way from Rotterdam, risking their lives to find a place to worship in freedom.

Freeman's sermon was filled with references to "God works in mysterious ways." It couldn't be faulted, not at all, yet David wondered if behind the theme was Freeman's way of insisting that he was bishop because of God's mysterious ways, not because he had switched the lots.

Then Freeman sat down and Marvin King stood to give the second sermon. There was nothing unusual about that. Visiting bishops or ministers were invited to give sermons. It was a privilege for the church members to hear the messages from other leaders. And then Levi took his turn to affirm the points made in the sermon. David's sermon, obviously, would have to be postponed to another Sunday. And then it was time for the closing hymn.

After the benediction, during the time of announcements and before everyone was dismissed, Abraham rose to his feet to say he was relinquishing his lot as deacon. Freeman only nodded and said he accepted his decision, because he was certain Abraham had been directed by God to do so.

A silence filled the church. A thick, enveloping, smothering silence. A waiting. David leaned forward on his chair, expecting—hoping, praying!—Freeman and Levi to follow Abraham's lead.

Nothing.

Freeman gave a closing prayer, then off he strode, through the kitchen door, Levi following on his heels. Marvin rose quickly and walked behind them. Usually, the ministers were the last to leave. Their work for the morning was done and they remained on the bench, a little spent.

Many in the church, though not all, had astounded looks on their faces as they watched the three men stride toward the door. Then they turned to look at David with their open, honest faces. God-fearing people, good people. He knew what they were thinking: Wasn't he going to do something?

David hadn't known what to expect from Freeman on this Sunday morning, but he hadn't expected . . . *nothing*. Acting as if everything was right as rain? Why, it was preposterous.

Amos Lapp sidled up to him and sat beside him. "Marvin's sermon kept circling around the block, didn't you think?"

David smiled. It was true. Marvin kept hammering home the same point: "For all have sinned, and come short of the glory of God." All.

David agreed wholeheartedly with Marvin's point. Many, many times he had experienced the Spirit's conviction of his own sin, faced fully the regret and remorse, and then, the sweet relief that came with confession. Yes, we all have sinned and fallen short of the glory of God. All.

Amos crossed one leg over the other and clasped his knee. "You know, don't you, that Marvin King is a Glick?"

"Wait. He's what? He's a Glick?"

"Marvin's mother and Freeman's father were siblings."

No. No, David hadn't realized the connection. Of course! Now the conversation he and Marvin had in his office a few days ago made complete sense. Marvin was laying the groundwork to excuse Freeman's actions.

David was disappointed—in Freeman, in Levi, in Marvin, in himself. He had hoped that giving Freeman the space to confess and repent would suffice, that he would seek the Lord's direction. What purpose did confession play when it was forced on someone? No, it needed to come from within to be genuine. But that strategy wasn't making much of an impact on Freeman and Levi.

During the fellowship meal, David tried to sit near Freeman, tried to get his attention for a private moment, but he was surrounded by his sons or relatives. There were enough Glick relatives, David realized today, to shelter Freeman and keep him in his role as an unrepentant bishop. And that would be a grave mistake. The root of all sins is the denial of sin, the refusal to admit sin.

But the reality of the situation was that David, alone, wasn't making much of a dent. He closed his eyes in exasperation. What next?

Abigail might have looked as if she was concentrating on the sermons during church, but her mind was miles away. She was thoroughly preoccupied by the Letter Identity Deception and wasn't quite sure how to proceed from here. She was uncomfortable with dishonesty. Dane was an innocent victim in the Letter Identity Deception and didn't deserve to be misled. He had no inkling that she was the writer of those letters and not her father. No inkling at all.

Briefly, she thought about telling Dane the truth, that she was the writer of the letters, not her father. Wasn't the truth always, always, the best plan? Absolutely. Always.

But not in this situation.

Her mind raced as she thought of all the things she had written in those letters to Francis/Dane. Admitting that she—posing as her father—had never felt as if she fit in, even in her own family. That she had never had a true friend, other than her sister. That she preferred books to people, because books were predictable. People were not.

No, the truth would be counterproductive in this particular situation. She created a mental list of reasons to not reveal the truth to Francis/Dane:

1. Her first priority was to break through the brick wall and discover the identity of the missing Glick ancestor.
2. Her second priority was to return to Ohio with the information so that her father would feel that his work was valued and important.
3. Francis/Dane might feel embarrassed if he knew the truth. Quite possibly, he too had revealed more than he intended to in their correspondence.
4. If Francis/Dane did know Abigail's true identity, he would reject her.

Somehow, she needed to stay on course, to see this brick wall through. She had an idea, but she needed help.

After the fellowship meal, she intercepted Dane as he walked to his horse in the parking pasture. "Yes."

"Yes?" Dane looked at her with unmasked delight. "Yes, what?"

Nervously, she fingered her apron edge. "Yes, I'll accept your help with my project."

He looked like he'd just been handed the moon. "Really?"

"Yes. I believe so." She bit her lip. "I think this might be an ideal solution."

"How can I help?"

"Have you heard about the Genographic Project?"

"No," Dane said.

"It was started in 2005 by the National Geographic Society." She explained that with a sample of DNA, scientists could trace his distant ancestry. He was fascinated. She was pleased with how she described the Genographic Project: Just enough information, but not too much. The Amish were fans of the National Geographic Society but would probably not be in favor of the computational technologies required to process and analyze the genetic information of Dane's DNA. She offered to have Dane's DNA processed through a kit. She hoped he wouldn't ask any specific questions about the kit. She had already bought it in anticipation of meeting Francis, but she hadn't read the directions yet. She wasn't entirely sure what might be required of Dane to collect his DNA. She had heard about the scraping of cheeks to collect a sample. Blood was better.

He was quiet for a moment, then a big smile wreathed his face. "I'm all yours."

Excellent.

⁓

David had intended to find a moment to introduce Birdy to his mother after church, but he was thoroughly preoccupied with trying, unsuccessfully, to find a moment alone with Freeman. And by the time he realized that wasn't going to happen, he couldn't find Birdy. Andy Miller was coming out of the barn as David was walking into it. "Andy, have you seen Birdy?"

"Katrina said Thelma wasn't feeling well, so the three of them left, about an hour ago."

Ah, a missed opportunity.

"David, have you had a chance to look through those leases?"

"Yes. I read through them. I'm amenable to this project, with one change. I want the leases to adjust from five years to three."

"Katrina told me how you felt about that."

"If that's something the lease company is willing to agree to, then I think there's no reason you can't go ahead."

"I'll follow up. I think it'll work." Andy smiled and put out his hand to shake David's. "This, *this* is going to be good for everyone in Stoney Ridge."

David returned his handshake. "I hope so too."

"If you don't mind, I'll get home to tell Katrina the good news. She'll be thrilled."

"And Thelma," David said. "Tell them both."

Dane gave Abigail a two-finger wave with a big smile as she walked past him with her grandmother and sister, uncle and cousins, on the way to their buggy. She looked away, pretending not to see him. She had already said goodbye to him. Why say goodbye twice?

Ruthie caught up to her. "How could you do that?"

"Do what?"

"Brush Dane off like that."

"I didn't brush him off. I didn't do anything."

"Exactly." Ruthie rolled her eyes dramatically. "Half the girls in town would swoon if Dane Glick made a point to wave goodbye to them. But not Gabby Stoltzfus."

"Abigail." How many times did she need to remind her? Between forgetfulness and eye rolling, she wondered if Ruthie might have some overlooked neurological issues.

Ruthie rolled her eyes yet again, then veered away abruptly to join her father. Uncle David drove his daughters home from church in the wagon, and Abigail, Laura, and Mammi followed behind in the buggy with Thistle. Laura took the reins, Mammi sat next to her, and Abigail climbed in the back.

"Listen, Gabby," Mammi said, turning her head slightly. "Ora Nisley is coming to supper this afternoon. Change into your blue dress."

"Who? Today? Why?" Abigail winced. It was starting. Mammi the Meddler's meddling.

"Ora Nisley. He's a widower. An eager-to-remarry widower."

Laura flicked the reins to get the horse moving faster. "Does he have children?"

Mammi mumbled something.

Laura leaned to her right. "How many?"

"Four."

"Mammi!" Laura said. "A widower with four children! That's not the kind of suitable man we had discussed finding for our Gabby."

"They're all grown. In fact, he has some—" She stopped herself abruptly.

"Grandchildren?" Laura said. "Were you going to say that he has *grandchildren*? Oh Mammi. That is definitely not the kind of man we had discussed for our Gabby."

Abigail completely agreed, though she resented being talked about in the third-person point of view while she was right here. Inches away!

"It's a perfect opportunity," Mammi said. "I asked Fern Lapp about him. She said that Ora Nisley has a thriving greenhouse business."

"I saw you and Fern talking," Laura said. "Did Fern have anything else to say about him?"

Mammi shifted uncomfortably.

"Mammi, what else did Fern have to say?"

She huffed. "She said that he might have a few unusual habits."

Abigail leaned over the front bench. "Such as?"

Mammi stiffened. "Such as he washes his hands rather a lot." She looked out the window. "There's nothing wrong with a man who values cleanliness."

Absolutely right. *She could have been describing me.* "Not unless it's untreated obsessive-compulsive disorder. The constant washing of hands is one of the top ten indicators. I've read all about this disorder."

Laura gasped. "Wait! I know the man you're talking about. He's the one who came into the kitchen after lunch to supervise how we were washing the dishes. Oh Mammi, he's so old!"

"He's not at all old! Only fifty-four."

Abigail gave a sideways glance at her grandmother, who was sixty-two.

Mammi noticed. "Age isn't important. Gabby likes things organized and so does Ora Nisley. I thought they might be very compatible."

"He's old and he's odd. That man's insistence on cleanliness bordered on the ridiculous. He drove us all crazy. We finally left him alone in the kitchen to clean up. And it was Sadie Smucker's kitchen!"

A trickle of pleasure rolled over Abigail. Her grandmother

had noticed that she was well organized. Compliments did not come her way very often. However, that didn't mean she wanted to be courted by a grandfather with obsessive-compulsive disorder. "He does sound as if he might be on the extreme side of tidiness."

"At least I'm trying, Gabby." Mammi sighed. "You're acting like I want this more than you."

"This? But what is 'this'?"

Her grandmother sounded exasperated. "For you to fall in love and get married."

Abigail didn't answer her right away. "Of course I want that. Of course I do." She had always thought she would get married, but after the Black Raspberry Incident, she was considering abandoning that assumption. Finding a compatible partner, for her, was proving to be highly unlikely. Too complicated. Too disappointing. She thought of the feedback she'd been given: too awkward, too blunt, too direct, too logical, lacking humor, unemotional, uncaring, unfeeling. "But I don't want to marry an old man."

It was as if Mammi had not heard her. "I expect you to be here for supper. Wearing your blue dress."

Dane like Rain, with that perpetual smile on his face, popped into her mind.

His interest in her, albeit surely temporary, might just be the solution to her problem. Not that she considered her single status a problem. But her grandmother did, and if she thought Abigail had a suitor, she might leave her alone to do her work. And in doing so, Abigail would help her father get back on his feet. Literally.

Abigail glanced down at the tips of her shoes. "Jesse asked if I would join him and a friend on a hike today." She had told her cousin a firm no, but she was suddenly rethinking that decision.

Her grandmother shifted in the bench to look at her askance. "With . . . a male friend?"

"Yes, in fact."

Her grandmother brightened.

"Jesse's friend Dane."

Her grandmother's eyebrows nearly shot right off her head. "Dane . . . ?"

"Yes. Dane Glick."

"Glick?" The light left her grandmother's face like a cloud covering the sun. "Dane Glick? The one who raises sheep? The one who came to supper the other night?"

Abigail clamped her mouth shut, wishing she hadn't reminded Mammi of his last name.

"Cancel it. You absolutely, positively must be home to meet Ora Nisley."

Laura turned slightly to give Abigail a wink, then smiled sweetly at Mammi. "Oh, she couldn't possibly do that. It would be rude. You don't want Gabby to get a reputation for brushing off one fellow to chase another."

Her grandmother was frowning. "I suppose you might be right . . ."

Laura had saved the day, as she often did, and found the opening for Abigail to slip away without any way for Mammi to object. This was an example of how intuitive and adroit her sister's people skills were.

But there was a glitch. Abigail wasn't trying to chase one fellow or the other.

Jesse could think of dozens of ways he would like to spend a sunny autumn afternoon. Instead, he was the acting chaperone for Dane Glick and his cousin Gabby as they hiked around Blue Lake Pond. Dane led them around the narrow trail and did 90 percent of the talking. Dane reminded Jesse of C.P., his horrible puppy: happy, lighthearted, eager for anything, and completely unaware that Gabby wasn't equally enamored with him. Gabby kept glancing at her wristwatch, as if she was either late for something or wanted to avoid something. He wasn't sure which.

Jesse looked behind him to make sure C.P. was following. Naturally, the dog had gotten distracted and was far behind, sniffing something. Jesse whistled and C.P. came bounding toward him, tail turning in circles like a whirligig.

Dane and Gabby were far ahead on the trail, and by the time Jesse caught up, he found he hadn't missed much. Dane was telling Gabby about what it was like to grow up on a dairy farm in an Amish community that didn't use any mechanical milking equipment. Each cow was milked by hand. "I was the youngest in the family, so it was my job to get up early and call the cows in." He put his hands around his mouth and shouted, "Whooee, whooee, whooee!"

Birds shot out of trees, C.P. barked frantically, and Dane laughed. "Had the same effect on the cows. Woke my brothers up too."

"So that ear-piercing sound would coax the cows to come in?" Gabby seemed amazed.

"Absolutely. They knew that hay was waiting for them in the barn. Each cow would head for her stall, and as soon as she was in place, with her head in the hay, I'd fasten the stanchion around her neck and put kickers on her hind legs."

"What are kickers?"

"Restraining chains."

Gabby looked puzzled. "Then they should really be called anti-kickers."

Dane howled with laughter over that, not at all sentient to the fact that Gabby wasn't trying to make a joke.

"My older brothers would make their way to the cow barn, groggy and bleary-eyed." He grinned. "Took us about two hours to milk the cows and get those big silver milk cans over to the milk-processing house. Morning and night." He rolled his eyes. "I don't miss it for a minute. Though . . . I do miss some of the cows. My brothers thought I was crazy, but I always thought each one had a unique personality."

He held a branch up for Gabby to pass under, then let it go, striding forward to catch up with her. The branch slapped Jesse in the face.

"I remember one time," Dane said, "a cow got into some bad water and we found her dead. We hitched chains to her legs and had the horses drag the body far to the edge of our property, out to the bone pile. All the other cows followed behind us, mooing mournfully."

"Oh my goodness," Gabby said. "Did they think they were going to a cow funeral?"

"Yes!" Dane grinned at her. "Exactly like that. It was their way of honoring their friend."

Dane and Gabby walked on ahead, talking about cow funerals, while Jesse waited for C.P. He couldn't see the puppy's black tail anywhere, so he backtracked, whistling and calling. He heard a familiar bark and took a shortcut down a steep embankment, sending rocks tumbling down to the beach below. There was C.P., wagging his tail in that big circle motion in front of a blazing fire. Bending down to pet him was Mim Schrock. And next to Mim was Danny Riehl, setting out a picnic. Jesse's archrival and, most unfortunately, a very nice guy.

This bleak afternoon outing just took a turn for the worse.

Abigail threw some bits of bread crust at a green mallard duck and his plain brown wife. They snatched at it, and she tossed more bread crusts at the ducks, but that only acted as an invitation to the flock. She started backing away as ducks emerged from the pond and waddled toward her. Duck after duck! Like a small army, they kept advancing on her. She turned to Dane, who sat on the beach, watching her. "Help!"

Dane laughed and rose to his feet. "You have to think like a duck." He took his sandwich and threw pieces of it into the water. Immediately, the ducks lost interest in Abigail and chased toward the water.

"Thank you," she said, keeping her eyes on those ducks, just in case. She looked down the shoreline of the pond and saw Jesse, sitting over at a bonfire, with two other people. When was he planning to return to them?

She stuffed more food into her mouth than she should have, trying to hurry things along and get the picnic over with, but then she had to figure how to chew and swallow without gagging.

Dane took his time. He was a man who seemed decidedly lacking in urgency.

Once he'd finally finished eating, Abigail was all for retrieving Jesse and going straight back to her uncle's house, but Dane wanted to walk around the lake. "Why?"

"Why?" He looked up, squinting against the sunlight that splashed through the trees. "Because it's a nice afternoon. Because it's probably one of the last autumn days we'll have before winter arrives." He reached out a hand to help her up, and she noticed that the corners of his eyes crinkled as he smiled at her. "Most of all, because there's no reason to hurry home. Is there?"

A breeze came up, brushing the surface of the pond into ripples, stirring leaves on the trees, rustling, whispering, crackling. She considered not answering him, assuming it to be a rhetorical question, but Dane seemed to be waiting for one. "My grandmother is bent on marrying me off. She's trying to match me up with an old widowed grandfather."

A smile lifted the corners of Dane's mouth. "An old man?"

"Yes. Extremely old. Fifty-four years old. She invited him to supper, but I told her I was going to the lake with Jesse and a young man. By now, I think, the old man would have gone home. Old people need to get to bed early."

Dane's smile grew larger. "So I'm your decoy?"

Honesty, she believed, was always the best policy. "Yes."

Dane burst out laughing.

Abigail felt the tips of her ears flush, and her heart thrummed in her ears. "Why is that so funny?"

His laughter faded, but his smile remained as he studied her. "You're quite fascinating, you know."

Fascinating? She had never heard herself described with that particular adjective. It was nice of him to say that, but she was sure he didn't mean it.

"I never know what you're going to say next."

Oh. That. That was not a new complaint. Her mother considered her candor as a problem of massive proportions.

"Think, Gabby. Think before you speak!" was a constant refrain. But the thing was, Abigail did think. She thought quite a lot.

As they ambled on down the trail that circled the lake, the dead leaves beneath their feet crunched as they walked over them, a carpet of dry leaves. In the late afternoon, as the breeze had died down, the lake became flat and still and solid as marble, with the setting sun shining off its surface. For a moment, there seemed no need to rush or plan.

Too soon, they were nearly back to their starting point on the beach. Abigail saw Jesse and his dog had left his friends' bonfire and returned to their blanket to polish off the remains of their picnic. Her cousin looked to be sound asleep; his black hat covered his face and his long legs were stretched out like a cat on a windowsill. His puppy lay curled up beside him with its head on Jesse's stomach. The moon was coming up over the treetops, competing with the last glimmer of light from the dying sun, as the day gave way to evening.

Abigail felt a little sorry the afternoon had come to an end. She had enjoyed herself. "Thank you for bringing me here."

Dane held her gaze a little longer than necessary. "You're very welcome." Then his face broke into that big, delighted grin. "I'm at your service. Happy to be your decoy any time you need one."

She felt herself smile in return and thought it was probably a very wide and foolish smile, yet she couldn't seem to help it. Then the worst possible thing occurred. The worst! She fought against it, but the pressure started building in her cheekbones, a tickling sensation built in her nose, making tears well into her eyes. Abigail squeezed her eyes shut, trying to force her sneeze under control.

Words of kindness had always been difficult for her. As far back as her memory could take her, she had coped with her mother's steady criticism, her grandmother's constant disappointment, and school peers' snubs by separating herself with detachment. Kindness, though, brought up feelings she couldn't control.

She pinched her nose to try to stifle the sneeze, but unfortunately that only made her feel as if her head might explode. She sneezed once—then sneezed again. And again. A triple threat, her signature sneeze attack. Finally, the tickling in her nose stopped and she had herself back under her control. Her eyes opened stealthily, halfway, as if she hoped to see that Dane hadn't noticed her sneezing attack.

He remained a foot apart, watching her with an expression of wonder, his hand stretched out with a handkerchief in his palm. He had noticed.

9

David tried not to let the situation with Freeman Glick haunt him, but he was still unsettled when he woke the following day. He hadn't slept well. He had let yesterday's events worry away at his subconscious.

After breakfast, he walked to the store through drizzle and depression that hinted strongly of winter's coming. He felt uncertain about what to do next. A Bible verse Freeman had quoted to him rolled over and over in his mind: "The lot is cast into the lap; but the whole disposing thereof is of the Lord." Could it be that trusting in the sovereignty of God might mean that the lot-switching business was ordained? Sanctioned, even?

He pondered that as he walked down the road.

Would it be so bad to let the lot switching slip under the rug? Freeman Glick was a powerful individual in this community. He was highly regarded, viewed as a patriarch. And David couldn't erase the fact that it was the prior bishop, Elmo Beiler, who had started the whole lot-switching business. If David had been under Elmo from the start, a man he admired and respected, would he have a different point of view about it? Might he have been tempted to participate? He hoped not, but he couldn't know for sure.

Another Bible verse floated to the forefront of his mind: "Be careful for nothing; but in every thing by prayer and supplication with thanksgiving let your requests be made known unto God. And the peace of God, which passeth all understanding, shall keep your hearts and minds through Christ Jesus."

David had a great deal to learn about the vocation of ministering, but he knew one thing for sure: prayer was at the heart of anything and everything. He stopped and tipped his head up to the sky. "What next, Lord? I don't know what to do. Guide my steps." Two little words in that Bible verse, so easy to overlook, filled his mind. *With thanksgiving.* He lifted his hands. "And thank you." *Thank you for bringing this situation to light, thank you for exposing it, for correcting our missteps, for providing a path through it.*

Even if he didn't yet know the path to take, even still, he was thankful.

He heard someone call his name and whirled around to find the source.

"Did you see it?"

Birdy! Her cheeks were ruddy from the cold and he couldn't hold back a smile. He walked toward her. "See what?"

"The great blue heron! He was standing on a fence post, not ten feet away from you. I thought that was why you had stopped."

David dipped his head. "I wish I could say that was the reason." How typical of him—to miss the natural world calling out to him because he was so locked up with his own thoughts.

"You looked rather solemn. Rather preacher-like."

An answering grin lifted his mouth. "Well, to be honest, I was praying."

Seeing his grin, her eyes sparkled. "Well, no one could fault you for that."

"I'll walk you to school." He wrapped his arm around her shoulder, bumping hips with her, clumsy and yet tender. This relationship with Birdy, it was still so new to him.

"Something must be weighing heavily on you, if you missed seeing the great blue heron. He could have practically reached out and grabbed your hat." They walked along awhile. "My hunch is that it had to do with church yesterday and my brother Freeman."

It could have been an awkward thing between them, a dividing point, though Birdy never made it seem so. Freeman was her oldest sibling. How could David talk honestly with her about her own brother's sin?

He stopped and faced her, taking her hands in his. "Birdy, I don't want to come between you and your brother."

"You're not. I was the one who brought it all out in the light."

"I was hoping it might resolve easily, but that doesn't seem to be the case." He looked down at their hands, joined together. "To be honest, I just don't know how to resolve it. That's what I was praying about."

"Perhaps it's time to seek help outside our church."

To involve another bishop is what she meant, and to do so would be a significant step. Each Amish church tried to solve its own problems, to keep everything "in-house." He tilted his head. "If I go outside the church, there's no turning back."

"I think we've already come to that point." She looked right in his eyes. "We have to leave the outcome with God."

He knew. He knew. "But Birdy, what will happen to us?"

"Well, that outcome belongs to God too."

He gazed at her for a while, and the most extraordinary feeling welled up inside him. He felt his heart lift into a place he did not think he had known before.

After they parted ways at the schoolhouse, he walked alone to the store. The gray clouds were breaking up and a stream of sunlight lit the road ahead of him. And then, like the sky above, his prayers for discernment cleared the air.

Later that morning, he finished his letter to Isaac Bender and placed it in the store's mailbox for the carrier to pick up. Indecision evaporated in that one act.

⌒

Abigail stayed up much too late last night making a list of all likely leads to pursue for the Bible project. Someday soon, when her father's well-being was restored, the two of them planned to spend a solid week at the National Archives in Washington, DC, combing through census records on microfiche. Some genealogists sought to exhaust all home sources before going to census records, but Abigail's father taught her to go to them first, accessible at the large Columbus, Ohio, public library. "Census records are a gold mine of information, Abigail," her father often said, "just waiting for someone like us to unearth them."

He showed her how census taking began in 1790 with six simple questions, only six, for the sole purpose of counting the nationwide population. In 1850, the census expanded to include more questions: age of family members, birthplace, occupation, race, immigration. By 1930, the census expanded to thirty questions. Vital records weren't officially kept in the United States until 1920, so the census records became the only source to find vital information.

Opportunities of abundance waited for the family history researcher, though you had to be savvy. Prior to 1850, the records were often inaccurate—census takers canvassed door to door, often missing remote areas, and those people they did question often withheld information or outright lied because they didn't trust the government's motives, vexing the census takers.

Abigail certainly understood those suspicions. The Plain People didn't trust the government, either. Why did it need personal information? Could information be used against them? Higher taxes? Military service? No. It was wise to be cautious when dealing with the government.

And yet, she was grateful for the collected information. And there lay the conundrum. Glad for the benefits provided by the government, reluctant to offer up anything more.

Abigail reined in her thoughts about the National Archives and set her mind to the task at hand. She combed through the books her uncle had loaned to her and categorized all the Glick primogenitors in Lancaster County. She was going to ask each primogenitor if she could see their family Bible. Old family Bibles, an accepted source of documentation for genealogical purposes, were usually passed to the oldest son. Family Bibles were held with high regard, considered the last tie to the Old World. Births, baptisms, marriages, and deaths were recorded with remarkable accuracy.

She would start with the primogenitors in Stoney Ridge and move out from there. First on the list: Freeman Glick.

~~~~

It was a fine morning. Jesse found it difficult to get out of bed quite as early as Fern Lapp expected, but he knew that the first few hours of light were the best part of the day, a time of freshness and optimism. "Die Maryeschtund hot Gold im Mund," Fern was fond of repeating. *The morning hours have gold in hand.*

Jesse particularly liked it when he knew Fern had left Windmill Farm for the day and he could turn on his transistor radio, kept tucked away, as he toiled on a challenging buggy. Those were his happiest moments. Of course it depended to a great extent on the buggy. He had dismissed Hank Lapp's complaints about the orneriness of certain buggies as sheer laziness and a fondness for fishing. But he had quickly discovered that there were, indeed, some buggies that made even Jesse despair.

Eli Smucker's old buggy was a case in point. Jesse had spent a great deal of time on that buggy and felt that he knew it quite well by now. It was not a difficult one to deal with, but it could not be kept going forever, and he wasn't sure whether Eli could accept that truth.

Jesse looked around at the other buggies that were waiting for attention. Billy Lapp had brought in a buggy that had no brake pads left to speak of. And there was Solomon Riehl's one with an axle that made an earsplitting squeal. Another buggy with wheels that needed some spokes replaced.

Jesse had a full day of work ahead of him. However, he needed to ask Hank a few questions, and as his former employer liked to say, "These buggies aren't dying. They'll still be there when you get back."

So he snatched his hat off the wall nail, slammed it on his head, and whistled for C.P. Companionably, his pup followed behind him to walk to the Bent N' Dent where they were greeted with a cheery welcome by the old codgers. Jesse grinned as he shed his hat and coat, happy to be in the store and out of the biting cold.

Hank dragged a chair close to the woodstove for him and pulled out a dog biscuit for C.P., who bounded toward him. "SIT DOWN AND WARM YOUR OLD BONES," he shouted in his everyday voice.

Jesse was too cold to point out that his bones were not old. He didn't have a chance to, anyway, because Eli Smucker leaned forward on his rocking chair and peppered him with questions about his broken-down buggy. "When is it going to be ready? I'm very fond of it. They don't make buggies like that anymore."

Jesse rubbed his hands together and tried to buy some time. The problem was that he wasn't quite sure how to repair Eli Smucker's ski sled attachments. They had rusty, brittle square head bolts—parts he couldn't locate to reorder. That was one of the reasons he had stopped by the store this morning. He wanted to ask Hank about it, but not in front of Eli Smucker, of course. Hank may not have been handy in the traditional sense, but he was a born inventor. He often came up with ingenious solutions. With a little "tinkering," as Hank called it, he could fix any problem.

For example, there had been a rash of scooter thefts on Main Street in Stoney Ridge. It was Hank's idea to suggest to scooter owners that they remove the handlebars and carry them into a store as they shopped. *Brilliant*. No more scooters were stolen.

Unfortunately, many scooter owners had trouble getting the handlebars back on. Apparently there was a tiny pin that popped out and was easily lost. It took a trip to the buggy shop, and a twenty-dollar repair bill for parts and labor, to get the scooter back into service. Nevertheless, Hank reminded them all, the problem of theft had been resolved.

The other reason Jesse stopped by was because he was ready to unveil the details of his plans for the Bent N' Dent to start a grocery delivery service. Yardstick Yoder, the fastest boy in Stoney Ridge, factored into these plans. He was released from school at 3:00 p.m. and could make those deliveries on his way home from school. "Call by three, arrive by five," was the lingo Jesse had invented.

Brilliant.

There were glitches in this plan, of course. Jesse anticipated accounting issues. He wasn't sure how his father would feel about people getting their groceries before they paid for them.

And then the biggest glitch of all: Yardstick Yoder. He was holding out for Jesse to offer him a more generous hourly wage.

Eli Smucker cleared his throat, waiting for a response. Just as Jesse was about to respond, the front door opened and in blew his grandmother on a gust of cold wind. His cousin Laura trailed behind her and gently closed the door. Mammi's steely gaze swept over the store and landed on the old men.

"Excellent!" she said, which Jesse knew was a trick. "You men can help us rearrange the store."

The old men stared at her, slack-jawed.

Mammi looked each one up and down, then narrowed her

mental telescope at C.P., who sat looking back at her with his tongue hanging out. "And why is there a dog in this store?"

Thus began Mammi's takeover of the Bent N' Dent. Her strategy for the store, as it was for her entire life, was to be helpful in the most unhelpful ways.

⁓

Abigail knocked on the door of the Big House and was surprised to find it opened by two very similar-looking women. Her first thought was that she might be having a stroke and seeing double. She had read about strokes. Then she remembered Uncle David had told her that Freeman and Levi Glick, brothers, happened to be married to sisters. She explained who she was and why she had come.

"You'll have to speak to my husband," one sister said. "He's out in the barn."

Abigail thanked them and went to the barn. She recognized Freeman Glick from his preaching on Sunday. Rather uninspired preaching, she thought, with a bad habit of rambling off topic, but that was beside the point. As was the lot-switching business that her grandmother was constantly stewing over. The only concern on Abigail's mind was how she could get a look at the Glick family Bible, assuming there was one.

Freeman was feeding a large bottle of milk to a calf when he saw her. "You. Here. Finish this up."

He handed her the bottle of milk and promptly walked away from her.

"But I have never fed a calf . . ."

He didn't seem concerned. Nor was he listening. He walked down the aisle of the massive barn and disappeared. She turned back to the calf, who looked at her with large, solemn eyes. She held the bottle out to it and it practically yanked the bottle right out of her hand. She could barely keep hold of that bottle! The tongue on that calf was like a powerful muscle, which, in fact, it was. The calf guzzled the rest of the milk, then looked at her again with those large, woeful eyes, disappointed that she had nothing more to offer. Fortunately, Freeman returned with a dose of medicine to give to the calf. He squirted a syringe down its throat and then turned his attention to Abigail. He looked her over, and he didn't like what he saw. "What do you want?"

His gaze was so piercing that she debated concealing her last name, but truth was always the best policy. "I'm Abigail Stoltzfus."

"I know who you are. I asked what you wanted."

Good. A practical person. "I would like to see your family Bible."

"Why?"

Ah! Judging by Freeman's suspicious reaction, there was, indeed, a treasured family Bible.

Down the long aisle of the barn came a boy of about nine or ten, as round as her cousin Molly, chomping gum and blowing large pink bubbles as he walked toward them. Freeman frowned and held out his hand. The boy spit the wad of gum into the open large palm. Freeman tossed the gum into a rubbish bin and turned his attention back to Abigail. "Why?"

Abigail had trouble keeping her eyes on Freeman because the round boy, directly behind his father, had reached into his pocket to get another piece of Bazooka bubble gum, unwrapped the wrapper, and popped the gum into his mouth.

"I'm working on a Glick family tree and I'm trying to fill in the blanks."

"There are no blanks." Freeman smiled, but there was no warmth in those dark eyes. He lifted a bale of hay as if it was feather-light and carried it outside to a wagon.

Abigail followed behind. "But there are. There's an important blank. A critical gap. I was hoping your family Bible might provide the missing information."

"There is no missing information."

Oh. He was a stonewaller. She would have to try a different tack. "How did your ancestors arrive here?" she asked him instead.

"My people came to the New World in 1748. The first wave of the Amish."

"But why do you think your ancestors came to the New World?"

"So they could own land. It wasn't possible to own land in Germany."

"How many ancestors came on that ship?"

"Peter Glick came over with a large family. They settled in Berks County, and all but one son, John, died when their house was burned by Indians. Every single Glick traces their lineage to John, who escaped the Indians by hiding in a hollow tree."

How interesting! A piece of history she had overlooked. "So who did John end up marrying?"

He stiffened. "His wife was Amish too, if that's what you're nosing around to find out."

"No doubt. My question is about a missing male name in the family tree a few decades later. I'm trying to track that individual down."

He narrowed his eyes. "My family is 100 percent Amish." He lifted a finger in the air and repeated, "One hundred percent!"

"Most likely. But you can't be certain unless I can confirm the identity of that unknown individual."

"We don't have anyone hiding in the woodpile, if that's what you're thinking."

"The only thing I'm after is the identity of your great-great—" she had to stop and count back—"great-great-grandfather. May I have your permission to look at your family Bible?"

"Absolutely not."

How exasperating! "But why not?"

"Because my word is good enough. I know who I am and who my people are. I don't need a Stoltzfus to tell me otherwise." He placed both hands flat on the wagon and turned away from her, signaling that their discussion had ended.

Incredible! A critical portion of family history was missing, and Freeman Glick didn't know about it or care to know the truth.

He walked off, muttering something she barely caught. "You Stoltzfuses are all alike. Always after something."

Abigail opened her mouth to protest, but thought better of it. She had assumed that the lot-switching business was not her problem. Apparently, like so many other assumptions she made about people, she was wrong.

10

The house was quiet, the children were asleep. This hour, before bedtime, belonged to David, and to the Lord God. Lamplight on his desk cast a halo of yellow-orange about the room. He scanned his bookshelves, looking for a book by Henri Nouwen, a Dutch-born Catholic priest, a brilliant thinker, who left the academic world to work with the mentally and physically handicapped. Gabby had reorganized his books in his bookshelves and he couldn't find anything. Where was it? He heard a foot-scuffling sound and turned around to see Ruthie standing there, hands on her hips, an angry look on her face.

"Dad, I can *not* handle Gabby's 'helpfulness' for one more day."

"What happened now?" David was a little perturbed himself. Where was that book by Nouwen?

"She alphabetized all the canned goods in the basement."

"What's wrong with that?"

"Because it's all her version of alphabetizing. Green beans and lima beans and peas are all together under a weird name."

He stopped hunting for books and looked over at Ruthie. "Legumes?"

"Yes! Whatever that means. And she put tomatoes in with all the canned fruit. She insisted that tomatoes are a fruit, even though I told her that was completely wrong."

Gabby was correct, actually, but David didn't think it would be wise to point that out to Ruthie right now. And then it occurred to him that she might have alphabetized his books. He looked through the titles but couldn't find it. "Have you explained your system to her?"

"I don't have a system! I just put the jars on the shelves as Molly and I finished canning them. That was good enough for everyone . . . until Gabby had to go and redo everything. And guess what else? She said that half of my jars weren't sealed properly and I was going to end up killing everyone. She called it something horrible. Bo-to, botch-o . . ."

What was it Dane Glick always said? To fully understand an animal, think the way an animal thinks. The same thing might work for people. How would Gabby, a very literal librarian, think to alphabetize books? Of course! By the author's name. And there it was, under *N*. He grabbed the book and spun around to Ruthie. "Botulism?"

"Yes! That's it. Why can't she just use normal words?" She scratched her head. "What does it mean, anyway?"

"It's a type of food poisoning."

"Oh." Ruthie's eyes dropped to the floor. Ohhhh.

David rubbed his stomach. Maybe that explained why he'd been having so much pain lately. What else could be the reason? But why did the pain come and go? He seemed fine when he was alone. He stopped himself. This was not the way to listen to his daughter. But then, did Ruthie truly try to listen to Gabby? She seemed to respond to Gabby with a filter of defensiveness, quick to take offense. Respectful listening was a learned skill, a key component to all harmonious relationships, and especially critical in our relationship with God. His thoughts strayed to how often he heard from Scripture only what he wanted to hear. No wonder James, the brother of the Lord Jesus, challenged his readers to be quick to listen, slow to speak. It was always better to listen than to speak. Always.

Suddenly he realized he had stopped listening *and* speaking to Ruthie. The very thing he had just spun around in his mind! He was here, but not here. Present but absent. His thoughts had left the room and wandered off, while his body remained. She could tell too. She stood before him, a deeply annoyed look on her face.

"Ruthie, did you tell Gabby how you felt?"

"Yes. I told her she was really pushing my buttons. She answered in such a typical Gabby way."

"How so?"

"She asked me where my buttons were. And she was serious! Dad . . . she's crazy."

"She's . . . literal."

Ruthie frowned. "Call it what you will, but I think she's weird. How much longer is she going to stay?"

"Honey, as long as she wants to. She's family." He put down his book. "Ruthie, do you know what the German word for hospitality is?"

"I have no idea."

"*Gastfreundschaft*. It means friendship for the guest."

"But is Gabby our guest? You said she was our family."

"It shouldn't matter. Hospitality is an attitude. By welcoming others into our home, we're sharing the love of Christ with them."

Ruthie frowned. "I don't think her mother sent her here to help. I think she sent her here because she needed a break from her."

There might be some truth to Ruthie's observation, but David knew what was really irking her. Earlier today, Gabby had spotted Ruthie and Luke Schrock holding hands on the way home from school and announced the news at supper in front of everyone, including his mother, who was horrified. Ruthie was mortified, then furious. To David, that news was worrying. Luke Schrock was the church's juvenile delinquent in the making. Again he struggled to stop his train of thought and concentrate on what Ruthie was saying.

"I don't understand why people think they need to fix us when they've got plenty of problems themselves." She turned to head to the stairs to go to bed.

David raised his voice a notch. "You don't mention Noah Yoder anymore." Yardstick had been Ruthie's latest crush—until recently.

She kept her hand on the doorjamb, though she did turn to look at him. "All he does is run. It's all he thinks about or talks about. Or does."

Yardstick was the son of Ephraim Yoder, who had died recently and left a pile of unpaid bills. David knew where he was running to—he had two part-time jobs after school. "Since when have you and Luke Schrock become friendly?"

"Since . . . this school year started." She looked down at her toes. Eyes still cast down, she pushed at the corner of the rug with her toes. "He's not as bad as everyone thinks. He just likes to have everyone scared of him."

"Why?"

She shrugged. "Luke says . . . it keeps life in Stoney Ridge . . . interesting."

A sharp pain shot through David's stomach.

⌒

Despite the disruption to her carefully ordered life in Ohio, Abigail was finding some positive experiences in Stoney Ridge. Even living with a houseful of young cousins was not as stressful as she had assumed it would be. They were pleasant girls, all but Ruthie, who had a very bad attitude.

Take yesterday, for example. Abigail was getting the mail at the mailbox when she saw Ruthie and the boy next door walking home from school, hand in hand. Abigail's attention was diverted from Ruthie's questionable behavior by a letter from her mother, and she opened it quickly, hoping to read good news about her father. Typical of her mother, Father was never mentioned. The letter was primarily filled with news about the people in their church and pointed suggestions for Abigail: There's no need to over-volunteer facts from the books you read, especially if no one has asked you about them. Try to be flexible when plans change without notice. Seek out ways to be thoughtful without being told.

How could anyone be thoughtful without being told *what* would be considered thoughtful?

She did try to put into practice her mother's advice. She spent the late afternoon reorganizing the canned goods in the basement and tossing out the jars that had bulging lids— probable evidence of botulism, which could cause food poisoning and risk horrific, lingering deaths for the entire family.

It was fortunate that Abigail had studied canning. Ruthie had clearly done minimal research on the topic.

At dinner, she remembered that she saw Ruthie and the boy next door holding hands, and thought her uncle might like to know. So she said it. Again, she was trying to be thoughtful.

Ruthie was no longer talking to her.

In retrospect, Laura told her, Abigail should have told him privately. Uncle David made up for Ruthie's bad attitude, though. Naturally, Abigail felt a familial attachment to him because he resembled her own father. Their voices, in particular, were eerily similar. But it was more than that. Her uncle was . . . unique among men. While it was true that her uncle ran a loose ship—very unlike the way he grew up, in Mammi's highly controlled household, and unlike the way you'd imagine he'd parent—there was something about it that was both surprising and refreshing.

Take family devotions, for example. Abigail was aware that each Amish community had their own way of carrying out family devotions. In her Ohio church, devotions were not considered necessary. Nor was reading the Bible. Nor was praying throughout the week. The bishop in Ohio felt that time spent in church sufficed.

But in Uncle David's home, after breakfast, each family member would push their chairs back, reach for a Bible from the stack in the corner, and kneel. Each morning, a chapter from the New Testament would be read aloud, with every family member taking a turn at a verse—a habit that Abigail thought was very wise because it held the attention of those little redheaded cousins.

But devotions didn't end at reading a chapter of the Bible. Uncle David would ask if anyone had questions. Questions!

About the Bible! And her cousins did have questions, especially—what a surprise!—Ruthie. That girl was skeptical about everything. *Everything.* Uncle David listened and answered each question, in depth. It wasn't a particularly time-efficient devotion, but it was rather . . . thought provoking.

Before bedtime each evening, the family would gather again around the kitchen table, push their chairs back again, and kneel. This time, Uncle David would read out of the black prayer book. Abigail's own father had the same pattern, but he only read the same prayer each night. Same prayer. Every night. Uncle David read a different prayer each evening.

Abigail found herself looking forward to these family gatherings.

Another unexpectedly pleasant circumstance was the absence of her grandmother for the middle part of each day. Mammi was preoccupied with the complete rearrangement of Uncle David's store and took Laura along with her to carry out the task. Abigail was entirely supportive of her grandmother's efforts to reorganize the store. She was a big advocate for efficiency and productivity, and the Bent N' Dent was in dire need of both. It was a truly appalling store—boxes were stacked in corners, fruit and vegetables were displayed right next to bags of BBQ charcoal. What if a bag broke open and the dust from the charcoal settled on an apple or a potato? Poisonous!

Don't even get her started on her uncle's cluttered office/storeroom. How could Uncle David find anything in that mess? Why, even his chair couldn't budge an inch. Abigail thrived on creating structure and order; nothing made her happier than to find a better, faster way to do something.

If her mind did not remain entirely focused on breaking through the brick wall, she would be at the store helping her grandmother and sister each day. But she couldn't allow herself to be distracted from her main objective.

Distractions, she believed, were the reason most people did not accomplish their goals. So even though she was sorely tempted to join her grandmother on the Bent N' Dent reorganization project, and she did feel a little concerned about the look of exhaustion on her uncle's face each afternoon as he returned with Mammi and Laura in the buggy, she kept her attention firmly focused on the brick wall.

⁓

Life had never seemed more out of control to David.

After his recent talk with Ruthie about hospitality as an attitude, he looked up the Latin word for hospitality, *hospes*, and noticed that *hostis*, the Latin word for hostility, was listed directly below it. A curious combination. He wondered who, centuries and centuries ago, had first coined those words, nearly identical but for two letters, and if he might have been inspired to think those words up during a visit from relatives. A visit from this old Roman's well-meaning but overly intrusive mother, perhaps.

David's mother had alienated nearly all the customers who came into the store, if not all. Fewer and fewer of the old codgers arrived before lunch to play checkers. His mother had dragged the rocking chairs out of the main room and stacked them in David's cluttered office. She even rolled up the braided rug that circled the woodstove and tucked it behind David's desk, so that his chair couldn't move. He had to climb over his desk to get into the chair.

Hank Lapp was outraged. "She treats our customers like potential shoplifters!"

"Not all of them, Hank." Just the old men who loitered all day. More importantly, since when did Hank consider himself a part-owner of the Bent N' Dent?

"And she's undoing all of Jesse's and my improvements!" he sputtered at David.

While it was true that his mother *was* undoing Hank and Jesse's doings, David was never convinced that the "doings" should be classified as improvements. Not to the bottom line of the store, anyway. But some of it had definitely been a plus to building community, and for that, he was full of regrets. "She hasn't undone everything, Hank," David said to mollify him. "We'll change things back after she goes home."

"WHOA!" Hank barked. He thrust a sandwich in David's face. "Is this going to leave when she leaves?"

David looked at the sandwich: sliced roasted turkey, fresh lettuce grown in Amos Lapp's greenhouse, generously lathered in homemade mayonnaise, all tucked between two slices of thick, crusty wheat bread. It looked delicious. It *was* delicious.

And that was the challenge, right there. The one change made by Jesse and Hank that his mother did approve of was the selling of fresh sandwiches. However, she had completely upgraded the selection, and Molly was no longer the bread maker for the store, which troubled David. His daughter needed this role. It had made her feel important.

Kind-natured, somewhat passive and pliable, Molly was often overshadowed by her siblings. She was right in the middle of the pack—Katrina and Ruthie were older than her, as was Jesse, the only boy, and the twins were younger than her. After his wife Anna died, food became a source of comfort for Molly, perhaps too much so, but David hoped that baking bread for the store might be the answer. She seemed so pleased to have the task, and her bread *was* improving. She hardly ever forgot to add yeast anymore.

But David's mother had been alarmed by Molly's portly appearance when she first arrived. She promptly shooed her out of the kitchen.

Hank was waiting for an answer, in between bites of sandwich.

"I'm going to see what I can do about keeping up the quality of those sandwiches," David said, nodding, but in a rather distracted fashion. It meant he would have to have an uncomfortable conversation with his mother about teaching Molly how to make better bread. His mother was so task oriented that she didn't have the patience to show Molly how it was done, much less to work at Molly's pace.

"Good," Hank said, raising his coffee cup to his lips and draining it noisily. "'Cuz Jesse and me, we've got some other ideas in the works. If you could keep one thing consistent, that would help."

And wasn't that the truth for just about everything in David's life?

Hank thumped his hat back on his head and seemed to mellow. He leaned forward to whisper, "A man like you can't be expected to stand up to a woman like that. It ain't in your nature."

Mystified, David watched Hank stride out the door. What was *that* supposed to mean?

He went back to his office to finish up some orders. He heard the bell ring and a customer come in, then he heard his mother's voice as she spoke to the customer. He waited for a moment to see if he might be called in to find something—that was the typical scenario each time a customer came in. Since his mother's reorganization had started, no one could find anything—but it sounded like things were being handled, so he turned his attention back to his order.

And then he recognized this customer's voice. Birdy. His pen stilled in the middle of an order. He was completely distracted.

Just outside his office door, he could hear his mother and Birdy having a conversation. An unexpected ripple of disquiet swept through him. His mother had no idea that Birdy was a Glick, nor that she was the one David had started to court. But Birdy would quickly figure out that Tillie was his mother. How would she react?

He heard a crash of glass, followed by silence, then Birdy's profuse apologies. She must be nervous. Whenever she felt nervous, she became clumsy. She referred to herself as "the most accident-prone Glick of all time."

David froze. He should go out there. Of course he should. He should introduce Birdy to his mother. This was the perfect opportunity. Just a casual encounter, nothing too formal. It would be the right thing to do, the right way to honor Birdy, the right way to handle his mother.

He should go. Absolutely.

He stayed in his office and let the opportunity pass.

⁓

Jesse walked up the driveway of Windmill Farm, deep in thought. He needed to find a certain kind of square bolt, just the right dimensions, to replace Eli Smucker's brittle old ones, and he couldn't locate them to order anywhere. He opened the door of the buggy shop and found Yardstick Yoder poking around his bench, helping himself to a plate of biscuits Fern had left for him. "Hey! What are you doing?"

Yardstick spun around, one half-eaten biscuit in his hand. "Waitin' on you. You're late. You said to be here right after school let out." He polished off the rest of the biscuit in one bite.

Jesse eyed him suspiciously. Yesterday more tools had gone missing. Had he stumbled upon the thief? A few days a week, Yardstick worked after school for Amos Lapp, doing odd chores around the farm. On those days, like yesterday, he would have access to the buggy shop. Jesse knew the boy and his mother were under a financial strain, though it was hard to believe a hammer or wrench could do much to help that. He walked up to Yardstick, checking for any odd bulges under his coat. He glanced at the pegboard but nothing was missing.

He looked Yardstick up and down, frowning. Schier gaar gfange un doch net grickt. *Almost caught but not quite.* He was going to have to keep an eye on this boy. Wasn't this always the way it turned out? The one you least suspected.

Yardstick jutted his chin out. "Have you thought about my terms for grocery deliveries?"

Appalling. Jesse very nearly caught him in an act of thievery, and the boy had the gall to demand a sky-high wage. "I've thought about it."

"Good, because I have something to add on to it."

Jesse stared at him. "You can't be serious."

"I'm always serious. I want running shoes thrown in. Good ones." He lifted one scuffed boot in the air, high enough that Jesse could see a hole in the sole.

155

"Yardstick, I am trying to do you a favor and give you a job at something you're obviously good at."

"I have a job. Two, in fact. If I have to give those up, it'd better be worth it for me."

"You're shoveling manure. I'm offering you a chance to run. To run!"

"I make more money shoveling manure than what you're offering me. And I don't need no new shoes to shovel." He walked up to Jesse, full of bravado. "Also, I want a percentage of every delivery. The way I figure it, the heavier the groceries, the more they cost. The more they cost, the more I earn."

Highway robbery.

Yardstick's thoughts seemed to wander. He walked around the buggy shop, looking things over, grabbing the last biscuit as he examined the tools hanging tidily on the pegboard. Jesse's biscuits! "And I want a free sandwich each day," he said, his mouth full. "The kind your grandmother makes. Your dad gave me one today." He rubbed his stomach in delight. "I don't want those sandwiches your sister Molly makes. I've tried one of those too." He made a face. "What do you say?" He shoved his hand out for a shake.

A silence fell while Jesse turned this extortion over in his mind. "What do I say? I say that you are nothing but a—"

The door to the buggy repair shop opened and in walked Miriam Schrock, followed by her brothers Luke and Sammy. C.P. jumped up to greet them as Jesse's mind went blank, completely empty, like a chalkboard that had just been erased.

"Are we interrupting?" Mim asked, ruffling C.P.'s ears. His favorite thing. How did she know?

Jesse was transfixed, rooted to the spot; he couldn't think a moment ahead. *Stunning.* That was the only word that came to mind. She was absolutely stunning. Petite and fine-boned, a striking dark-haired beauty.

Yardstick tensed and kept one eye on Luke, who kept an eye on him. "Jesse and I were just agreeing to the terms of my employment at the Bent N' Dent. And otherwise." He reached out and grabbed Jesse's hand to give it a shake. "Isn't that right?"

Jesse gave a brief nod. He thought he did, anyway. His mind and his body seemed misaligned. Strangely out of kilter, the way a loose axle affects the glide of a buggy.

Yardstick dashed out the door, leaving an awkward silence. C.P. left Mim and wandered over to Luke. He made a little buzz-saw growl in his throat, which Jesse admired. His puppy had a fine sense of discernment. He called C.P. to his side, all the time unable to take his eyes off Mim.

She was so lovely, queen-like, with all that black raven hair. Did Danny Riehl appreciate her? he wondered.

Mim pushed her glasses up on the bridge of her nose. "Are you all right?"

"Yes." His voice came out in a crack and Luke gave a snort. Jesse threw him a look. There was a devilish half grin on that boy's face. Jesse cleared his throat and turned his attention back to Mim. "Never better." He was having trouble keeping his thoughts in order. *Pull yourself together, man!* "How can I be of service?"

"I'm working on a Christmas gift for my mother. I want to fix up an old wooden wheelbarrow to put some flowerpots in it, and I wondered if you ever came across old hardware." She walked around the repair shop, stopping to peek into Eli Smucker's buggy. "Maybe not. I suppose I could go see if the old sisters have something in their garage. They've got so much stuff in that place, it could be a museum."

Jesse nearly keeled over. "Miriam! You're a genius! Thank you, thank you!" He saw Amos drive up the driveway and ran to meet him, to borrow his horse and buggy for an errand. He was halfway to the Sisters' House before he realized he had left Mim waiting for an answer in the buggy shop. And C.P.! He had forgotten about him entirely.

He squeezed his eyes shut. Gabby's single-mindedness was catching.

11

Outside the house, Abigail was intercepted by her grandmother, whom she generally avoided due to the probability
of some sort of complaint.

"Ora Nisley is willing to give it another chance. He'll
be here for supper tonight. You must be here." As Abigail
opened her mouth to object, Mammi lifted a hand in the
air to stop her from continuing. "You must. No excuses."

"Mammi, I don't think your matchmaking is a good idea."

"Ora Nisley is different. He's highly motivated to find a
wife." Mammi extended her hand toward her. "I think you'll
find if you just try harder—"

Try harder? In what way? When it came to working with
people, particularly male people, Abigail made mistake after
mistake after mistake. That's why she preferred deceased
people in old family trees. Much easier. But her grandmother
wasn't able to comprehend a thing like that.

"—and focus on the ones who are here and now, not long
gone. That is a far more valuable pursuit than tracking down
old letters and diaries."

"That's it!" Abigail clapped her hands together. "Why, Mammi, you've given me a wonderful idea! I can interview the oldest inhabitants of Stoney Ridge and see what information I can track down."

Molly walked past them and stopped to chime in. "Oldest inhabitants? That would be the sisters of the Sisters' House. They're as old as the hills. Older. But don't listen to Emma. She's kinda—" she whirled one finger around her ear—"loopy."

"I really want to finish this genealogy for my father. *This* one. I need to do this for him."

Mammi had been listening to her, head cocked, eyes narrowed. "Is it for him or for you?"

Maybe both. "Just let me finish. I started it and I need to finish it. I need to see this through."

"Why? Why is it so important to complete it? You've already done plenty of work on it. What does it matter if it's got some holes?"

"Because . . . this client needs the whole picture. Everybody does. You can't just pick and choose the parts you want to."

Mammi laid a hand on her arm. "I didn't realize you felt so strongly about it."

How could she have missed that? Mammi didn't realize anything! Abigail tried another tack. "Finishing this family tree will make all the difference to Dad."

"I'm sorry, Gabby, but the well-being of your father is not up to you."

"Then to whom? Who else? Sometimes I think I'm the only one who believes that my father will get well."

Mammi's head rocked back a little, as if she'd just been slapped. She looked at Abigail as if she didn't quite know who she was anymore. Her eyes grew suspiciously shiny. "Gabby, life isn't as simple and logical as you think it is. As much as you want something, it doesn't mean it's going to happen." She turned to leave the room, but stopped at the jamb to turn back. "I only want you to be happy," she said, almost like a command. "Be here for dinner."

Abigail grabbed her coat and went outside to take down some laundry, stiff in the cold. As she unclipped the laundry pegs and folded the frozen sheets, she made a mental list of the problems that had accumulated in the past forty-eight hours and which now required urgent attention:

1. The Meddling Mammi Problem. Tillie Yoder Stoltzfus was a one-woman hurricane: unexpected and everywhere.

2. Then came the Ruthie Laundry Problem, which had now escalated to include the Ruthie Canned Goods Problem. Apparently, Ruthie was no longer speaking to Abigail. Molly had to tell her that late-breaking news because Abigail hadn't noticed. There was an obvious reason for Ruthie's quick-to-take offense attitude. In Abigail's mind, and in the mind of most, no doubt—Ruthie had in her veins a fair measure of Yoder blood.

3. The Glick Family Bible Problem. This issue was of serious concern and occupied every waking moment. How would Abigail be able to get a look at that Bible? True, as a Stoltzfus, she was viewed with suspicion by Freeman Glick, but he also seemed to be a man who might enjoy having someone show interest in his heritage. Why would he be so resistant to letting her look through it? Unless . . . unless he had something to hide.

Interesting.

Her father often told her she could find the solution to any problem in her own unique way. That was always an extremely helpful remark to hear; however, it often struck her as a polite way to wave her away and failed to address any immediate dilemma.

⁂

Jesse was flabbergasted. He had never in his entire life seen a house that was filled with more objects, bits and pieces, and junk, than the Sisters' House. It was like walking through the basement and attics of the Smithsonian in Washington, DC, a place he'd never actually been to, but his cousin Gabby spoke of it so often, and in such infinite, exhausting detail, he felt as if he had.

The sisters were delighted to have someone show interest in their belongings and suggested that he start his hunt for square bolts in their carriage house, the most likely place for old hardware to be. "Papa saved everything," Sylvia assured him. "He said things today weren't built of the same quality as they were years ago, when he was young." When that would have been, Jesse could only guess. The sisters were as old as Methuselah; which century would their father have lived in when he was a young man?

He spent a few hours hunting and pecking through bags, boxes, jars, old chests. It was apparent that someone had started to organize things—Bethany Schrock, he recalled, had begun the massive task but then was offered a job at the Bent N' Dent, so she happily abandoned the cleanup project for the old sisters and he could see why. Organizing the Sisters' House was not for the faint of heart. It was overwhelming.

He had come across quite a few mouse skeletons, two shed snake skins, and something flattened and furry he didn't dare try to identify. But he did find an old wooden trunk, filled with junk, that might be of interest to his cousin Gabby.

By suppertime, his stomach was complaining and he hadn't found the bolts, but he wasn't at all discouraged. Just the opposite. He felt like he was a detective, on a hunt for clues. He was confident that square bolts could be found in this carriage house and, even better, the hardware Mim Schrock needed for her wheelbarrow, which would make her indebted to him. He blew out the kerosene lantern, determined to return tomorrow for more happy hunting.

Life suddenly seemed to be brimming with possibilities.

But when he got back to the buggy repair shop, he was met by a hungry puppy that had chosen the interior of Eli Smucker's buggy as the site to relieve itself. And Jesse's favorite screwdrivers had gone missing.

David was engrossed in a book, swept off to the time of the Reformation, when he heard someone clear her throat. He looked up to see his daughter Ruthie in front of his desk in the living room, waiting to be noticed, fists at her hips the way his mother often stood, a strident pose. In fact, she looked remarkably similar to his mother. It was a startling thought.

"Dad, what are you going to do about Molly?"

He put his book down. "What do you mean?"

"Didn't you notice how much she had to eat for supper tonight?"

Yes, in fact, he had noticed. Three helpings of Amish

Haystack, two of sweet potato pie. "Did something happen at school to upset her?"

"One of the horrible boys made up a song about her. 'Molly, Molly, 2x4, can't get through the kitchen door.'"

Oh. His heart sank. He remembered something Anna used to say: "A mother is only as happy as her saddest child." A father too.

He had been aware that the fragile confidence Molly had gained as the Bent N' Dent's sole bread maker had slipped away in the last two weeks. In its place was an insatiable appetite. A source of comfort, he realized.

"I can't *believe* what Birdy is doing about it."

"What?"

"Nothing!"

"Nothing?"

"Nothing of any impact. She's having Molly come to Moss Hill tomorrow afternoon to bake cookies. Molly is going to leave the cookies on the boy's desk."

"I see. And you think that won't have any impact?"

"No. They'll just tease her all the more. If I were the teacher, I would have that boy clean out the outhouses for the rest of the year. And wear a sign on his back saying I AM A BULLY. That would stop him."

As David pondered Birdy's strategy, he was suddenly filled with a great sense of pride. She was helping Molly to attack the bully with kindness. There were some teachers who would be only too eager to shame that boy. Shame could be a very strong means to encourage children to behave well, but was it a lasting lesson? Would it truly change a child's heart? He thought not.

"Let's give Birdy and Molly a chance to solve the problem

their way. The outhouses will always be there, and if that boy had to wear a sign that proclaimed his sins, it wouldn't be long before everyone would eventually have some sort of sign." Besides, this way Molly would be getting extra attention from Birdy, someone who could be very beneficial. That was reassuring to him, evidence that Birdy knew what she was doing about this teasing problem. "Ruthie, is Luke Schrock behind this?"

"No!" She glanced at her feet. "He used to tease her, but he's stopped. It's Leroy Glick. He's the one who teases Molly. He's awful."

Leroy Glick. Freeman's son. Why wasn't David surprised that Leroy would be part of this?

She lifted her head abruptly. "But I could ask Luke to take care of it."

He turned sharply to look at her. "What does that mean?"

She hunched her shoulders and squinted at the lantern light on his desk. "He could just scare him. He doesn't have to beat him up."

"Ruthie." The word came out in a hoarse whisper. He looked at his daughter, the one who most resembled his wife, and couldn't believe those terrible words had come out of her mouth. She'd said it so easily: *He could just scare him. He doesn't have to beat him up.*

"Violence is never justifiable," he said, his voice nearly shaking. "Vengeance belongs only to the Lord."

Ruthie frowned. "I'm trying to do something to help Molly. That's all." She spun on a dime and left the room.

David leaned back in his chair and let out a deep sigh. The lantern on his desk hissed and sputtered as the small flame died out, throwing the room into darkness.

What kind of influence was Luke Schrock having over his daughter?

⸻

Mammi answered the door to warmly welcome in Ora Nisley. He was fiftyish, trim, silver-haired, and quite earnest. "I'm glad you could come, Ora." Mammi waved a hand in Abigail's direction. "Here is my granddaughter Abigail, whom I've told you so much about."

Abigail forced a tight, fake smile and offered her hand to shake Ora's, but he seemed startled by the action and flinched, lifting his hands slowly in the air as if surrendering. An awkward moment followed until Abigail realized that Ora didn't intend to shake her hand. Ah yes! He was germophobic. She could understand his concern. Uncle David's household was teeming with germs.

Mammi stepped in. "Abigail was so sorry to have missed meeting you last Sunday."

"Not really," Abigail said, and Mammi's eyebrows shot up.

"May I see you in the other room?" Mammi said to her, which meant that Abigail had made a social blunder. She followed her grandmother to the living room. Mammi glared at her. "You must be more polite to Ora."

Polite? How was being honest considered to be the opposite of being polite? Laura had tried to explain it to her once—that little white lies could be used to avoid hurting someone's feelings. But what was the difference between a little white lie and a giant black lie? Where was the line drawn? It was always a conundrum to Abigail. But from the look on Mammi's face, now was not the time to pursue an explanation. She nodded and followed Mammi back into the entry hall. Ora was no longer there.

They found him washing his hands at the kitchen sink. As he reached out for the soap, Abigail gave a shout. "Ora, stop! If you think shaking a hand is germy, you wouldn't believe what kind of bacteria is on a wet bar of soap!"

Ora dropped the soap on the floor. "I had no idea!" He reached for a rag on the counter to wipe his hands.

"No! Not a rag! Filled with microbes."

Ora held his hands in the air, panic-stricken. "I don't know what to do!"

Abigail hurried over to tear off a paper towel to hand to him. "There. This is safest."

Again a look of warning from Mammi, but less severe this time.

12

Toward the end of that week, construction workers began to drill the oil wells on Moss Hill. David stopped by to see the work commence and joined Andy, Katrina, and Thelma at a distance from the equipment. Andy Miller had assured him that the dust and gravel and traffic would disappear as soon as the pumping units were installed. "Once everything is built," Andy had promised more than once, "there will be very little impact."

David hoped so. Right now, the hillside was a flurry of noisy, dirty, chaotic activity, with trucks rolling up and down the hastily built dirt road. The air was filled with sounds of drills, cement trucks were pouring cement into pipes sent into the earth. It was disturbing.

Moss Hill was an unusual spot in Stoney Ridge—it was the highest point in Stoney Ridge, set apart from most of the town, covered in rocks . . . and moss. Thelma and Katrina had made quite a business out of that moss. Had the hill any tillable acreage, David wouldn't have gone along with the plans to drill for oil, though he knew of plenty of farmers who leased portions of their land to oil companies and continued to farm around the pumps. Considering this was the first time the church had allowed oil drilling, he was grateful it wasn't a controversial piece of land. The entire process was already inviting jibes from the locals. Yesterday, in the store, the old men had scrounged up chairs and were gathered around the woodstove. Hank Lapp asked David for a cup of Texas Tea. David poured a cup of Lipton tea and held it out to him. Hank Lapp started laughing so hard he had tears rolling down his cheeks. David didn't know that Texas Tea was a term for petroleum, which brought howls of laughter from the men.

"They're going to drill down four thousand feet," Andy said. "The drilling goes pretty fast. It'll only take about a few weeks to get the two pumpjacks in place and working. Then you'll hardly be aware of the drills. These trucks will be gone. A portable generator will keep the pumpjacks going."

"Why are they called pumpjacks?" Katrina had to shout over the sounds of the drilling equipment.

"It's got all kinds of names," Andy said. "Oil horse, donkey pumper, nodding donkey, rocking horse, dinosaur, Big Texan, thirsty bird. They all refer to the same thing—it's the piston pump in an oil well."

"I like rocking horse," Katrina said.

"As do I," Thelma said. "We'll call those two pumps our Moss Hill rocking horses."

David turned to Andy. "So how does the oil company get the oil?"

"See those holding tanks? That's where the oil goes until it gets picked up."

David had to cup his ears to hear Andy. "Who picks it up?"

"That's another company. Think of it as being similar to a dairy. Whenever the holding tanks are full, the truck arrives to siphon out the oil. Or to dispose of the salt water in the water tank." Andy pointed to the last tank. "That's a water tank."

"Why would there be salt water in an oil well?"

"It's a by-product of drilling. It comes up from deep underground aquifers along with the oil."

Katrina's head bobbed up. "You mean, ocean water?"

"In a way," Andy said. "It's seawater trapped in the land, from a time when the earth was covered in ocean water. But salt water is ten to thirty times saltier than ocean water."

"Why?" Katrina said. David was impressed with her curiosity about this venture. She wanted to know every single detail. That was a marked difference from the girl he had raised, a girl who had little patience for learning. Once something was difficult, she had lost interest and moved on. She was changing, he realized. Maturing into adulthood, and it pleased him to no end.

"Underground aquifers are in contact with all kinds of minerals. The water ends up more saline than seawater, even though it's far from the oceans." He pointed to a tank. "That's the saltwater tank. The water has to be disposed of carefully so it doesn't contaminate the soil and render it sterile. Some larger wells pump it back underground, but these are too small to warrant that kind of equipment."

David gazed around the hillside, his mind ruminating over a verse in Genesis: "And God said, Let the waters under the heaven be gathered together unto one place, and let the dry land appear: and it was so. And God called the dry land

Earth; and the gathering together of the waters called he Seas: and God saw that it was good." There was so much still to learn. So many hidden things left to discover.

"Thelma and Katrina's moss farming can carry on without disruption." Andy smiled at David. "I'm glad you were willing to try this. I think there's enough benefits to outweigh the negatives, if there even are any negatives."

"Yes. I'm sure you're right." He hoped Andy was right. David was relying on the young man's vast and varied knowledge about oil traps, his skills and judgment for this project.

David walked down the hill and noticed a tall man standing on the road, watching the construction. Freeman Glick.

"You're welcome to go up the hill so you can see it up close," he said as he approached Freeman.

He was staring, looking at David with his usual inscrutable glare. "This is as close as I want to get."

Freeman had spoken a metaphor. The two men stood a yard apart, each waiting for the other to speak.

David carefully composed his face into a calm and mild expression. "Freeman, you can't pretend the lot switching didn't happen. It's not going to go away. You are in need of repentance."

"I was following Elmo's directions. No different than Abraham."

"But it is different. Abraham didn't know that the lots had been switched so that he would become deacon. You knew. And you did three times—for your brother Levi, for Abraham, and again for yourself."

"I did what I did for the benefit of the church. That's what my role is."

"What do you think your role is as bishop?"

"To guide and instruct the community. To lead them in worship."

"But not to interfere. Not to take over."

"The church needs help."

"And we do need help. No one would argue with that point. I'm not accusing you of being self-serving. I realize your intention was for the good of the church. But Freeman, you took it upon yourself to decide what was best for the church."

"And you?" He lifted an arm toward the construction site of the oil wells. "You don't think you are guilty of that same thing? You are pillaging the earth for oil—and why? To sell it. To make money. And what will that oil be used for? Cars. Airplanes. Electricity. Things our people don't even use." He shook a large finger at David. "How dare you lecture me when you are doing the exact same thing."

"This land belongs to Thelma Beiler."

"And will one day belong to your daughter."

"Yes. Thelma made Katrina her heir, but that day won't come for many years."

"And you are dallying with my sister's affections. Perhaps one day, you will be the owner of this land."

Dallying? Dallying with Birdy? How insulting. David ignored that outrageous implication. "It was Thelma's and Katrina's decision, together, to allow the wells to be drilled. Since when have we stopped someone from starting a business?"

"When it contradicts biblical principles."

"As for the argument about how the oil will be used after it's sold—is this business venture so different from Daniel Fisher's? He hires out as an electrician. And Mose Smucker grows tobacco to sell—though no one in our church smokes cigarettes." None that he was aware of, anyway. Probably Luke Schrock did.

"Those oil wells will contaminate the land."

"From everything I've read and studied about, I don't agree. Thelma's hillside is untillable."

"The water will be fouled. I've done some research too."

"But there is no fresh water on her hill. There's water deep in the earth that is a by-product of drilling the wells, but it's salty water. Undrinkable. And that water will be hauled away."

"You've got a ready answer for everything, don't you, David?"

"I'm listening to your objections, Freeman. If there are any negative consequences to the oil wells, I will stop production. I did insist on a short lease for the oil wells, to allow for flexibility. But you can't compare allowing oil wells to lot switching."

"At their heart, they're the same thing. You think you know best. I think I know best."

David felt like he was banging his head against a wall. "Switching lots was a direct violation of trust. Freeman, you bungled your work terribly. It was a sin."

"And you—you're no different than Aaron, the first high priest, who built a golden calf and presented it to the people to worship." Freeman lifted his eyes toward the oil wells. "Time will tell who has bungled his work."

⸰⸱⸲⸳

On a gray afternoon, Abigail was standing in line at the Sweet Tooth Bakery, trying to decide which cinnamon roll she wanted in the case.

"Pssst."

Abigail swatted a fly or mosquito that was buzzing around her head, so small she couldn't see it.

"Pssst. Behind you."

She turned to find that round boy who liked to chew bubble gum. "What are you doing here?"

"You want to see my father's family Bible?"

She squinted at him. "Aren't you Freeman Glick's son?"

He blew a bubble at her. "Yup. Leroy Glick is the name."

"How old are you, Leroy?"

"Nine. Nearly ten."

"When's your birthday?"

"Next October."

Why, that was eleven months away! He was either extremely poor at arithmetic or he was . . . shrewd. She strongly suspected the latter. "Why are you asking me about your family Bible?"

He wiggled his eyebrows in a knowing way. "Because I can get it for you."

Abigail froze. "How?"

"Next Saturday, after Thanksgiving. My dad will be gone all day. I can meet you at the Bent N' Dent and pass it to you."

"How long could I keep it?"

"Keep it? You can't keep it. You can just look at it. Maybe . . . for an hour. I have to get it back before my dad gets home."

That was somewhat disappointing news. Abigail hoped she could spend hours, days, weeks, perusing the Bible's records. Well, as her father often said, "Don't look a gift horse in the mouth." She put a hand on his shoulder. "Leroy, that would be wonderful. Thank you."

"It'll cost you."

"How much?" She would pay whatever he asked.

"One box of Bazooka bubble gum. The big box, the type that a store orders. Unopened. You can get it from your uncle at the Bent N' Dent."

"Leroy, you realize that bubble gum isn't good for your teeth, don't you? You know you'll end up looking like a withered apple doll one day."

He blew a gigantic bubble at her, so big that she could barely see his face behind it. Then he popped it with his fingers and held the wad in his hand. "First, I'm going to get a lifetime supply of bubble gum by finding the winning wrapper in the bubble gum contest. Then I'll worry about ordering a set of wooden choppers."

Abigail had never heard of bubble gum contests and thought it sounded extremely counterproductive to good dental hygiene in children. However, Leroy's teeth erosion was not her most pressing concern. Getting a chance to look at that Glick family Bible topped her list. While she realized that Freeman Glick would not approve of his son's actions, she could justify her willingness to accept Leroy's bribe on the basis that any genealogist would jump at the chance to break through a brick wall. Better still, this might hold the key to help her father break through his melancholia.

But it would be wrong to encourage Leroy's deception, accept the bribery, and provide the demanded bubble gum ransom. If not strictly illegal, it was doubtless immoral. He was only a nine-year-old boy.

Her grandmother would not have approved of this. At all.

She watched Leroy practice blowing more bubbles. After he popped an enormous bubble, she said, "What time shall we meet?"

13

After the very unproductive attempt to see the family Bible at the Freeman Glick household, Abigail decided she needed to go about her interviews in a different way. But she also decided she needed reinforcements. On Saturday afternoon she found Molly baking bread in the kitchen while Ruthie sat at the kitchen table, leafing through a magazine that Abigail was quite sure Mammi would shred, if she happened to be home, which she wasn't. "Ruthie, would you come with me to the Sisters' House?"

Ruthie gave her a curious look. "Why?"

"Molly said that they are the oldest inhabitants of Stoney Ridge. I'm hoping they might be able to shed light on a genealogy project I'm working on."

"I don't know why you enjoy this genealogy stuff. It looks boring."

Boring? Boring was one thing it wasn't. "I don't think boring is the right word."

"Dull? Dreary? Unexciting? What would you call it?"

"Thrilling."

"I think it sounds mind numbing," Ruthie said. "Trying to keep track of who's related to whom and how families all link together."

Mind numbing? Boring? *Incredible.* "You take all those dates and names, and start to fill in the blanks of a person's life."

Abigail could see in her eyes that Ruthie wasn't impressed. How could she make her understand the importance of genealogy? Then she forgot everything she wanted to convey because standing right there at the kitchen doorjamb was Dane Glick, grinning, with his squared-off cleft chin and eyes the color of root beer. When had he arrived? How long had he been standing there?

"Door was unlocked," Dane said, answering the question in her eyes, "and I saw you all in the kitchen, so figured I'd just come on in." He sat down at the kitchen table. "I'm a hobby genealogist too, for the same reasons you just described to Ruthie." He reached out for a red apple in a wooden bowl and polished it against his coat. "Genealogy is the story of the people we come from, who they were, what they cared about. It's a way to record the lives of ordinary people."

In one deft move, Ruthie closed the magazine and slipped it under her bottom on the chair. "If they're so ordinary, why does it matter?"

"Because they're part of us. We're pretty ordinary too. I like to study genealogy to see what in my ancestors resembles what I've experienced. Sometimes, I've found that my interests match my ancestors' interests. It's making history personal." He took a loud bite of apple.

Ruthie looked at him blankly. "But why? What does it matter?"

Dane chewed, then swallowed. He had all the time in the world. "You start to understand what you're made of, the kind of stock you come from."

Abigail hadn't considered genealogy from that angle. To her, it was like piecing together a puzzle, a mental exercise. It also startled her to hear Dane refer to himself as a hobby genealogist. What did that mean?

Ruthie still looked blank.

"Look at it this way, Ruthie," Dane said. "When I want to breed one of my sheep, I would look carefully at the bloodlines for multiple past generations—to find out if there are any health concerns, or personality issues. Will a sheep be healthy? Will it be stable?"

"Oh! You want to find out if you're going to die young."

"No. No! I'm just trying to show you that there's a link to how bloodlines—or people—develop."

Molly was thumping her dough over at the counter by the stove. She held the dough up—which seemed to always have a slightly gray tinge, which Abigail found rather alarming—in the air. "Like this! The starter is super old."

Why, Molly was correct! "Yes, Molly!" Abigail said. "An excellent illustration from the natural world. The yeast in bread dough could be likened to bloodlines. A little bit of the past continues on into the future. Same with a person's DNA."

Ruthie remained unconvinced. "So you're saying that my life is fixed. That the personality and interests I have are kind of . . . genetically determined into me."

Fixed? Abigail looked at Dane, who looked back at her. Genetically determined? She didn't know how to respond to that question, mainly because such a question had never occurred to her. She saw things in black and white; Ruthie seemed to only see gray. She was a baffling teenager, Ruthie was, and she clearly could not understand the critical value of genealogy.

The silence grew immense, maybe twenty or thirty seconds long, until Dane finished his apple, set down the whittled core on a napkin, and took charge. "There might be something to that in animals, Ruthie. When I breed a horse, I'm looking for certain traits and characteristics to carry forward. But God gave human beings free will. It's the driving force behind who you become. Genetics certainly are a factor, but you can either reinforce a genetic bent or not reinforce a genetic bent. No one lives a fixed life—every person has choices about how they're going to live their life. It's how you respond to those choices that makes the difference."

An interesting point. This was exactly the sort of input that Abigail valued—subtle explanations in areas that she was not skilled in, not conscious of, nor felt any need to bother with.

And then there was Dane. He was interesting too. He might be more focused than Abigail had initially presumed him to be. Perhaps with a higher intelligence, as well.

Which prompted another question. Why was Dane here?

He seemed to read her mind. "I wondered if you might want to go on a walk with me." He looked out the window. "It's a beautiful fall afternoon."

Abigail's mind went blank. Completely empty.

"She'd love to," Ruthie volunteered, a little overly eager and overly loud.

"It's not possible. I have a meeting scheduled at the Sisters' House."

"They don't know you're coming," Ruthie said, "so they won't be expecting you."

Yes, but Abigail's mind was entirely focused on interviewing the sisters. It wasn't possible to shift lanes of thought so quickly.

She hesitated, trying to come up with a rational explanation to politely turn down Dane's offer, but he jumped right into the opening. "I'll take you there. They live across town." He jumped up, took a few steps, and stood at the doorjamb, waiting for her.

Ruthie grabbed Abigail's arm. "Go with him!" she whispered. "And try not to act so funny."

Funny? Abigail had been called many things, but never funny.

This turn of events was incredibly annoying to Abigail, but she could not think of an excuse that would satisfy anyone. Dane helped her into his buggy, then ran around to the other side to climb in. He picked up the reins and flicked them to get the horse moving. His large hands looked roughened by hard work, but he held the reins with a touching gentleness.

Abigail rolled down her window and breathed in the smells of fall, the crispness in the air, sweet as apple cider on her tongue. Unfortunately, she could think of nothing to say. Then she remembered Laura's basic rule of asking a man to talk about himself. Dane had already raised the topic of training difficult horses, so she asked him to elaborate. This was an excellent move and Dane seemed quite, quite pleased by her interest.

A memorable moment.

When he finished with that topic, he kept up a running description of every farm and field along the way. They passed weather-beaten barns and outbuildings, a few cows grazing at pasture that would look up at them curiously. In all directions were brown, withered fields, empty of crops. He was quite an enthusiastic talker, that Dane. She nodded and smiled as he talked, so he would know she was listening. Laura had often said that was just the way to encourage a young man to talk. Nod and smile.

But Dane seemed to realize he was the only one who was doing the talking because he stopped abruptly and his cheeks reddened.

"So . . . I've got some questions for you about genealogies," he said.

Relief! Abigail took a deep breath, finally able to relax. She was back in the world she knew.

⌒⌒

Dane pulled the buggy up to a weathered, white-framed two-story house. Paint peeled off the wooden clapboards, the roof was missing shingles, a downspout hung perilously from the gutter, but the garden looked well tended. "This is the Sisters' House," he said, as he slid open Abigail's door. "They've lived in Stoney Ridge most of their lives."

"How many sisters are there?"

"Five, I think. Ella is the oldest." He hesitated, then added, "I have to warn you. Her memory isn't very keen. Or her mind. You can't take everything she says as fact. Or to heart."

"Understood."

"Sylvia is the youngest. She's the heart of the family. They all count on her." He grinned. "Funny how birth order has a way of catching up with you."

"How so?"

"Well, I'm the youngest in my family. No one ever listened to me. Maybe when my brothers are all old and gray and toothless, then they'll listen."

"I'm the middle one in my family, and no one ever listens to me."

"Well, that shoots a hole in my theory." Dane laughed. "Maybe it's us." He knocked on the front door a few times, waited, then knocked harder. Harder still. Just when they thought no one was at home, the door slowly opened. Four wrinkled faces with shoe-button eyes peered at them.

"Visitors!" one old sister said. Her back was quite stooped, as curved as a question mark.

"Hello, ladies. I brought David Stoltzfus's niece with me," Dane said. "She had some questions about your family tree."

"Oh, do come in," another sister said. "We were just having our afternoon tea. Won't you join us?"

"That one is Sylvia," Dane whispered. "Follow her lead. She's the boss."

Inside, clutter filled the living room, floor to ceiling, in such a way that Abigail stopped abruptly and gasped. "Oh, we've come at a bad time. You're in the midst of moving!"

"Moving?" Sylvia gazed around the room. "I suppose we've gotten too accustomed to our clutter. Our eyesight isn't what it used to be."

"We like to think of ourselves as historians," one sister volunteered.

"Savers," said another sister.

"That's Ada," Dane said. "I think. Maybe Lena."

"Hoarders," said another in an accusing voice.

"That one is definitely Fannie," Dane whispered.

A diminutive woman sat hunched in an armchair, knitting

needles clenched in her gnarled hands. The center part of her scalp was balding beneath her prayer cap, worn out from a lifetime of hair twisted tight and neat and pinned into place. She lifted her head to reveal milky eyes. "One never knows when one might need something."

Abigail felt Dane glance her way. "That'll be Ella."

Sylvia still seemed embarrassed by the condition of the room, though the other sisters didn't seem to mind at all. "Bethany Schrock was helping us get organized, but then she started working at the Bent N' Dent. Without her . . ." She hesitated.

Fannie leaned in. "Without her constant pressure and nagging."

Sylvia frowned at Fannie. "I was going to say, without Bethany's gentle encouragement, we seem to have gone back to our messy ways." She lifted some *Budget* newspapers out of a chair. "Do sit down." She moved a knitting project out of another chair. "Dane, you sit there."

Dane waited until everyone found a seat, then he sat down and yelped. He bolted up, turned, and found a stray knitting needle on his chair.

"Ah, there it is," Fannie said. She took the knitting needle from Dane and stuck it down the front of her dress. She looked at Abigail. "Now, David Stoltzfus's niece, what name do you go by?"

"I'm Abigail. I'm here because I'm trying to research the Glick family tree."

"Why, we have Glick blood!" Sylvia said. "We were all Glicks, until the turn of the century."

"The last century," Fannie said. "Not this new one."

"At that point, our branch of the tree split off." Lena sighed

. . . or was she Ada? "And now we're the last leaves on our branch. None of us sisters married."

"Ada nearly did," Lena said. "Remember that fellow who came around that long, hot summer? It was the drought year. The well ran dry that summer."

Ada's eyes sparkled. "Oh, he was a handsome fellow." She twirled one capstring, lost down memory lane. "But he wanted to move to Texas and I couldn't leave my sisters."

"No, that was asking too much," Fannie said. "Too, too much."

Abigail could see how conversations among the sisters might seem like five balls of yarn, unrolling at the same time. Prudently, she decided to veer the conversation back on course. "I was hoping you might have some information about the Glicks. Information that goes back into the 1700s and 1800s."

All five sisters lifted their heads at once, like baby birds in a nest, and talked at the same time, offering up partial names and calendar dates and confusing details, correcting each other on misinformation, of which there was an abundance.

Abigail sighed. Relying on the old sisters' sketchy, drafty memories was going to take some work. And patience. "Actually, I hoped you might have some paperwork I could look through. Old diaries or letters. Or maybe a family Bible that I could look in."

The sisters looked around the living room, cluttered from floor to ceiling with books, newspapers, boxes. A silence fell.

"It might take a little looking," Sylvia said. "We'll add it to our to-do list."

Abigail's heart sank to her shoes.

The old codgers had gone home for the day, Bethany had left early for a dentist appointment, and David was alone in the Bent N' Dent. Snatches of solitude were something he had always treasured, even more so in the last few weeks. These moments were becoming increasingly rare.

He walked around the store. His mother's reorganization was in full swing. Boxes lined the aisles. Shelves had been emptied. The hardwood floors had been rubbed with lemon oil. The next time Jesse dropped by, the two of them would move the shelving around the store. His mother had drawn a revised floor plan to allow for more shelving space, as well as a much easier flow of pathways for customers pushing carts. He stopped in the middle of the store and turned slowly in a circle.

She was right. His mother was right. The store's floor plan was going to be significantly improved. It already was. She had moved small single-purchase items close to the register at the counter, like gums and candies and breath mints, and sales for those items had quadrupled in the first week.

This, this was the side of his mother that he admired. She had a business savvy that far surpassed his own meager ability. She could see things he couldn't see, whether it was his clumsy store layout or better product placement.

Tillie Yoder Stoltzfus was not an easy woman to work with. She steamrolled over people, unaware of her effect on them. But the truth was that she *did* often know best. That was the challenge, right there.

After all, she had picked out Anna for him.

He remembered as if it were yesterday. He was twenty-two years old and painfully shy, downright tongue-tied. He'd hardly ever spoken to a girl other than his sisters, much less dared to ask one out. His life consisted of working in the family store and reading books. Until one day, his mother decided it was time he start thinking about a wife. They were alone in the store, on an afternoon much like this one, and she insisted that he invite their new neighbor's redheaded daughter to a volleyball game at the youth gathering. "She's not interested in me." She hadn't even noticed David. Hardly anyone did. And everybody—every single fellow!—had noticed Anna.

"You have to try, David. There's someone for everyone."

"Ken Schuh basst alle Fuus." *No shoe fits every foot.*

His mother lifted her finger in the air. "Let's try my way first. Ask Anna out. Then decide if there's no one for you."

So he did. He gathered every ounce of courage he could muster, stammered a weak request to drive her home from the volleyball game, and to his surprise, she smiled brightly and said, "Why, I thought you'd never ask." As if she had just been waiting for him to ask. And it turned out later, indeed she had.

That moment changed his life. That pivotal event was the very reason he was willing to accept and adjust to the things his mother insisted on, as annoying as they could be. So often, without a doubt, she was right.

A horse's loud, nose-clearing snort cut into his thoughts, and he crossed the room to look out the window and see who had arrived, so late in the day. He saw his son Jesse tie the harness reins of his horse to the hitching post with a practiced motion, then run a hand down the horse's mane in a small show of thanks to the animal, something David always did. He was growing up, Jesse was, in leaps and bounds. It filled him with pleasure to see his son make these small steps forward into manhood.

Then he felt his heartbeat give a hitch as he realized Jesse wasn't alone. Birdy Glick climbed out of the passenger side and clapped her hands together. Jesse's puppy leaped out of the buggy and sped toward the bushes as Birdy slid the buggy door shut. She took a few steps to join Jesse; they were laughing over something, and he wondered what could be so funny. He felt curiously left out.

He opened the door for them. "Jesse, Birdy, come in from the cold."

"Dad! I was heading to the store to check on a delivery, and picked up Birdy along the way."

"Hello, David!" Birdy said, smiling wide, as she came up to him. "Isn't that the most beautiful sunset you've ever seen?"

He looked past her toward the setting sun, a glowing red ball. "It surely is." It *was* glorious. How had he missed it? The puppy came flying out of the bushes, leaped up the store steps, and darted past David.

Jesse had gone behind the counter and returned with a brown package in his hands. "Got what I came for. Some new parts for Eli Smucker's rickety old buggy." He walked up to them. "Birdy, come for supper," Jesse said. "Meet my grandmother."

Birdy, always eager, said, "Why, I'd love to."

David blew out a startled breath. Meet his mother? Without any preparation, any warning? For either of them! His mother, no doubt, would drill her with questions, and Birdy would be especially sensitive to pleasing her, which would be impossible.

"Molly's not cooking anymore," Jesse said. "You'll be safe."

Birdy looked to David and her smile faded. "Perhaps another time?"

David quickly masked his concerns with a smile. "Tonight would be fine. Just fine. I'll go get my coat and we can head home." He gave her a warm smile, which she returned, relief in her eyes.

In his office, David felt a jab of pain in his gut. He reached for the Tums that he kept in his top desk drawer, grabbed a few, and chewed them rapidly as he slipped an arm through a coat sleeve. "Lord, let me feel your presence." To *feel* it. The Word of God said that his presence was always with him, that it could never be separated from him, but right now he needed to feel it, to sense it. He paused for a moment, expectantly. Waiting for something. Anything. If not a feeling, then perhaps . . . a word? Again, he waited.

Honesty. That was the word that came to him.

At the house, Jesse took the horse into the barn while David and Birdy went inside. His mother saw them approach and came to open the door. "Birdy, meet Tillie Stoltzfus. Mom, this is Birdy." *Honesty*, he sensed again. "Birdy Glick."

David's mother had a fixed expression on her face, but he knew her quick, determined mind was connecting the dots. She peered up at Birdy, who towered over her. Birdy blinked down at David's mother.

"Glick?" His mother's voice was flat.

Birdy stepped forward and tripped over the doormat, barely catching herself by grabbing onto the doorjamb to avoid stumbling into his mother. "Oh, clumsy me," she said with a girlish giggle.

"Let me take your coat," David said.

Birdy spun around sharply to face him, not realizing he was closer to her than she had assumed. He took a step back to avoid her, just as Jesse opened the door after coming in from the barn. In the next instant, David tripped backward over the open threshold and elbowed Jesse hard, knocking the wind out of him.

"You're a Glick," his mother repeated, before spinning around and heading into the kitchen. "Good heavens, they're everywhere," she grumbled, loud enough for all to hear.

Jesse wheezed for air like a dying man as he stumbled toward his chair at the table. David gave him a look to cut the dramatics. Birdy remained frozen against the entryway wall, a look on her face as if she wished she could be anywhere but here.

He smiled at her. "Come, Birdy. There's a place for you at the table."

But there wasn't.

There wasn't an inch to spare at the table and his mother was unconcerned about setting another place. She'd gone straight to the oven to remove the roasting chicken and cover it with foil. David crossed the room and opened the silverware drawer to pull out a fork and knife.

"You should have told me you were bringing someone home, David. I would have added a leaf to the table." Again, she spoke in a raised voice, just loud enough for Birdy to hear.

By now David was steaming mad. He went to the table and pushed Gabby's plate over so that she would be squeezed against Laura. The girls watched him, wide-eyed, unaccustomed to seeing David riled up. "Ruthie," he barked. "Go get the chair from my desk."

Ruthie jumped up and hurried to fetch the chair.

"David, perhaps—" Birdy started.

"Sit."

Birdy sat. They all sat, including David's stony-faced mother, as he offered a prayer of thanks for the meal. In that blessed and brief silence, he asked the Lord for an extra measure of patience tonight.

The moment heads lifted, hands reached for bowls of mashed potatoes, gravy, string beans, applesauce. Birdy jumped right in, accustomed to fending for oneself in a large family.

"Where's the chicken?" Jesse asked, fully recovered.

"I wanted to let it rest a few minutes," Tillie said. She cast a sly look at Birdy, who was scooping a second spoonful of mashed potatoes onto her plate. "I do hope there's enough."

"There's always enough," David said.

Birdy jumped up. "Let me get the chicken, Tillie. I'm closest to it."

Tillie rose to her feet from the far end of the table. "No! I want to carve it first." But Birdy was already in the kitchen, tearing off the foil that covered the chicken and lifting up the platter. She spun around with the platter in her arms just as Tillie hurried to intervene. Birdy collided with Tillie and the slippery chicken slid off the platter and went sailing. It hit the wall, leaving a greasy mark on the pale green paint, before dropping to the floor with a thud. Jesse's dog leaped on the unexpected bounty as all eyes at the table watched, dumbfounded.

"Oh dear," Birdy said. "I'm terribly sorry."

"Terrible is just the right word for it," Tillie snapped.

David felt as if he was watching a sled go downhill, pick up speed, then hit a rock and fly out of control.

⌒﹏⌒

After David had taken Birdy home, listened to her profuse apologies about the flyaway chicken, and provided equally profuse reassurances that all was well, he returned to a quiet house and an empty kitchen. Everyone was in bed, for which he was very grateful. He loved the silence of this time of day.

A piece of cake waited for him on a plate in the middle of the cleared table. He found a fork and carried the cake to his desk in the living room. He added a log to the woodstove and sat in his chair, stretching out his legs. It had been a long day.

David took up his slice of cake. It was a sponge cake as he had never experienced before: light and moist. He supposed it was the freshness of the eggs. His mother's cooking, it was . . . heavenly.

"I don't like her."

His fork froze in midair. He looked up to see his mother, standing by the jamb, arms crossed against her chest. Her face registered disapproval.

"Birdy." His mother puffed out her chest. "I don't like her."

"And why not?"

"She's ungainly, awkward, oversized. Clumsy too."

"I'll pretend I didn't hear such shallow words from you."

"She knocked over a box of spaghetti sauce jars in the Bent N' Dent. An entire box! I saw it happen with my own eyes."

"I suspect you made her nervous."

"She nearly did you in tonight. You and Jesse both."

"It was just an accident. Too many people standing at the door."

"And how do you explain the chicken mishap?"

"She was trying to help."

"Nonsense. She's completely unsuited to be a bishop's wife."

David put his fork down and pushed the plate away. The cake no longer appealed to him.

"I don't approve."

"Of what?"

"Not what. Whom. I don't approve of Birdy Glick."

"Did I *ask* for your approval?"

"I'm your mother, David. Sons should always listen to their mothers."

"If they're fourteen. But I'm forty-four. Soon to be a grandfather. I think it's time for me to choose my own friends."

"We're not talking about a friend. You're thinking of marrying her, aren't you?"

"Mother, that's really none of your business."

"I can see the writing on the wall. You're in for more heartache."

David sighed. "And why is that?"

"She's a Glick. Blood is always, always thicker than water."

He should have spoken up. This was the only way with his mother. One had to be firm with her. One had to stand up to her.

The difficulty, of course, with standing up to his mother was that it appeared to make little difference. "You don't know her at all, Mother. You don't know the kind of person she is. You haven't given her a chance."

She raised a hand to interrupt him. "David, you must be wise about this. You'll be tarred with the same brush as Freeman Glick. Everyone will assume you were all in this lot-switching business together. You need to be careful."

What did that mean, to be careful? Her next remark made this clear.

"You need to break things off with her."

"I don't want to do that," David had intended to say, but for some reason the words came out as, "I'll think about it."

14

Children were never simple, Abigail knew that, but she had not expected to find such diversity among siblings as there was in Uncle David's home. Though she and Laura were closest in age to Katrina, there was very little contact. Katrina was rarely over to visit at Uncle David's—to avoid getting cornered by Mammi might be the reason—but even when she was, she seemed preoccupied and distant. Abigail felt she hardly knew her cousin anymore. Jesse came around frequently, mostly at mealtimes, with the black puppy trailing behind him. He always had a smile and a quick joke.

Ruthie was inclined to be on the moody side. Sometimes, she would sit there, staring out of the window, and say nothing at all.

"What are you thinking of?" Abigail would ask.

Ruthie would shake her head and reply, "Nothing."

That couldn't be true. Nobody thought of nothing, but it was difficult to imagine what thoughts a girl like Ruthie might have. Sulky and sullen ones, most likely. Molly's thoughts,

Abigail had no doubt, would be quite pleasant and most likely have to do with food, which she thoroughly enjoyed. Eight-year-old Lydie was what Mammi called a social butterfly, while her twin, Emily, was happiest in her own company. She was indifferent to others, unlike Lydie, who was always invited over to friends' homes to play. Emily preferred to be home with a book.

On a Saturday afternoon, some girls stopped by to play with Lydie, who wasn't home at the time, but Ruthie intervened and invited the girls to stay and play with Emily. Emily simply stared at them and said nothing. Abigail understood Emily's reluctance to be expected to be sociable just because little girls had stopped by to play. Before she had a chance to say so, Ruthie jumped in.

"You should talk to these girls," Ruthie admonished Emily. "They are your guests, and you should go play with them."

Emily mumbled something, and all three girls went off to the yard together. But when Abigail and Ruthie looked out of the window not twenty minutes later, they saw the two visiting girls playing happily while Emily was nowhere to be seen. Abigail found her in her room, reading a book.

Ruthie was indignant and insisted she go outside with her friends.

"Leave Emily to do what she wants to do," Abigail said. "She can't help it. Remember where she comes from. Remember your people. She has their blood in her veins."

Ruthie looked at her in horror. "*What* are you talking about?"

"Books, of course. Look at how your father loves his books. Emily is her father's daughter. She takes an interest in books that most other children, or adults, would not ever bother reading. Books are in her blood."

Emily smiled up at her as Ruthie helped her get her sweater on. "I like that. Books in my blood."

Ruthie rolled her eyes. "Don't listen to Gabby and her family tree nonsense." She opened the door to shoo Emily out.

Ruthie's skepticism about the merits of genealogy was not new to Abigail. Her own mother and grandmother shared similar doubts. Abigail knew from experience that she could not sway a doubter's views. However, a few days later, she found the means to succinctly prove to Ruthie that the study of genealogy was vitally important.

It happened as Abigail was doing a favor. First for Mammi, then for her uncle. Mammi had asked Abigail to pick up a few spices for dinner at the Bent N' Dent.

Donning boots, mittens, and a warm coat, she set out for a chilly walk. The day was sunny, but the wind was brisk. Molly had given her a shortcut to get to the store, but it required cutting through a cornfield. As she crossed through the farmer's field, avoiding the spiky severed brown cornstalks, a heron rose and sailed low over a stand of pine trees. Dane Glick, she thought, would enjoy the sight of that heron. Perhaps he had already seen it swooping around Stoney Ridge.

And thinking of what Dane might like surprised her.

She came to a road, looked up and down, and saw the store in the distance at the corner of an intersection. Molly's directions, despite being the muddiest possible course, were excellent. After getting Mammi's spices, Uncle David asked her if she wouldn't mind dropping a small box of groceries off at Moss Hill on the way home. "Thelma isn't feeling well. Birdy called and asked if someone could run a few things over."

"Of course I don't mind," she told him. "Of course I don't.

I'm here to help." She had missed supper on Saturday and the chance to meet Birdy, but Laura filled her in on every detail, particularly Mammi's chilly hospitality.

Abigail hadn't realized that Moss Hill should more accurately be named Moss Mountain. It was practically vertical. She climbed up the winding driveway, up and up, so steep that she was perspiring by the time she reached the landing. Once there, she easily found the modest, well-kept house and knocked on its door. A tall, sturdy, intelligent-looking woman answered. She had brown hair and dark brown eyes, and a rather long nose, and was perhaps a few years older than Abigail. She smiled, which made her somewhat ordinary features quite pretty. If not pretty, then definitely merry.

"You must be Birdy."

"That's right."

"I'm Abigail. Uncle David's niece from Ohio. You met my sister Laura Saturday night."

"Oh, yes. Yes, of course."

"Uncle David sent a few groceries over for Thelma."

"Did he? I thought David might drop them off on his way home." Birdy blushed and looked down awkwardly. Abigail followed her gaze and noticed Birdy's hands. They were work-worn hands, strong and dependable. "Do come in." She stepped back and Abigail wiped her feet on the mat and followed her into the entryway.

"Let me see if Thelma is up to a visit. She caught a dreadful cold. Katrina is in town, at a doctor's appointment, and I just got home from teaching school."

While she waited, Abigail glanced idly around the entryway, noticing three different-sized black bonnets hanging on pegs near the door. Then she looked through the open door into a very, very tiny kitchen. A pot of sautéing onions sat simmering on the stove, sending a savory aroma throughout the house.

Birdy reappeared and said, "She's sound asleep."

"That's all right. Thelma doesn't know who I am anyway."

"That wouldn't bother her one bit. She likes to meet new people." Birdy sifted through the box of groceries. "Thank you for dropping these off. You saved me a trip."

A strange sound of metal against metal filled the air. "What in the world is that?"

"I think that's the drill," Birdy said. "For the oil well." She looked up. "I'd take you up there if I could, but I've just got dinner started and I don't want to leave Thelma. You can go up and watch, if you're interested. Just stay at a distance. Andy is up there. Tell him I sent you."

"How will I know who he is?"

Birdy smiled, and again Abigail noticed that the warmth of her smile could light a room. "Andy Miller is Amish. He'll be the only man up there who's not wearing a hard hat."

Abigail was very interested in these oil wells. She had heard her uncle discuss them, but she had no idea what they might look like. She followed the dirt path until she came to the construction site. She saw enormous pieces of equipment that were clearly designed to dig deep into the earth. The drill bit brought up soil and rock and dumped it into a pile. Curious, Abigail got as close as she dared to the dump pile.

And there—there it was!—she found the perfect illustration to succinctly make her point to Ruthie about the importance of genealogy.

Unfortunately, Ruthie was only sporadically speaking to

Abigail. On again, off again. After this morning's incident, it was off again.

Before breakfast, she had grabbed Ruthie's coat off the wall peg to go feed the chickens. She thought the coat was hers, an innocent mistake, as all coats were black. On the way back to the henhouse, she put her hands in the pockets and felt something odd. It turned out to be a tube of lip gloss. Hot pink! As she had walked into the house, she held it up in the air to ask Ruthie about it.

Reflecting upon that moment later, Abigail realized she should have waited until she was alone with Ruthie to ask her about it. Unfortunately, the entire family, *especially* Mammi, sat at the kitchen table and witnessed the sight of lip gloss. Ruthie was furious.

Well, Ruthie might not be *speaking* to her, but she didn't say anything about listening to her.

Abigail hoped there was a difference.

⌒

Early the next morning, before his girls left for school, David walked to the store. Restless with so much uncertainty in his life, he tried to concentrate on something altogether more enjoyable than church problems, something like Birdy, but found his thoughts about Birdy were equally unsettling. He was ashamed of himself for avoiding her ever since the dinner at his home.

Today was an example. He had seen Birdy walk down the road toward the schoolhouse. He could have shouted hello, could have shared a good morning like they often did as he dropped his daughters off at school, but instead he hid behind a tree until she went into the schoolhouse and shut the door.

Good grief. He was a grown man. What was wrong with him? For the last few weeks, he hadn't even found time to teach the Bible memorization classes for Birdy's scholars as he had been doing. Was that not a sign of sin in his own life? He rubbed his stomach against a mild but persistent gnawing pain. He was letting all kinds of insecurities eat away at him. Why? Why couldn't he fully embrace this new relationship God had brought into his life?

Multiple reasons, he mused, as he trudged on toward the Bent N' Dent. One was Freeman's insinuation that he was dallying with Birdy—such a careless word, "dallying" was—for his own benefit.

Could he be dallying with Birdy? Maybe he was. His mother used to say that he could sit on a fence and watch himself walk by.

But the other nagging reason stemmed from his mother's strong, *strong!* disapproval. As much as he kept trying to push away his mother's remark about blood being thicker than water out of his mind, in some center place of him, he had the same doubts. Who knew what kind of ramifications a Quieting could bring to the church in the months and years to come. Would it eventually come between him and Birdy? As hard as he tried to convince himself otherwise, it sat there nonetheless. Doubt had settled in for a stay.

❦

Abigail poured herself another cup of tea, sat down at the kitchen table, and for a brief moment, allowed her thoughts to wander. For several reasons, the kitchen was a good place to be. First, there was the view, that of a small valley with a creek running through it, an Amish farm—Eagle Hill—across the road, all bordered by a ridge. A stand of trees made a sound like ocean waves when the wind and rain blew through the tree limbs. Or that, at least, was the sound which Abigail imagined the ocean to make. She had never been to the sea, which was far, far away from central Pennsylvania. But she could imagine it, if she closed her eyes tightly and listened to the trees swaying in the wind. Perhaps one day she would visit it, and would stand on the sandy beach and let the cold salty water wash over her toes. Perhaps.

The other advantage to sitting at the kitchen table to work was the fact that there was always something to watch out the window. Like now, for example: Jesse had left his puppy with them for the day. C.P. was out in the yard, chasing a foolish rabbit that dared to venture into the yard. The rabbit made a dash for the thickets and C.P. chased behind, only to stop abruptly at the thickets, ears pricked, baffled by the rabbit's disappearance.

Abigail raised her teacup to her lips and looked out over the brim . . . and practically choked on her sip. There was Dane, waving happily to her, standing in front of the kitchen window.

She opened the kitchen door and looked up into his eager face. Their eyes held for several beats while her cheeks warmed. She tucked a stray lock of hair behind one ear. "Why are you here?"

"The rain has stopped and it's going to be a beautiful day! I thought it'd be fun to show you something special."

"Not possible." She had a long to-do list.

"It's entirely possible." Laura appeared out of nowhere and spoke over her shoulder. "Gabby'd love to go with you, Dane."

"I can't. I have my afternoon all planned out."

"Plans are made to be changed," Dane said with a grin, as Laura grabbed Abigail's coat and bonnet off the wall peg and gently pushed her out the door and toward him.

No, Abigail thought, plans were made to help one accomplish her tasks. But she seemed to have no choice in this matter. There was no point in throwing up one's hands in despair. Her father was always doing that—throwing up his hands with a shrug. Abigail followed Dane down the path toward his buggy. She assumed he was going to take her to the Sisters' House, but Dane drove the buggy in the opposite direction of town.

"Where are you taking me?" Abigail asked.

"Just be open to something different." He must have seen that she was resisting. "Relax. There's nothing wrong with a little spontaneity. It keeps a person young."

She was disturbed by Dane's logic. He was remarkably perceptive about her. She had never mentioned this to him, but she had often been accused of acting like a little old lady.

Was she turning into her father? He refused to go anywhere new, to try new food, to meet new people.

"So?" Dane said, turning right on a road Abigail had not traveled. "You're doing okay?" He was watching her in that intense way he had, the way that made her feel as if he was reading her thoughts.

Abigail took a deep breath and gave a quick nod. "Carry on."

Dane drove the buggy up a long, steep driveway, so steep that at one point he jumped out of the buggy and asked her to get out too. "It's easier for the horse to pull the buggy," he said, which she thought was very humane, though she was feeling increasing anxiety as they walked up a gravel road. The trees on each side of the road were so thick that it felt as if they were entering a national forest. When they came to the crest of the hill, Dane helped her back in the buggy, and flicked the reins again to get the horse moving along. Finally, they came to a cleared flat area, ringed by tall conifers.

"Welcome to my home."

Dane had described his property as untillable, and that was a very apt description. It was much like Moss Hill, nearly vertical. He explained it was land that belonged to his grandfather, part of the Big House's acreage, and when his grandfather died, his oldest son—Freeman—divided up the land and parceled it out among his brothers. This untillable hilltop went to Dane's father, the youngest son. He tried to farm it and gave up, moving his family west to Somerset County. Dane had no interest in farming, but he did like the idea of raising sheep. This property wasn't good for much, but it would work for sheep. So with his father's blessing, Dane was set free from a farmer's life and came back to claim the neglected hilltop.

A large fenced paddock filled the yard, and in it were his sheep, a dozen or so, milled together in a tight clump, wide dark eyes staring out at them from ruffs of beige wool. There was a small wooden cabin with a tall brick chimney, and a smallish barn, more like an outbuilding. The cabin looked extremely old, as if it might topple over in a strong wind. There was a blue plastic tarp on part of the roof.

As old as the cabin looked, the barn looked newly constructed. The pinewood siding was still yellow and the green metal roof was clearly modern. Dane pulled the buggy to a stop and turned to Abigail. "I want to show you my world."

15

Surely, Bishop Isaac Bender must have received David's letter by now. He'd been coming to the store early for the last week, hoping there might be a phone call from Isaac. He assumed Isaac would be like most Amish farmers, who went to the phone shanty sometime each day to handle messages. He wanted to speak privately to Isaac, before the store opened and the old men arrived to play checkers, though few of them came now that his mother was reorganizing the store.

David had met Isaac Bender at last year's ministers' meeting. Isaac was in his midseventies, though he didn't seem at all old. He stood over six feet, with thick, tousled hair, a chest-slapping beard, and outsized hands that you could easily imagine holding an ax to split firewood. He was calm and confident, a man used to fixing things.

Isaac had become a bishop when he was young, only twenty-seven years old. He had a reputation for meddling in church districts, in a good way, and was often consulted when problems couldn't be solved. He believed it usually came down to problems with the leadership.

"Even a saint is tempted by an open door," Isaac had told the men at last year's meeting. "Ordained leaders are susceptible to all kinds of temptations. But when leaders succumb to sin, our churches tend to be almost entirely unequipped to do anything about them."

Isaac had observed that some ordained leaders were often not recognized to be dangerous until far too much damage had been done. Even if problems were identified, the follow-through was frequently abysmal. He wanted to do something about this. He wasn't shy about telling churches when they had let a problem fester too long. He didn't agree with the typical Plain way: Don't ask, don't tell. He was willing to do what everyone else was extremely reluctant to do: To take to task a fellow minister. And he did it more thoroughly and dispassionately than others could.

David vividly remembered points Isaac had made last fall, never thinking he would be experiencing them: "Disasters do not simply occur. They evolve. A single failure rarely leads to harm. Just like in anything else, decisions compound themselves. No sooner have you taken one fork in the road than another and another and another comes upon you."

Yes. Yes! That was just what had happened in Stoney Ridge. One decision made by Elmo set Freeman down a path that led to more of the same.

Isaac had tried to persuade the ministers to take warning signs seriously. "When you have suspicions about someone, you must pay attention. 'He's a fine minister,' people will say, 'but sometimes he has his moments.'"

What are those moments? Isaac pressed the group of men to consider that question, but no one volunteered anything. "There are certain kinds of behavior that should alert people that something may be seriously wrong with a person. Outbursts of anger, neglect of responsibilities, abusive behavior, overstepping boundaries. Too often, those behaviors are shrugged off. The facts are hard to stare in the face."

And that's where David was now. Staring such facts right in the face. Freeman Glick's stone-cold face.

On this afternoon, after a morning of cold rain, it had turned into a beautiful, sunny day. David held the store's door open for the UPS driver to maneuver the box-laden dolly inside, when he heard the phone ring in his storeroom. It rarely rang, especially late in the day. He scribbled his name on the UPS receipt and bolted to his desk, rushing to grab the phone. "Hello?"

"Isaac Bender here." David instantly recognized his gravelly, no-nonsense voice. "I received your letter."

"Hold on a minute." David closed his storeroom door behind him, climbed over his desk to sit in his chair, and leaned back. "There. Thank you for calling, Isaac."

"Tell me more," Isaac said. "Tell me how this all started. From your perspective."

"About a year and a half ago, I moved to Stoney Ridge from Ohio."

"Why there?"

"Two reasons. First, I sensed . . . God's call to come. And then, the bishop—who, at the time, was Elmo Beiler—wrote and asked if I would consider moving here. I'd met Elmo years ago, and we'd kept in touch."

"So, you moved your family to Stoney Ridge."

"Yes. I purchased the old Bent N' Dent store from someone Elmo knew, and he welcomed me into ministry. I'd been a minister for six years in Ohio."

"All was well under Elmo's leadership?"

"It was. It seemed to be, anyway. For the first few months, everything seemed fine. And then I began to get a feeling that something might not be quite right."

"Go on."

"It had to do with the working relationship between Freeman Glick and myself. We were both ministers. Elmo and I had grown close, and it seemed as if Freeman resented our friendship. Freeman was Elmo's nephew by his sister, so I found it hard to believe that he would have any reason to feel competitive with me. Anyway, that's not important."

"It might be, David. What made you feel as if he was competing with you?"

"Well, one example might be my sermons. Usually, after a sermon, the other ministers affirm what the minister says. After a few months, instead of affirming, Freeman would correct my sermons and point out what he felt were errors."

"Was he correct?"

"Every minister should be open to correction." David fiddled with the pencils sitting in a mug.

Isaac persisted. "Did he have valid points?"

"Elmo didn't think so. He tried to put an end to it, but Freeman ignored him and continued, every Sunday, to publicly correct my sermons. It became apparent that Elmo didn't have a way to control Freeman. Then . . . Elmo died last summer. And Freeman became bishop."

"And what's happened since then?"

"Freeman picked up where Elmo left off. Over the last year, the church had been losing families and it concerned Freeman, far more than it had bothered Elmo. Freeman began to cut corners to keep young people in the church. He became mildly dictatorial, and wouldn't tolerate any differing opinions."

A few months ago, Freeman had used church funds to purchase a tractor for the farmers to use, thinking it would bring benefit to them. Whether or not the use of a tractor would be allowed was one issue, but far more important was the fact that Freeman had used church funds without discussion. David suggested that Freeman confess to the church that he had used the funds, to admit he had done wrong, even if he meant it for the right reasons. Freeman vehemently disagreed. He warned David to never intimate that an ordained leader could be at fault, lest it end up tainting all of them. David had argued with him on that point, stressing that public confessions by the ordained leaders were the most important confessions of all. "We're fallible human beings," David had told Freeman. "Possibly, the most fallible of all the church members."

"At most," Freeman argued back, "you may say that you're sorry things didn't go as well as you had hoped."

That conversation about confessions was the moment when David fully realized what Elmo had meant when he warned David that there was a "snake in the garden."

Isaac cleared his throat, snapping David from the past to the present. "In your letter, you said that Freeman's sister revealed that she had seen him switch the lots."

"Yes. It was a practice started by Elmo, years ago. He switched the lots to include Freeman, then his wife's cousin Abraham, then Freeman switched the lots to bring in his brother Levi as a minister. And finally, five or six months ago, he did it again, when it was time to choose a bishop to replace Elmo."

"Who ended up in those lots?"

"Freeman and I."

David thought Isaac would be stunned speechless, but he didn't seem at all shocked.

"You don't seem surprised by this information."

"Ministers are struggling human beings. Every minister has things he ought to know but has yet to learn, capacities of judgment that will fail, a strength of character that can break. We should expect to be in better company than this, but we shouldn't be surprised when we encounter sin among us."

No. That was true. David was well aware of his own sins and shortcomings.

"And since the practice has been revealed, has Freeman shown any repentance?"

"None that is apparent. The Sunday after the revealing, he arrived to preach like it was any other church morning."

"Then he is trying to manage sin on his own. The only effective remedy for sin is the forgiveness of sin—and only God can forgive sin."

Yes, David agreed with him. Confession is the way out. No excuses, no rationalizations, no denials.

"So," David said. "What's next?"

Isaac cleared his throat. "Saturday is a ministers' meeting. We will need to bring this up for guidance and discussion."

"Freeman will be there."

"And so will I." Isaac let out a deep sigh. "David, no matter what measures are taken, ministers will always falter, always fail. It isn't reasonable to expect any of us to be blameless."

True, David thought, *but what is reasonable is that we never cease to aim for it.*

Dane Glick's barn was spotless. Even the tack room was in perfect order. There was a place for everything and everything was in its place. Abigail was quite impressed.

Until they went to his cabin.

In front of it were the remnants of a female's touch: randomly sprawling rosebushes that had managed on their own to survive, a faded whirligig, a pile of stones. Dane noticed what she was looking at. "Memory stones. My mother collected them."

"Memory stones, as in, from the Old Testament?"

Dane beamed. "Yes. Each one represents an 'Only God' event my mother wanted to sear onto our memory."

He had her hooked. Abigail would like to know more about those memory stones, each one, and about the woman who collected them.

The cabin had steps that led up to a covered porch. Inside, a combined kitchen and den made up the largest room. Along one wall sat a sagging sofa covered with a dark green slipcover. The room was alarmingly cluttered, dusty, and messy, revealing a priority of very poor housekeeping. Cobwebs draped the lines where wall met ceiling, and the wooden floors were as scratched and scarred as those in any one-room schoolhouse she'd ever been in.

And the *kitchen*. Ora Nisley would be breaking out in hives if he saw this. Dirty dishes piled in the sink, on the tabletop, even on the floor. When had Dane last washed up?

Far more distressing was the condition of Dane's desk, if you could call it a desk. It was actually an old wooden door placed on top of cinder blocks. Bills were tossed everywhere, a ledger was opened but had only one entry in it, and she gasped when she saw a shoebox filled with uncashed checks. Checks! Made out to Dane Glick.

"But . . . this is your business, isn't it? Your livelihood?"

"Yes," he said, removing his hat. "I haven't quite worked out the kinks in my accounting system." He rubbed his nose with his knuckles, and his cheeks reddened, which she was starting to diagnose as evidence of embarrassment.

Abigail released a long-suffering sigh. Order was the greatest love in her life. Order and structure. It was unthinkable to her that others didn't hold those values in similar esteem.

He lifted his eyes to the clock on the wall. "Do you mind if I leave you here for a moment? I need to tend to my animals."

"Can I help you?"

"No. Those sheep of mine, they spook easily. A stranger might frighten them. Every afternoon, I like to check on each one of them, run a hand over them, make sure they haven't gotten into anything or hurt themselves. Sheep—they're not the brightest." He thumped his hat on his head. "I won't be too long," he said as he went out the door, leaving Abigail alone in his cabin.

She was aware that it would be inappropriate to start reorganizing Dane's muddled mess. She should leave it all alone. But all she could see before her was chaos.

She could hear her sister Laura's voice in her head: "Do not touch anything. This is not your problem. Fixing his accounting system, without his permission, would be considered a major social blunder." And Laura would be correct. Abigail suppressed the desire she had to bring order out of chaos.

She stepped up to the window. Her breath fogged the glass and she had to wipe it with her elbow. Dane was walking across the yard, a lightness to every step. She thought she had never known anyone who seemed so thoroughly content. Downright happy, rain or shine, all the time.

Dane hopped over the paddock fence with a bale of timothy hay on his shoulder and started to call his sheep, one by one. She studied him for a long while. Banded together in a tight clump, his sheep lifted their heads at the sound of his voice. She could see the moment it registered in their little sheep brains that they knew this voice, because all at once, they stumbled over each other trying to get to him. A Bible verse danced through her mind, something Uncle David had read aloud that very morning during devotion time: "My sheep hear my voice, and I know them, and they follow me."

She had heard those words before, knew them by heart, but they jumped off the page and came to life as she watched the way Dane's little flock of sheep recognized him. He knew each sheep, and each sheep knew him. She could hear her uncle's deep voice: "This, this is the way Jesus loves us, you and me. He is the good shepherd, we are his sheep."

That was the effect Dane Glick had on her. Things previously left on a page, closed away in a file or a box, kept springing to life. It made her . . . uncomfortable. As Dane scattered the hay around for the sheep to munch on, she turned from the window and felt another jolt as she surveyed the room.

Dane Glick was not a lazy man, but it was remarkable to reflect how he did not care for his home the way he cared for his animals. She had not thought about this before now, but it was rather interesting to think that Dane might believe structure and organization and cleanliness just happened along. Perhaps there was always a woman in the background, a mother or a sister, who had ensured that these important things occurred for him.

For a few moments she paced nervously around the room, wondering what to do while she waited for Dane to return. She really should just keep pacing and leave the desk alone. *Walk away, Abigail. Ignore it. This is not your problem.*

She started with the unpaid bills.

16

Nearly an hour passed before Dane returned. As he walked in the door, he was already apologizing. "This new horse of mine kicked a hole in the stall and cut herself. I had to clean and bandage her cut, then fix the hole in the—" Barely through the threshold, he stilled and looked around his cabin. "What in the world happened?"

Abigail was standing on a chair in the kitchen. She looked around the little room. Dane had been in the barn for a very long time. After she had finished tidying up his desk, she noticed the chaotic condition of the bookshelves—and she was pleased to see that he liked to read substantive books, unlike her cousin Ruthie, who preferred vacuous romance novels—so she alphabetized them by author, then she finished the rest of the room. When he still hadn't returned, she rearranged the few pieces of furniture in the room, so that they wouldn't block the pathway to the kitchen. Then she started to clean up the kitchen, to wash and dry the stacks of dirty dishes. As she put away the dishes, she found the cupboards were not efficiently organized, so she had pulled the chair from his desk into the kitchen and had just begun pulling things out of the cupboard and onto the counter. As Dane walked around the room, stunned, Abigail felt a spike of concern that she might have gone too far. He stood in front of the bookshelves in a daze. She climbed down from the chair to stand beside him, which took only three steps. Dane was silent for a while, taking in all of the changes she had made.

"If you'd prefer, the books could be categorized by topic rather than by author. It's not the official way to categorize, but it is possible."

"No, no," Dane said, his voice distant and far off.

"I didn't touch your bedroom." Her voice, she knew, held a tinge of panic.

Then he turned toward her. "Abigail . . . I don't know what to say . . ."

She nodded. He didn't need to explain. She knew what the problem was. It was something very basic within her, something that made her different from anyone else. She was an excellent problem solver, a clear and logical thinker, but when it came to people, she always made incorrect assumptions about what was appropriate and what was not. Like now, for example.

Dane was still staring at her, a look of complete amazement on his face. It reminded her of Ben Miller after the Black Raspberry Incident. She had gone too far, once again.

"You, Abigail Stoltzfus, have been sent to me on angel's wings." He leaned down and kissed her on the cheek.

She fought against it, but the pressure started building in her face. Her inappropriate reaction to overwhelming emotion was about to begin. She sneezed once—a painful explosion that came from within her cheekbones instead of her nose—then she sneezed again. From out of his pocket, Dane handed over a handkerchief as white as new paper. Within minutes, she had sneezed several more times into it. The pressure in her cheekbones made tears well into her eyes. She covered her nose with Dane's handkerchief and waited for the attack to pass.

Looking down, she crumpled the cloth inside her fist. "I'll wash this and return it to you."

"It's no bother."

She found his eyes. "Why are you so nice?"

"How could I not be nice when you've done me such a great kindness?"

Out blasted another sneeze, window-rattling loud, fully expressed before she could muffle it.

❦

It was Thanksgiving. Before the sun of that Thursday morning was up, the Stoltzfus house was a heady heaven of mouthwatering scents. No easy thing to endure on a morning set aside for fasting. David wasn't sure if he felt sorry for the family who happened to host church on Thanksgiving morning, or pleased for them. It was a morning when no one lingered to visit. Everyone, including all the Stoltzfuses, made a beeline for their homes the moment the church service ended, led by their gnawing, growling stomachs. Katrina and Thelma came straight over from church, as did Jesse and Andy Miller. Waiting for them at home was a feast.

For the last few days, David's mother had set aside her

massive reorganization of the store—left it in utter dishevel-
ment—so that she could set her mind to prepare for Thanksgiving dinner. Last night, the girls helped Mammi prepare
the cooked turkey into a delicious *roarscht*, turkey mixed
with broth, bread, herbs. Potatoes to mash were boiling on
the stovetop. Pumpkin bread, rolls, and four kinds of pies
sat on the top shelf of the pantry. The refrigerator was filled
with vegetable casseroles and a green Jell-O salad. And the
pudding! His mother's specialty. He felt as if he were a boy
again.

"Dad," Jesse said, eyeing the sour cream cut-out cookies on a platter on the kitchen counter, a specialty of his
mother's, "I wonder if you are aware that the rest of the
Stoney Ridge Amish aren't fasting on this day."

"Son, I do know. Every settlement observes Thanksgiving
in a different way, but this is how we do it." But my oh my,
those cookies did look good.

"And why do we fast?"

"To focus our minds on giving thanks for the bounty the
Creator has given us."

"Now, Dad, aren't we supposed to do that every day?"

David sighed. He was too hungry to walk right into a
semantics trap set by his silver-tongued son. "Jesse, just wait
a little longer. Mammi's almost ready for us." He went to
his desk in the living room to remove himself from visual
temptation. Gabby and Laura had set places for everyone
at a long table in the room and were engrossed in creating
place cards. They didn't even notice David as he sat at his
desk, but he couldn't help overhearing the girls.

"Laura, do you remember the names of the other children
in your class in school?"

"Yes. Why?"

"So do I. Dane Glick said he couldn't remember them, apart from one or two very close friends. But horses were different, he said. He remembered virtually every horse he had ever handled, from the first buggy horse his family had, to each of the field horses. The way he described them, full of quirks and character, they were like old friends to him, comfortable and reassuring." She turned to Laura. "Does that seem odd to you?"

"No. It sounds like someone who loves horses. You know, Gabby, not everyone has your memory for detail."

"True."

"You've been spending quite a bit of time with Dane Glick."

"We're trying to determine the identity of his missing ancestor."

"That's all?"

"Yes." Gabby looked out the window. "Though it seems that he has an assumption that there is more between us than ancestor sleuthing."

"Is that such a bad thing?"

Gabby leaned toward Laura to whisper to her. "Er lacht iwwer's ganz Gsicht." *He is all smiles.*

"What's wrong with that?"

"Don't you think he smiles too much?"

"How could anyone be accused of smiling too much?"

"What if he's . . . too happy?"

Laura burst out with a laugh. "Gabby, listen to yourself. How could anyone ever be too happy?"

"No one can be happy all the time. What if someone were to make him . . . unhappy?"

Laura stilled. "So that's what you're worried about. Hurting his feelings?"

"Possibly."

"That's excellent, Gabby."

"I don't know what you mean."

"I mean that you're concerned about his feelings. And you're enjoying your time together?"

"Immensely," Gabby said. As David watched her, she had a look on her face as if she might have just realized it for the first time.

"And is Dane enjoying himself?"

"Apparently. But he—"

"Then stop fretting and fussing about it," Laura said, cutting her off. "Stop overanalyzing everything. For once, just have a little fun."

The girls finished the name cards, set them at each place, and went into the kitchen. David watched them walk away, pondering the mystery of love. How remarkable, to think that Gabby might have found love, right here in Stoney Ridge, with a Glick.

A Glick! Birdy. He'd forgotten all about her today.

David jumped from his desk and went into the kitchen. Through the window, he saw Andy Miller and Katrina, laughing at Jesse's puppy as it chased its own tail in a tight circle. He glanced at his mother, who was at the kitchen sink with her eyes fixed on Katrina and Andy. As David grabbed a coat to hurry outside, his mother caught him. "Who is this Andy boy?"

David put an arm through a coat sleeve. "He's hardly a boy. He works at Moss Hill as a farmhand for Thelma."

"But what do you know about him? Is he the one who's behind all this oil well nonsense?"

David put his hands on his mother's shoulders. "I know that he is our guest on this fine day." He left her at the window and strode across the yard to reach Katrina. "Did you happen to invite Birdy for Thanksgiving dinner?"

Katrina's eyes went wide in surprise. "No. She left right after church. She said she had someplace she had to go, and I just assumed she was going to her relatives." She tilted her head. "Dad, I'm sorry. I guess I thought you would have asked her if you wanted her to . . ." She tipped her head toward the house. Toward his mother.

David shook his head. "You're right . . ." His voice drizzled off. He knew, *he knew*! Freeman and Levi's family would not have included her in today's gathering.

But then, he didn't include her, either. She would be spending Thanksgiving dinner, at Moss Hill, alone. Andy spoke up. "I'll go over to Moss Hill and bring her back."

Katrina nodded. "We'll both go."

"No," David said. "You stay here. I'll go."

Mammi called to them from the front porch. "Dinner's ready." She pointed toward them with a long, accusing finger. "You, Andy Miller, are to sit next to me."

Andy paled. "Why do I just feel as if I've been targeted by the Grand Inquisitor?"

David leaned toward Katrina. "Tell Mammi to start the meal without me. Not to wait. Tell her that something has come up. She'll understand." She wouldn't, of course, but he would have to deal with that later.

He harnessed Thistle to the buggy in record time and drove the horse over to Moss Hill, but as the buggy crested the hill, he could tell the little house was empty. No buttery glow from the kitchen, no smoke from the chimney. He knocked on the door, but there was no answer. He went to the greenhouse—the mossery, as Katrina renamed it—and into the barn, peered into the henhouse, and retreated quickly as the hens squawked at the interruption. He walked up to the construction site of the oil wells and called out for Birdy, but there was no answer. She was nowhere in sight on Moss Hill. Where could she be? On a walk? Or . . . he knew.

David drove down the road toward the schoolhouse and slapped the reins to hurry the horse when he saw a wisp of smoke curling from the chimney's pipe. He stopped the horse and moved toward the door of the schoolhouse in long, unhurried strides, feeling the awesome gnaw in his stomach, wondering what to say when he reached her.

He opened the door and let it thud quietly behind him. She was in the front of the classroom, writing on the chalkboard, and she went on writing, her attention riveted to the board.

"Birdy," he said, as he took a few steps up the center aisle. "Birdy, I'm so sorry."

She turned to him in surprise. "For what?"

For being so neglectful. For being such a coward, such an avoider. "Please come. Come to our house for Thanksgiving dinner."

Birdy dropped her chin and looked down at the piece of chalk in her hands.

He stood a few yards away from her, watching, wondering, waiting. "Birdy"—spoken softer this time.

Her head snapped up, revealing dark brown eyes shimmering with unshed tears. "Thank you for the invitation, David, but, you see, I've already eaten." She spread her hand, palm up, toward her desk. "And I have so much work to catch up on here. Please give everyone my regards." Then she spun back to the chalkboard to continue with her task. She was hurt, so hurt.

David scraped a hand down his face and continued staring at Birdy as she wrote on the board, coming to grips with the hard fact that he was the cause of this pain. She had showed immense kindness to him, to his daughters, and in return, he had hurt her. And for what reason? Because he was concerned about the flak he would get over his growing relationship with her—from the church, from Freeman, from his mother.

She deserved so much more.

He turned slowly, walked down the aisle, and left the schoolhouse. On the way home, David felt an ache in his gut that had nothing to do with an empty stomach.

Late on Thanksgiving afternoon, just as the sun had slipped down behind the ridge, taking its light with it, Abigail searched around the house for Ruthie and found her out in the barn, getting ready to milk the cow. Moomoo. What an odd choice to name a cow. Imagine if everything was named for the sound it made: Trumpet for an elephant, Wheeze for a hippo, Screech for a peacock. But then, it occurred to her that none of those animals would be candidates as farm pets, and she dismissed the mental conversation as trivial.

Ruthie sat on a three-legged milking stool, the pail between her legs, and leaned forward. The cow's udder was heavy with milk and swayed as she swabbed it with disinfectant.

"Are you still filled with dubiousness about genealogy?"

Ruthie looked up, surprised by the question, perhaps because it had been a few days since they had previously discussed it. "Dubiousness? What exactly does that mean?"

"That you're still filled with doubt about the merits of genealogy."

"Oh, not *that* again," she mumbled, sulky. She turned back to milk the cow, pulling and squeezing, as milk hit the bottom of the empty metal bucket with a *ping! ping!*

"Perhaps you've never thought of yourself as being particularly brainy, but I've heard you ask your father quite challenging questions after family devotions. And I've also seen the way you help Molly and the twins with their schoolwork. I believe you underestimate your intelligence."

Ruthie gave her a sideways glance, eyes narrowed.

In the palm of Abigail's hands was a handkerchief, filled with dirt she had collected from the well site at Moss Hill. "Do you understand how oil is created?"

Ruthie sighed. "Well, sort of. I read a little about it after Katrina told me about the oil trap on Moss Hill." She looked up at Abigail and hurried to add, "But I can't explain it in the detail that you can." The cow slapped Abigail's legs with a manure-caked tail, and Ruthie giggled, a rare occurrence, then went back to her milking.

Abigail moved around Ruthie to avoid the cow's tail and unfolded the handkerchief. "Each geological layer tells a story—biological material has been trapped underground, embedded in dirt and water and millions of microorganisms. Given enough time, and enough heat, and enough pressure, that matter turns into oil. Nobody ever sees that depth, that dimension of the earth, but neither does anyone doubt that it's there. What connects the earth that you can't see to the air above is the soil's crust. The evidence of all of those years is what you're looking at now in that pile of dirt and rocks and water and oil."

Ruthie pushed away a lock of hair that had fallen in her eyes. "So?"

"It's the same with a person. When you dig into the past, it's like you're finding genealogical layers that tell a story." Abigail wrapped up the handkerchief. "Now do you understand?"

"Understand what?"

"The story of this little patch of earth is right here, under our feet." She tossed the handkerchief to the ground. "It might seem invisible to the untrained eye, but it's all there. You just have to look for it."

Ruthie kicked the handkerchief with her toe. "Personally, I think that dirt is just dirt. What's in the past should stay in the past."

And Abigail was told that she was the literal one! But, on a brighter note, it appeared that Ruthie was speaking to her again.

17

Abigail arrived at the Bent N' Dent at 10:56 a.m. on Saturday. Her cousin Jesse had set aside an unopened box of bubble gum for her, adding in a 10 percent fee for himself, though she didn't really see the necessity for a fee, especially among family. She was in no position to object, though. And a fortuitous sequence of events meant that her uncle was not planning to be at the store this morning. She would be able to meet Leroy, privately, in her uncle's back office.

When she walked into the store, she was happy to see that the old men, those who normally loitered around the woodstove for hours on end, had not arrived yet. She wondered if that might be her grandmother's influence. Jesse said that the old codgers scattered like buckshot whenever they saw Tillie Yoder Stoltzfus coming through the door.

Bethany Schrock was restocking shelves as Abigail went behind the register to get the box of bubble gum. There it was, with her name on it, just as Jesse had promised. When she saw that Bethany was up on a ladder to fill a shelf, she called to her, "I'm going to use Uncle David's office for a little while."

"That's fine," Bethany called back. "You know, your grandmother started this whole reshelving project. Shoot-fire! She has me frazzled down to my last stitch. And where is she now?" Bethany continued to mutter disparaging comments about Mammi from high up on the ladder, but Abigail couldn't take time to listen to them now.

She went into the office and cleared off the desk, carefully placing things in a pile so she could replace them when she was finished. Her heart was racing with excitement. She had high hopes that today's discovery would solve the riddle, but she held many doubts that a nine-year-old boy could be a reliable informant.

She glanced at the wall clock. 11:04. Leroy Glick was late. It was very frustrating to her how often people, even a nine-year-old person, did not respect others' time. Then she heard the bell ring on the store's door and she hurried into the front room to see Leroy walk in with a large square bulging from his coat.

She glanced at Bethany, still on the ladder. "I'll handle it, Bethany."

She motioned to Leroy to follow her and they went into Uncle David's office. "Put it on the desk," she said.

"Not until I get my bubble gum."

Abigail pointed to the box on the floor and Leroy's face lit up. He unbuttoned his coat, then his shirt, then his undershirt. There was the old family Bible!

He set it on the desk and bent down to pick up the bubble gum box. He put it right on the desk, *this close* to an exceptionally valuable centuries-old Bible. She gasped. "Leroy, you mustn't allow bubble gum to be anywhere near this Bible."

"I need to get the gum wrappers! One of them has a ticket

225

for a lifetime supply of bubble gum." He ripped open the box and started to pull out the little gum bundles.

To Abigail's way of thinking, Leroy already had a lifetime supply of gum, right there in the box. "Can you please take the box and go over to that chair? I need to work and I don't want to be distracted by your bubble blowing."

"Fine. But I don't have much time. I need to be home for lunch."

"What?" She glanced at the clock. 11:15 a.m. Fine. She would have to work fast.

She sat at the desk and pulled out her white gloves, then carefully opened the Bible's heavily worn leather cover, delicately turning the pages until she came to the section between the Old and New Testaments, a place for records and registers. She scanned the pages quickly, pleased to see that the handwriting changed many times. Excellent. That was an indication that this was an original record, not copied.

She started at the beginning of the record, dating from 1741. She read down an orderly list of names and dates, marriages, baptisms, births, and deaths.

Abigail's mind was churning backward in time. She wondered about those earliest immigrants, those first ones who came from Europe on a leaky, bobbing high-masted ship. Did they have any idea what the future would look like for them? From what she'd read, Penn's Woods was thickly forested. The immigrants claimed their land and then had to clear it of trees to farm it. Imagine the work they did to claim their property, the disappointments and hardships and sorrows they endured. It was a life filled with risk and reward, most likely more risk than reward. She'd read once that monograms had first been created so that the children of mothers who died in childbirth—and there were many—would be sure to receive their mother's belongings.

She turned a page as thin and brittle as onionskin and saw that the handwriting had now changed. It became delicate, spidery yet feminine, with curious little unconnected notes scrawled in the index, as if the writer couldn't help herself from recording important events.

HOR hung on May 15, 1881.

All Saints' Day, 1881, Elizabeth's child born today. A boy.

Then the handwriting changed again, to someone else's penmanship. No additional notes were found in the indexes. She squeezed her eyes shut. Her father had taught her a valid investigation required three confirming facts. She had just found the first piece of evidence.

"I gotta go."

Abigail looked up to find the entire box of bubble gum had been opened, wrappers littered the floor. Leroy's pockets were filled with unwrapped gum. "Leroy, I'm just getting somewhere. You've got to let me have it a little longer."

"Can't. Gotta go."

She glanced at the wall clock. "You promised me one hour. It's only 11:43."

He sighed. "Yeah, but I'm bored."

"Not an acceptable excuse. I get seventeen more minutes. Clean up the wrappers while you wait."

She ran her finger down the delicate pages to find records dating in the 1830s. She skimmed farther down and saw Elizabeth's birth date and her parents' names. She scribbled the information down on a Bent N' Dent notepad she found on her uncle's desk.

Elizabeth's marriage was never documented. Her living child had a birth date, but no known father.

She read through those dates again, wondering who HOR might be. Was he the father of Elizabeth's child? Obviously, he was not approved of by the family. Most likely, not a church member.

She turned another page to learn what had happened to Elizabeth's surviving son, Mose Glick. The handwriting changed again, this time to what seemed like a man's penmanship: bold, slanted, no-nonsense. Perhaps Mose himself recorded these events. He married, had four sons, then his wife died and he married again and had four more sons. He became a minister, then a bishop. She turned the page again and realized that Freeman was a direct descendant of Mose Glick. Somehow, just the handwriting alone revealed their common ancestry. Bold, slanted, no-nonsense.

Leroy stood right in front of her, blowing bubbles. Highly distracting. "Five more minutes, Leroy. That was our agreement."

"Can't. I gotta go." He reached out and grabbed the Bible, stuffed it under his coat, and hurried out the door. A precious, ancient, beloved Bible, jammed against the unwashed body of a bubble-gum-chewing nine-year-old boy. Disgusting.

Bubble gum wrappers littered the floor. Appalling.

Oh no. No, no, no, no. An appalling realization struck Abigail. She *had* to see that Bible again. The Bent N' Dent notepad she had used to record her observations was jammed inside.

David Stoltzfus sat in complete silence, reflecting on all that this particular Saturday represented. He was in the back of the barn, watching men greet each other with a firm handshake and a kind word, pleased at the turnout for this annual ministers' meeting. Twenty-one ordained leaders had come to the barn of Mahlon Mast—three from each of the seven church districts. He recognized most of them from last year's meeting. There was Monroe Smucker, a small, bald man with a crumpled face like a baby. Then there was Enos Bontrager, a thoughtful student of the Bible who was prone to depression. On the bench next to him sat Lucas Lehman, a minister who was rather too dour for David's taste. And of course there were Freeman and Levi Glick.

Mahlon Mast had prepared his barn for the meeting with meticulous attention to every detail. There wasn't a spider to be found; the barn had been swept and cleaned that thoroughly. Kerosene heaters were placed at the end of each row of benches. Bishop Henry Hershberger, a small, thin man with quick-moving eyes, led the day's agenda.

David treasured these gatherings. Ministers belonged to a world that even their own families had trouble understanding. Anna certainly hadn't understood, David recalled. She resented the time he spent away from the family, the middle-of-the-night knocks on the door, the confidences he kept from her. David was not only removed from normal give-and-take friendships, but he was also alone. Friendships were few.

Once a year, at these ministers' meetings, there was a place full of men who understood, who longed to make contact with each other and belong to a community of a few. They may each have had their own reasons for coming, but in the end, David had come to discover, the fellowship filled and fortified them for the year's work that lay ahead of them.

The men would meet to discuss the troubles and concerns they encountered in their churches. This little group, David mused as he watched them, was a microcosm of the church as a whole, promoting the faith as best they could. Sometimes they bungled it, sometimes they handled it well, but they did their best to hold firmly to their beliefs and values in a world that wanted to steal them away.

So far this morning they had discussed, at length, the ongoing cell phone dilemma. Did the benefits of cell phone use outweigh the drawbacks? For every negative story—like the one shared by Mahlon Mast about how many young men whipped out their cell phones to take pictures at his daughter's recent wedding—there was a positive story. One farmer got his hand caught—mangled!—in the wheat thresher, and his son was able to call for an ambulance immediately, avoiding the delay of a long run to a phone shanty. The farmer's hand had been saved. The cell phone dilemma was put on the wait-and-see list, to be discussed again next year. Privately, David thought it was too late; once the cell phone had been introduced, it would be very hard to get rid of.

And then there were smaller issues discussed—some vandalism in nearby Leola that was targeted at the Amish. Some benefits planned to help replenish the drained reserves of the Amish Aid Society. Marvin King was particularly enthusiastic about the benefits because of the barn fires in his church. He had the money earmarked.

If it weren't for the oil wells on Moss Hill, David would feel alarmed by Marvin's presumptions, but he felt that God was providing the means to handle Ephraim Yoder's hospital bills in a different way. David had already gone to the hospital's billing office with the lease bonus to start the process of repayment.

Isaac Bender had recommended that David wait until after lunch to address the dilemma that plagued the church of Stoney Ridge. Isaac felt it would end up derailing the meeting for any other conversation.

As the men reconvened after lunch, Isaac stood strong and tall in the middle of the floor. "There is something else, something that must be confronted."

David waited until Isaac gave him a nod, then he stood, his stomach twisted in a tight knot. "The church of Stoney Ridge has been dealt a blow."

The room fell silent. Heads turned toward him as David continued. "It's been discovered that Elmo Beiler, who has passed, had switched the lots during an ordination. That practice has continued on two more times." He did not mention Freeman's name, hoping he might stand and repent. But Freeman did nothing. He watched David but with an air of complete detachment on his face.

"When brought to light, unrepentant sin has resulted." David paused and looked right at Freeman. "The sin came from our bishop."

All eyes turned to Freeman. He slowly rose to his feet. "Most of you have known me my entire life. You've known my parents, my grandparents, even my great-grandparents. You've known the kind of people I come from, the kind of stock I belong to." His voice conveyed a calm confidence, a man used to fixing things.

Funny how sometimes people undergoing the worst kind of discord in their lives can look so calm. But David could see. Freeman's bearded chin jutted out firmly, but his eyes were far from certain.

"I'm sure you even know that my ancestor is Peter Glick, who emigrated with his family to Pennsylvania in 1748. You all know the dramatic story of the Indian attack that killed Peter Glick's family. One son"—he waved a finger in the air to prove the point—"only one son, John Glick, escaped the Indians by hiding in a hollowed-out tree. I, along with every other Glick, can trace their history to John. That is the truth." Freeman dropped his chin on his chest and remained silent for a moment. "There is another truth to be told, my brothers. Stoney Ridge has a very jealous minister who is creating discord in our church." Levi and Marvin bobbed their heads in agreement. "The church did not have problems before David Stoltzfus moved in." He lifted his head and gazed slowly around the entire room, meeting each pair of eyes. "You can all attest to that."

Freeman pointed at David. "This man has created conflict from the moment he arrived. Every single thing, he objects to, unless it personally benefits him. Just ask him about those oil wells he's digging. Never once did he ask the church if digging for oil would be appropriate." He wagged a finger in the air. "Not once!"

Levi nodded vigorously. "Never one single time."

"He has stooped so low as to toy with my own sister's affections, influencing her to betray her family. To lead her on with hopes of marriage, only to drop her—" he snapped his fingers "—when she no longer served his purposes."

David had expected this kind of bait-and-switch response. Still, his stomach was shooting out arrows of pain. He pressed a hand against his belly, trying to absorb the pain. He had to get through this. "Freeman, do you deny that you switched the lots to become bishop?"

No one spoke. No one moved. A silence filled the barn so dramatically that you could hear the wings of the swallows, zipping around in the rafters. Each man's eyes were on Freeman, waiting for his response to David's question.

And then a blast of severe pain ripped through David's middle, one spasm after another, until he doubled over.

Abigail was leaving the Bent N' Dent as her cousin Jesse drove his buggy into the parking lot. "Gabby, I've been meaning to tell you something."

"Please call me Abigail."

Jesse whistled for his puppy to jump out of the buggy. "I've been digging through the carriage house at the Sisters' House, looking for some spare buggy parts." He grinned. "I can't believe I'm actually saying this, but I'm starting to understand how you like sifting through old people's junk."

That wasn't exactly the way she perceived her genealogy work, but she realized Jesse was trying to be affirming. "Did you find what you needed?"

"Actually, yes. Square bolts! And I came across something I thought you might find interesting. A wooden chest that's filled with old papers from around Stoney Ridge."

Abigail's heart started pounding. "How old?"

"Seriously old. I saw one receipt for a saw that was dated 1889."

"1889?" Don't get excited, she told herself. It might be nothing. But it might yield something too. "Do you think they might let me go through it?"

"Absolutely. I already told them my cousin Gabby might be dropping by."

"Abigail," she corrected quietly, but her mind was spinning. This could be a bonanza!

Out of nowhere, Leroy Glick hurtled himself between them, gasping for breath. "I kept shouting and you never heard me." He picked himself up and started toward the store.

"What's happened?"

Leroy turned his chin to shout, "It's Jesse's dad! He dropped dead at the ministers' meeting!"

18

Jesse sat by his dad's hospital bed in the emergency room, feeling rather shaken up. It was disturbing to see tubes and wires connected to his dad, to see him lying in a bed wearing a flimsy hospital gown. He never thought of his father as . . . a mere mortal. It never occurred to him that he could die. Jesse had already lost his mother. What if something happened to his dad? His father was the rock of their family. Jesse wasn't ready to be the rock. He couldn't even take care of a puppy. How would he be able to take care of his sisters?

Jesse felt the wind knocked out of him, as if someone had punched him in the stomach, really hard. *There's a word for this*, he thought: *despair*. It happened to everyone, but you felt it alone. Disconsolate. Wretched. Despondent. A shocking loss that couldn't be shared.

He thought of others who had faced this kind of terrible grief—Yardstick Yoder, for one. Maybe, he looked up at the ceiling, if God would heal his father, Jesse would spend a little time getting to know Yardstick and turn him from his life of crime. Take him hunting, for example, or teach him something about buggy repair. He kept his eyes on the ceiling. "What do you think? Would that be a fair deal?"

His father stirred as he spoke that prayer aloud, his eyes fluttered open, then closed again.

What would his father think about trying to make a bargain with God? Probably, he wouldn't be in favor of it. But Jesse had always loved bargains, deal making, gambling. He hoped God would be a little understanding, given the dire circumstances. There were examples in the Bible of men brashly striking a bargain with God—Abraham, for one, when he tried to negotiate God's peace for Sodom, a corrupt city where his nephew Lot lived. Barren Hannah, who pleaded with God for a son and promised to give him to God's service. There were others too.

Wouldn't his father be pleased to know that Jesse actually listened to his sermons?

The curtain pulled back and in came Birdy. She bent down to wrap an arm around Jesse's shoulder and give him a squeeze, awkward but tender, then sat in the chair next to him. "Has the doctor told you what the problem is?"

Jesse shook his head. "Not yet. They've run some tests. Nurses keep coming in and out to check on him."

"So all you know is that he collapsed at the ministers' meeting?"

"That, and he's in a lot of pain, so they gave him something to knock him out." He glanced up at her. "How'd you get in here?"

Birdy grinned. "There's a very large amount of people in the waiting room. Your grandmother and your cousin Abigail made a few suggestions to the nurses about how to improve the efficiency of the waiting room, which made the nurses rather upset, voices were raised, and I found the hullaballoo created an ideal diversion to slip in."

Jesse lifted his thumb in the air. "Smart move, Birdy." He looked down at his dad. In a whispered voice that shamed him with its cracking, he said, "Birdy, is he going to die?"

Birdy's eyebrows lifted in surprise, almost amusement, but she answered him in all seriousness. "Goodness, no. Look at how strong and steady his heartbeat is on the monitor. And notice how normal his color is, how steady and regular his breathing. Those machines are a little frightening, but we don't need them to see for ourselves that he's going to be all right." She patted Jesse's knee. "Your father has had a lot of stress in the last few months. I suspect his body is trying to tell him he's had enough."

His father shifted in bed, woken by their voices. His eyes fluttered open. "Birdy? Jesse?" His gaze covered the room, then he made a vague upward gesture with one hand and slowly lifted himself up on one elbow. "Help me get out of here."

Birdy laughed. "Not quite yet, David." She leaned toward Jesse. "See? His stubborn streak is already up and going. He'll be fine."

A doctor came in, a woman in a white coat, her strawberry blonde hair held tightly in a bun, reading through his chart. "The test results from the scope came back in. Looks like you've got yourself a peptic ulcer, Mr. Stoltzfus. We're going to give you some medicine that should help and put you on a very bland diet. Very bland. If you cooperate, you'll be just fine."

An ulcer! That wasn't the ticket to a fast death that Jesse had feared. He turned to his father, expecting to see great relief on his face. An ulcer . . . not great but manageable. His father didn't seem to be absorbing the good news. He was staring at the doctor with a stricken look on his face.

"Ruth?"

The doctor looked up from the chart, then inhaled a tight gasp of air. "David?"

Again, the curtain was yanked back and Mammi burst into the room. "Will someone please explain what is wrong with my son? David, you're finally awake." She noticed Birdy. "Birdy Glick! How in the world did you get in here? I was told family only!"

Birdy jumped to her feet. In her haste, her elbow knocked over David's breakfast tray. Jesse felt as if he was watching everything in slow motion: Utensils clattered to the ground, a cup of water splattered on the wall.

All eyes moved to Mammi. And lingered there. Everyone's back seemed to stand a little straighter.

The doctor broke the silence. "Hello, Mother."

⟶⟵

It had been a long day. Uncle David could be released from the hospital as soon as the pharmacist filled the prescriptions, and most everyone who had arrived to stand vigil, with the exception of Abigail, Jesse, and Mammi, had to get home to care for children or livestock. Impatient, Abigail took it upon herself to retrieve the drugs rather than wait for them to be delivered, and was appalled at the inefficiency of the pharmacist. An elderly, bespectacled man, he moved as if his feet were bogged in quicksand. She found it helpful to stand at the counter rather than sit in a plastic chair and watch every move the pharmacist made—he seemed to move faster under her keen observation, though it was alarming to see his hands tremble.

By ten o'clock, they were in a taxi and on their way home. At last! Uncle David was weak with relief, grateful but subdued, exhausted by the day. He went straight to bed when they arrived home. Mammi and Abigail followed suit.

Abigail wore socks to bed because the night seemed unusually cold, and was almost asleep when she heard an odd sound—*ping!*—like hail hitting the window. She listened for a moment but only heard Laura's whiffling snore, so she rolled over to try to go back to sleep.

Ping!

She got out of bed and went to the window to look at the sky. Clouds covered the stars, but there was no hail.

Ping!

A pebble hit the window. She looked down and saw Ruthie flapping her arms. She waved to her and Ruthie flapped twice as fast. Something was wrong. She grabbed her robe and hurried down the stairs to open the door. "What's wrong? Are you hurt? Are you having a seizure? Shall I call for an ambulance?" The thought of two hospital visits in one day was horrifying, but . . . she was here to help her uncle's family. And *sweet molasses!*, did they *ever* need help. It was one problem after another.

"A seizure? *What* are you talking about?"

"Your arms were flapping uncontrollably."

"I was trying to get Laura to come downstairs. I didn't know you were home yet. Someone locked me out."

"But how could that have happened? You should have

gone to bed hours ago. And why were you outside all alone on a cold night?"

Standing rigid, eyes on the ground in front of her, she leaned slightly in her direction. And when she spoke, it was in a whisper. "I wasn't alone, Gabby."

She looked outside and saw the Juvenile Delinquent walking down the hill. Oh. Oh!

Ruthie gave her a look. "You won't tell Mammi or Dad, will you?"

"No." If Ruthie wanted to keep company with a Juvenile Delinquent, that was her business. "You'd better get upstairs and get to bed."

"Laura said Dad has an ulcer. That he'll be okay."

No wonder Uncle David had an ulcer. Ruthie was a pain in the gut. "Yes. He's upstairs in bed, sound asleep." *Where I should be. And you.*

Relief covered Ruthie's face, and for a brief moment, she looked like the girl she was. She started up the stairs, then stopped halfway up and turned back. "Thanks, Gabby."

"Abigail," she corrected, but Ruthie had already crested the last step and was tiptoeing down the hall to her bedroom.

⌒〰⌒

After several attempts at reading, David finally sighed and returned the book to its place. Simply wanting this day to end, he reached over to turn down the oil lamp . . . and paused.

His thoughts jumbled and raced. So much had happened in the last twenty-four hours. The ministers' meeting, the announcement of Freeman's deception, then . . . the ulcer—an ulcer! What a pathetically weak example he was of a minister.

But God was at work, even in David's weakness. How else

would he have ever known that his sister Ruth was working at the Stoney Ridge Hospital? He laid his head on the pillow. What a remarkable discovery. A memory stone moment, Gabby called it.

And then his mind took another turn: Birdy. It was heartwarming to find her at his side when he woke up in the hospital. It was different from the way he felt with anyone else.

But after he had been released and everyone who had come to keep vigil had left to head home, all except Gabby and his mother, and after Gabby had volunteered to go hurry along the pharmacist to fill the drug prescriptions, his mother read aloud the material the hospital had given him about managing a peptic ulcer. The list of forbidden foods left very little to eat, he noted with dismay. He had a feeling that his future would be filled with beige food: oatmeal, grits, rice. When she came to the last page, his mother let the papers drop in her lap and turned to him. "David, at the next opportunity, you must turn Birdy away. She's all wrong for you."

As he had looked at her, his mother's expression seemed to soften. "It would be the kind thing to do."

He had no response to give her. Nothing that would be polite.

How could his love life be on the top of her mind on the evening that she had seen her youngest daughter for the first time in years?

It was a pity that his mother had no husband. If she had, then maybe she would be spending her concern on his behalf instead of trying to manage her son.

David let out a long sigh, turned out the light, and then settled farther into bed. Still, sleep refused to come. Needing a lift in his spirits, he turned to an unfailing remedy. Aloud, in the pitch black of the night, he repeated Psalm 23 over and over, his mind focusing on each phrase of the beloved psalm, until sleep finally overcame him: "The LORD is my shepherd, I shall not want. He maketh me to lie down in green pastures: he leadeth me beside the still waters. He restoreth my soul: he leadeth me in the paths of righteousness for his name's sake. Yea, though I walk through the valley of the shadow of death, I will fear no evil: for thou art with me; thy rod and thy staff they comfort me. Thou preparest a table before me in the presence of mine enemies: thou anointest my head with oil; my cup runneth over. Surely goodness and mercy shall follow me all the days of my life: and I will dwell in the house of the LORD for ever."

⌇

Abigail woke early, bundled into her coat, and stepped out on the porch. Snow! Uncle David's hillside looked like it had been dusted with powdered sugar by a heavy-handed baker. Each of her breaths did a smoky dance before her. All was so quiet she could hear the soft whisk of a sparrow hawk as it circled overhead. The kitchen window threw a soft light onto the frosty lawn. This house, she realized, didn't feel unfriendly anymore.

Ruthie came outside to join her. She slurped loudly on her cup of tea. "Have you always been the way you are?"

"Yes. How?"

"Bold. Audacious. Impudent."

"I'm not trying to be bold or audacious or impudent." But she was impressed with Ruthie's vocabulary. She sat down in the chair and rubbed her elbows.

"Then . . . let's call it . . . confident. Sure of yourself."

Curious. "I don't think of myself as all that confident."

"You sound confident when you talk back to Mammi."

"I don't talk back to her."

"Sure you do. Like the other night, when she asked if you might be growing fond of Ora Nisley and you said that would be impossible."

"I was simply answering her question." Abigail looked out at the snow. "Is that so wrong?"

"I was raised so you don't talk back to elders." She frowned. "Sometimes I ache to talk back to Mammi."

"Maybe it's not about talking back. Just talking honestly." Recently, Laura had observed that Ruthie was coy, sneaky, indirect. Unlike Molly, who was willing to tell everybody everything, Ruthie was more circumspect. Laura said Ruthie had more on her mind than she would say. That was an example of Laura's insights about people. Abigail had just assumed Ruthie was permanently sulky.

Ruthie swirled the rest of the tea in her mug. "Has it ever occurred to you that your dad might be depressed because Mammi wore him down?"

This woke Abigail up. "Wore him down?"

"Yes. Think about it. He was the oldest when his father died, but just a boy himself. Imagine how much Mammi expected out of him! Work at the store, mind the younger children, behave himself, be an example to others. Why, I wonder if he ever had a childhood. Work, work, work. No fun, no joy. Just endless expectations."

Like Thistle, the first horse Dane Glick trained. He had told Abigail that Thistle's first master was too hard on her, and the horse finally gave up. She had never understood why her father was the way he was, but maybe Ruthie's

243

perspicacious assessment was correct. He just gave up. *That*, Abigail thought, explained a lot.

"Did you know we have another aunt? She's not Amish, so she's never spoken of."

Abigail did know. "She was at the hospital last night."

"What?!"

"Yes. Apparently, she's an emergency room doctor."

"Did you talk to her? Has she been in Stoney Ridge all this time? She hasn't tried to find us?"

"There wasn't time for much of a conversation. She was called away to another patient."

"What did she look like?"

"It was a motorcycle accident." Abigail shuddered. "Very bloody. Very grisly."

"Not the patient! Dad's sister."

"Oh. She looks like . . . well, like a female version of your father." *And mine.*

"Did you find out anything about her? Anything at all?"

"Let me think. She's new to Stoney Ridge. Took the job just last month, in fact. She said she's still living in boxes, but she didn't happen to say where those boxes resided." Abigail rubbed her elbows, feeling chilled. "I suspect your father will make an effort to contact her once he's back on his feet."

"Her name is Ruth," she said softly.

"Like you."

Ruthie nodded. "I can't imagine anything would ever have stopped my mom or dad from acknowledging me. Even if I didn't get baptized. But Mammi would shun me like that." She snapped her fingers. "She's sure she's right about everything. She might have been a preacher if the job was open to women. Instead she just preaches at me and anybody else who will stand still five minutes."

Abigail could not disagree with that assessment of their grandmother. Mammi never used five words when she could use thirty. "She does like to parcel out advice."

"Everything sounds like a lecture, not advice. I can never usually make out the point of what she tries to say."

You learn. Abigail got up slowly, legs a little numb from being motionless so long.

"Gabby, I don't think I want to be Amish."

Ruthie never ceased to surprise her. "Is that something you need to decide this morning?"

"I guess not. It's just that . . . I want to do something with my life. Something big, like Aunt Ruth did. I want my life to start."

Mammi rapped on the kitchen window and motioned for them to come inside, impatience writ large on her face.

"I guess it's time to get ready for church." Ruthie tossed the tea out onto the snow and it made a mark. The first mark on the powdered sugar landscape. "Thanks again for last night's rescue, Gabby."

"Call me Abigail, please," but Ruthie was already inside by the time she finished the last word of her sentence.

⁓

During the night, several inches of snow had fallen. David knew that Birdy would be out walking on this morning, the first true and lasting snowfall of the year. She liked to make the first tracks through the top crust, to fully appreciate the stark beauty of this annual event.

Emily, Lydie, and Molly peeked into his room to see if he

was awake. He motioned to them, and they lunged toward him in a fierce, possessive hug. He looped his arms around them. "I'm fine, girls. Just fine."

Ruthie came into his room with a cup of something steaming from it. "You girls go and get ready for church." As they clambered off his bed, she handed him the cup. "This is from Mammi."

Ah, coffee! David took a sip and nearly spit it out. "What is it?" It tasted like fresh-cut grass.

"Chamomile tea. It's the first day of your new diet."

David set it down. "No coffee?"

"Never again."

David cringed. This new diet was going to take getting used to. He felt a vague sense of deprivation, then chided himself for such thoughts. Had he kept going through his wife's passing, his church's corruption, and all that happened in between, only to be felled by a bleeding ulcer?

"So how *are* you feeling?"

"Not so bad."

"You gave Molly and the twins a scare last night."

And you, David thought. He could see relief ease over her face. "Merely an overreaction."

"Doesn't sound like it." She ran a finger along the night table by his bedside. "I forgot to tell you that Birdy's strategy seemed to work."

"What strategy is that?"

"Making cookies for the boy who teased Molly. Each day, Molly has left cookies on his desk." She snapped her fingers. "Voilà. It worked. They're not even calling her names any longer."

"Luke Schrock didn't have anything to do with it, did he?"

"Nope. I decided to take your advice and give Birdy a chance to solve the problem her way." She rose to her feet. "Mammi is making you some kind of pasty-looking food. I can bring it up to you before we leave for church."

"No. I'll come down."

"Mammi said you are not to leave this bed."

He gave her a weak smile. "I'm feeling fine today. Truly I am."

Ruthie hesitated at the doorjamb. "Gabby said that my aunt Ruth was working in the emergency room."

"Yes." David watched his daughter for a long moment, knowing she had been working up to this. "It was quite a surprise to wake up and find her at the foot of my bed. Then she was called away and I didn't see her after that. But I'll follow up."

"Promise?"

"Absolutely. Nothing happens by chance. There's a reason I was in the emergency room last night." He looked at the weak, watery tea. If God used a stomach ulcer to get him into the hospital at just the right moment to cross paths with his missing sister, then he had found something to be thankful for over it.

19

Jesse thought things through as he made his way home, leading his horse home by the reins. There was just enough snow on the ground to safely deliver Eli Smucker's buggy on the sled attachments, and Jesse was pleased that the recycled square bolts had held tight.

He had brought C.P. with him so that the dog could have a good walk on the way back. The walk would wear him out, and that was one of the first lessons Jesse had learned about puppies. A tired puppy was a good puppy. There were times when Jesse realized that everyone could learn much simply by living with a dog.

Overall, canine companionship had become an unexpected pleasure for Jesse. There were times when C.P. ignored firm boundaries—such as when he got into Fern's garden and dug up some old carrots to gnaw on, only to throw them up in her kitchen—but those times were coming far less often. Jesse was even finding some qualities to admire in the pup. While other people's dogs yapped and leapt up and slobbered and barked, C.P. kept quiet and close to Jesse, even in town.

But raising a dog was not what was burdening Jesse today. It was Yardstick Yoder. Jesse had made good on his promise to God to spend time with Yardstick if his dad would get well. He even agreed to Yardstick's demand for an outrageously high hourly wage. But then Yardstick told him he wanted to learn how to repair buggies. He wanted to apprentice to Jesse. For the same hourly wage as he was being paid to deliver groceries!

Jesse was barely beyond the apprentice status himself, and scraped along on a modest income. In his mind's eye, he saw his meager earnings evaporate like a puddle on a hot day.

A buggy was approaching from behind, so he stepped off the road to wait until it passed. The buggy slowed, then stopped. Dane Glick leaned out the window and called to him. "Buggy man, how 'bout a lift? You can tie your horse to the back of the buggy."

Why not? The temperature was dropping and Jesse had forgotten his gloves. He whistled to C.P. and slid open the buggy door on the passenger side. The silly puppy leapt into the open buggy door to greet Dane, wagging his tail furiously. Dane leaned over to scratch the pup behind both ears, his favorite thing.

C.P. settled as Dane flicked the reins. He had a look on his face as if he'd just had an encounter with an angel.

"What's up with you?" Jesse said.

"I want to marry her."

"Who? Your new horse?" He grinned, then his grin faded. "Wait . . . you're talking about Gabby, aren't you." He vaguely remembered that Dane and Gabby had come to the hospital together the other night. It was still astounding to him that Dane was infatuated with his cousin. "Dane, are you sure? Gabby's . . . I don't know . . . she's not your typical girl."

249

"That's what I like about her. Abigail's not silly, like most girls. She's someone you can have a real conversation with."

"I'll say."

"She's straight to the point. Straight question, straight answer."

Being straight to the point was what people generally didn't like about Gabby. "But have you given this some thought? I mean, I can think of a dozen girls you might have more in common with than Gabby."

"Nope. Abigail's the one for me."

Jesse could not imagine a more unlikely pair than Gabby and Dane. Whereas Gabby was serious, Dane was light-hearted. Gabby preferred solitude, Dane hated to be alone. Whatever Dane did, he did with his whole heart. Gabby approached life with great caution. She was inflexible; Dane's whole life was driven by spontaneity. He was passionate about his horse-healing business and spoke of his horses as if they were family members. Gabby avoided any and all relationships, people or otherwise. "I think you need to slow down. Take your time. Get to know her."

"There's just something about her, Jesse. I realize she's your cousin, but even you can't deny that she's a beautiful woman."

"Gabby? Beautiful?" In a certain light, Jesse supposed that Gabby could be considered attractive. "Dane, I have to be honest—Gabby isn't right for you. In fact, she's all wrong."

Dane's face fell. "You're trying to let me down easy, aren't you?" He frowned. "Did she tell you something? I come on too strong, don't I?" He squeezed his hands into fists and pounded the dashboard. "I knew it! I scared her off."

"No, it's nothing like that. It's you. You need someone who can match your energy. Your . . . enthusiasm."

Dane relaxed a little. "Perhaps you underestimate her."

"But . . . she's not . . . average."

"Average sounds pretty bland. It sounds . . . like my sheep."

"She tends to think she's the authority on most subjects."

"Yes! Yes. Abigail has a natural authority."

Jesse took off his hat and scratched his head. "Why is it you sound like you're describing one of your horses?"

"A horse? That's ridiculous. Why, Abigail is . . . breathtaking. Yes, exactly that. She takes my breath away." Dane pulled the horse off to the side of the road as he approached the Windmill Farm mailbox at the base of the driveway. "You'll keep this conversation to yourself, won't you?"

Distracted by the sight in a passing buggy, Jesse barely nodded as he climbed out. In it were Mim Schrock and Danny Riehl, laughing together, as if one of them had just told a hilarious joke. Or perhaps they were laughing at Jesse. "Don't worry, Dane. Your secret is safe with me."

Besides, whom would he have to tell?

At last, Abigail felt she was making progress breaking through the brick wall. Her grandmother could soon set her meddling focus on someone else, and she would return to Ohio to report her findings to her father. All would be well.

She had driven Thistle over to Dane Glick's hill in the afternoon and found him in the horse barn. "Have you eaten in the last thirty minutes?"

He swept his hat off his head and bent over at the waist in an exaggerated bow. "And a pleasure it is to exchange a warm salutation with you, Abigail."

251

His words and actions flustered her, so she ignored them. "Have you? Eaten anything, I mean."

"Nope."

"Brushed your teeth or used mouthwash in the last thirty minutes?"

He shook his head.

"Excellent." She held out the sample collection tube for Dane. "Spit into this."

"Excuse me?"

"You promised to help me. Don't you remember?"

"Yes. Of course. Of course I remember doing that. It's just . . . why?"

"To provide a sample for the DNA kit. Your saliva will be analyzed to determine your ancestry." She was relieved it didn't require a blood sample.

Dane looked at her, then at the plastic tube. Slowly, he took it from her and spit into it. "Okay, here you go."

She peered at the line on the tube. "Spit some more. You have to fill it to that line."

Dane spit into the tube again, until Abigail was satisfied. She clicked the cap onto the sample and put it into the bio-hazard bag, sealing it shut. "I'll get it out in today's mail. It should take anywhere from one week to four weeks to get the lab results."

Dane smiled, listening to her.

She paused, then peered up at him. "What's wrong?"

"Nothing. Please continue."

"You're laughing at me."

"I'm not laughing at you."

"You're smiling."

"I'm simply moved by how much you seem to love what

you do. And you do, don't you?" He held her gaze a little longer than necessary.

She wished she didn't genuinely like this man as much as she did.

She sealed the box to drop off at the post office. "Dane, there's something else. Would you be willing to ask Freeman for a favor?"

"Certainly. What kind of favor?"

"I'd like to see the Glick family Bible."

Dane looked up and down the aisle of his barn. He glanced at the wall clock. "There's no time like the present."

"Now?" You'd think she would be growing accustomed to Dane's spontaneity, but it always took her by surprise.

"Now. We can drop the spit box in a mailbox down the road." He took her hand in his and led her out to where Thistle was patiently waiting in the buggy. After helping her in, he climbed inside and paused, a cat-in-the-cream look in his eyes. He reached into the backseat and retrieved a bag. In it was a small, thin box, carefully wrapped, which he handed to Abigail. "This is a present for you," he said. "I was going to drop it by later this week. I hope you like it."

Abigail looked at the box. "Why? Why did you get me a gift?"

"It's a small thank-you for organizing my cabin." He grinned. "Go ahead. Open it."

Abigail tore open the paper. Inside the box was a pen.

"It's for your important genealogy work."

It was the most beautiful thing she had seen, and she struggled with her tears. He was a fine man, Dane Glick was, a good man, who noticed things she thought were important. He was very kind to her. Very kind.

She looked at the beautiful pen in her hands. She could not speak.

And then she sneezed.

❧

Twenty minutes later, Dane and Abigail were knocking at the door of the Big House. Freeman opened the door. His piercing gaze shifted from Dane to Abigail, back to Dane.

Dane took off his hat. "I'd like you to let Abigail see our family Bible."

"Why?"

"Her father has a reputation for helping people trace their family roots. I'd written to her father a while back, and he's been creating a family tree for the Glicks. For all of us. No one has done that in our family, correct?"

"There's never been a need for it. We know the people we come from."

"No doubt. And not everyone is interested in genealogy, but I am. I suppose it's because of my work with horses. I can see how pedigrees play out over the years."

Freeman's expression indicated disbelief. Abigail started to think about escape plans. "Meaning what?"

"Just that it's fascinating to discover the history that re-peats itself. For example, do you have any idea how many ordained leaders there are in the Glick line? That kind of information is interesting."

Oh, excellent point, Dane.

Freeman softened, just a little. His shoulders dropped, the set of his jaw relaxed.

"So Abigail is trying to finish up the project for her father and needs to confirm a few dates."

"I can answer any questions you have. The Glicks suffered for their faith in Europe, and were the first to come to the New World."

"Yes, yes, we know all that. She just wanted to confirm a few things. It won't take long."

Freeman looked at Abigail. "Why would I do a favor for the niece of David Stoltzfus?"

"Because you're not a spiteful man."

Actually, Freeman *was* a spiteful man. But Abigail was quite impressed with how Dane was conducting the interview. His approach appeared sound and well considered, calm and credible. That was fortunate because Abigail was struggling to focus. Her mind was still reeling from the hand-holding incident back in Dane's horse barn. She wasn't accustomed to having her hand held by a young man. Did it mean something more to him than just helping her to the buggy? Was it significant? She wished Laura were here to help analyze the situation.

Dane seemed unaware of the importance of the hand-holding incident and remained focused on persuading Freeman to bring out the family Bible. "Abigail has nothing to do with what's going on in our church. Nothing whatsoever. An innocent bystander."

Freeman had yet to take his eyes off Abigail, as if he knew all the jumbled thoughts that were running through her mind and disapproved of them. Suddenly he gave a brief nod, his mouth so tight it all but disappeared into his beard. He opened the door for them and pointed to the kitchen table. "Sit."

They sat.

Freeman turned to go up the stairs. If Abigail was lucky,

Freeman would not open the Bible before handing it over to her.

She wasn't lucky. She was never lucky. But then again, she didn't believe in luck.

Dane winked at her. "Relax."

She tried, but it was difficult to relax in the Big House. Eyes were everywhere. Freeman's and Levi's wives bustled in the kitchen, small children slipped in and out of the room. No one said a word, but everyone watched them.

Then in the front door came Leroy, blowing a bubble. His eyes went huge when he saw Abigail. He snapped the bubble. "What are you doing here?"

"We're here to see the family Bible," Dane said.

Freeman returned to the room, set the Bible carefully on the kitchen table, and stood back. Something fluttered out of the Bible and Abigail gasped. Freeman bent down and picked up some bubblegum wrappers. He looked at Leroy, who was tiptoeing out of the kitchen toward the front door, then he looked at Abigail. Dots connected in his mind. Abigail could see it happen as clearly as if he was drawing a picture on paper. The front door slammed shut.

Freeman marched to the front door, opened it, and boomed, "Leroy Glick! Get back here at once."

Abigail could see Leroy running up the hill that led to the Hanging Tree—the same refuge spot for Dane as a boy. When she turned her attention back to the table, she saw that Dane had opened the Bible to its bulging center, found the Bent N' Dent notepad, and was peering at it curiously. Slowly, he lifted his head and handed it to her. "Perhaps this is what you were looking for."

Yes. Yes, exactly that.

Winter arrived in its completeness. Even in the middle of the days, bright with sunlight, the temperature barely hovered above freezing. A crumbling ridge of snowbanks, built up by the snowplows, nearly closed in the driveway leading to the Stoltzfus farm.

David had been working half days since his hospital visit, but today he felt well enough to last the full day at the store. However, the snow returned once more in the afternoon, covering the roads with an icy crust where any movement could be hazardous. No customers would be venturing out today, so he decided to close up early.

The wind was raw and cold, so David carefully secured each footstep against a fall, eager to escape mishap and get home from the store. Such careful responsibility was a far cry from his childhood enthusiasm for sledding with his sister Ruth on the hill. Back then, when he was a boy, danger was a thrill, but now he preferred to use the wintry conditions as an excuse to stay at home and concentrate on his next sermon.

Ruth.

So many memories of his sister had come flooding back to him in the last few days. She had a rebellious streak from the start, that sister of his. Most of the trouble he got into as a boy was started by Ruth. Playing hooky from school together, fishing in the lake on a summer afternoon, hiding from his mother after they broke a window while playing ball. He smiled to himself as he walked down the road. Ruth had confessed that she had thrown the ball that broke the window—she hadn't, he had—and took the punishment for him so he could go to a friend's birthday party.

A few years later, Ruth's independent streak took her down a different path. She wanted to go to high school. Their mother refused, insisting she start work in the family store. She demanded that Ruth become baptized, along with her friends. His mother was convinced that defining Ruth's path would squelch her rebellious attitude. Wrong, wrong, wrong. She only pushed it underground.

Secretly, Ruth studied for her high school proficiency test, the GED, and passed it. He would never forget the cold, hard, silent response of his mother on the morning Ruth announced that she had been accepted to a private college with a full scholarship, and that she was going.

And she did go. She left and she stayed away. His mother never mentioned Ruth's name again, as if she had died.

For the last few days, David had called the hospital to leave a message for his sister, but she had yet to return his call. His mother had yet to mention her name. What more could he do to try to reach out to her? It was no coincidence that Ruth was working the afternoon David was in the emergency room. Nothing happens by chance. Surely, God was at work to bring their family back together. He looked up at the gray skies. "In your time, Lord," he prayed aloud. "Your time. Not mine."

As he walked across the quiet, snowy meadow, his thoughts strayed once again to Birdy, as they often did when he had moments alone. He wondered what she might be doing, and when on earth he was going to see her again. He missed her far more than he had anticipated, and wished she were with him. And yet he had made no effort to see her, to spend time with her, since he had seen her in the hospital. He hadn't dropped by the schoolhouse; she hadn't stopped by the store.

Things were put on hold between them. Could they drift on as they were, or would things have to be decided one way or another?

This situation was far from straightforward. As Isaac Bender and his team slowly made their way around Stoney Ridge to gather information about Freeman, David heard rumors of what he had most feared: a simmering feud was developing between the Glicks, of which there were many, and David. Birdy was smack-dab in the middle of it. She might not think her loyalty lay with her family, but when push came to shove, how could it not? As his mother said, blood was thicker than water.

The questions Isaac's team posed to the church family were wrenching. For the last few days, they went from home to home, interviewing each member. It had to be done, Isaac reminded him, to gather truth, but the toll on everyone was profound. No one wanted to be disloyal to church leaders, but the truth had to be discerned.

How hard it must be, David pondered, to be pulled in a tug-of-war between two loyalties, family and church, at the same time. But then, wasn't duality also at the heart of Christianity? He had to be both a man and a Christian. David was not at all confident how he had been at doing this. Perhaps he was too sensitive to his own flaws, but he worried how far he fell short of living in God's image. It was his duty to put his identity as a minister above his own desires. He was a minister first.

And there was his answer. His relationship with Birdy needed to be set aside until this church matter was resolved. That realization made him sad and he stopped for a moment to consider what that meant.

All around him, snow fell in an unhurried quiet, as if there could be no stopping it. He held his hand out for fragile white flakes to softly make their rest.

Not long ago David had read an essay by astronomer and mathematician Johannes Kepler called "The Six-Cornered Snowflake." A snowflake was the perfect Christmas gift, Kepler mused, because it came from the heavens and looked like a star. Then the scientist went on to ponder why a snowflake always had six corners. Why not five corners? Why not seven? No two snowflakes were alike, but each one was a hexagon.

To David, the answer was obvious. An epiphany. *Epiphaneia*, a visible appearing of something hitherto invisible. In ancient Greece, the word was used to describe a sunrise. On this wintry afternoon, David's epiphany was an illustration from the natural world of the sovereignty of God, extending from the heavens to the snowflake.

Perhaps Kepler's thoughtful muses were an answer to his prayer this morning. Nothing, from the infinite to the minute, happens by chance in the economy of God.

20

A few days after the unfortunate Notepad in the Bible Incident, Abigail sat on the floor of the living room and began wrapping Christmas presents. She tied the last present, sat back, and leaned on the heels of her hands. Christmas was weeks away, and she was hopeful she would be back in Ohio by then, but Mammi was abundantly clear that they would leave only when the time was right and she was the only one who knew when that time would be. Abigail felt it would be wise to be prepared for every possible scenario.

She heard a rapping at the door and went to answer it, finding Dane with a troubled look on his face. "Dane! What's wrong?"

"Freeman is rather upset," Dane began.

Abigail nodded. "That is, if I may say, his natural condition."

Dane's face softened, and amusement came into his eyes. "I meant he's rather upset that you had seen the Glick Family Bible without his knowledge. So I don't think it's going to work out to get another look at the Bible."

"I realized that after he told us to leave his house. But I

have another idea. I thought it might be wise to check with the sisters at the Sisters' House and see if they might have found anything. They said they would look."

"That's right. I forgot about that." He thumped his hat on his head. "So let's be off."

"Now?"

"Why not? There's no time like the present."

By now it was well into afternoon. Darts of sunlight came through the windshield, and Dane had to lower the brim of his hat to shade his eyes from the glare. His hands briefly tightened on the reins.

Abigail was glad her face was partially shadowed. "Thank you, for—" her voice caught—"doing this for me."

"It's for me too. I started this whole thing. I'm as curious as you are."

"I haven't received the DNA sample results yet, but I'm hoping they'll arrive within the week. If everything goes according to plan, I'll be home for Christmas."

Dane's smile faded. She watched his fist clench around the reins, watched his hand and wrist turn rigid. "You're not planning to stay for Christmas?"

"If I can wrap up this case, it will be a wonderful Christmas gift for my father."

"But you'd come back after Christmas, wouldn't you?"

"No. No reason to." Not unless Mammi intervened, and Abigail doubted she would object. She had been thoroughly preoccupied with Uncle David's ulcer lately. She hadn't even gone to the store. The Bent N' Dent reorganization project had ground to a halt.

Their gazes met, and lingered, and parted. He gathered

up the reins and slapped the horse's backside to pick up its pace, but he remained quiet for the rest of the ride.

At the Sisters' House, Sylvia opened the door with a look of delight. "How perfect! I've been meaning to send a note to you, but this snow has rendered us housebound." She opened the door wide to make room for them. "Come in, come in out of the cold."

The other four sisters sat in the living room, each occupied with her own task. Clearly, Abigail saw with dismay, no one seemed to have done much organizing since she had last been here. She had to clasp her hands behind her back to keep from tidying up. The four sisters started to talk, all at once, asking about David's ulcer, offering suggestions for mild, easy-to-digest food.

"Stewed crackers," Lena said.

"Soaked in milk," Fannie said.

"Epsom salts," Ada said. "Makes a fine liver flush."

"Liver?" Fannie said in an annoyed tone. "Liver? David's got an ulcer."

After a few moments, Sylvia raised a delicate hand, forefinger slightly extended, and a hush fell over the room.

Abigail made note. So that's how it was done. "My cousin Jesse told me he found a wooden chest in the carriage house that he thought might be useful."

Sylvia tilted her head. "Have you ever heard of Fraktur?"

"The art?"

"It was a common way to record family documents among the Penn Dutch, back in the 1800s. My great-grandmother was quite fond of decorative Fraktur. She was known for her skill and was commissioned to paint for families. She painted the interior of her trunk. That's the chest. That's the one Jesse found for us."

Abigail gasped. This was just the kind of find she had been hoping for! She looked to Dane and he grinned. "I'll go with Sylvia," he said. "You stay here with the sisters."

Sylvia and Dane returned from the carriage house. In Dane's arms was a large chest. He set it down, huffing and puffing. Sylvia lifted the lid. Inside was a beautiful painting with familiar motifs: distelfink birds, hearts, and someone's wedding date. Abigail moved in closer. She didn't touch anything, didn't lift anything out, but she did peer closer into the dark corners of the chest. She could see stiff leathered baby shoes in one corner, and in another, a stack of newspapers. She felt eyes resting heavily on her.

She looked up to see all five sisters, plus Dane, watching her. "Abigail, we should be heading home soon," he said cautiously.

"Perhaps you'd like to take the chest home with you, dear?" Sylvia asked. "You could take all the time you'd like to go through it. We don't mind, do we, sisters? It's just gathering dust and mold."

Abigail's hand flew to her chest. "Oh, yes. Yes!"

⁓

It was cold. Wind howled through every chink in the house. Abigail sat on the floor of her bedroom, wearing her black sweater over her nightgown, sure she could see her breath. Now and then, she heard things scuttle in the wall and wondered why Uncle David didn't get a cat to chase those mice.

Laura had insisted on turning out the light so she could go to sleep. She had been up at the crack of dawn this morning so that she could be in the phone shanty, waiting for a call from Tenacious Tim. That was their habit, to meet early each day to talk to each other.

Unfortunately, Tenacious Tim seemed to be losing his tenacity. He missed calling two days in a row. Laura, who waited patiently for the phone to ring in a dark shanty on those freezing cold mornings, was growing concerned. She even mentioned that she might be returning to Ohio sooner than expected. Abigail thought it might have something to do with Tenacious Tim's excuse that he had a new neighbor, someone named Ruby, who needed help moving in. He was exhausted, he told Laura, and had slept in the next morning.

Abigail gave Laura her best advice: "Girls named for jewels are always trouble." That helpful insight seemed to only increase Laura's anxiety. She said she would give Tim one more chance, she would wait one more morning for his phone call.

"And then what?" Abigail asked. "What will you do if he doesn't call tomorrow?"

Laura had glared at her. "You just don't like Tim, do you?"

"I don't have an opinion about him one way or the other," Abigail said. Other than his caterpillar eyebrows. Those were dreadful.

Laura blew out the light, turned to the wall, and pulled the sheets over her head.

That was why, in a darkened room with only a flashlight for illumination, Abigail sifted alone through the old sisters' chest. With each new musty object she pulled out, her excitement grew, as if she was on a treasure hunt. And in a way, she was.

Inside this old chest was exactly the kind of treasure trove she hoped to discover in Stoney Ridge. But what an odd assortment of things! A pair of leather baby shoes, never worn—what was the story behind those shoes? Spectacles that looked like Mammi's. A horseshoe, a small cast-iron fry pan. She dug farther. Toward the bottom of the chest were old receipts, neatly bound with a piece of twine. A handwritten cookbook, full of ingredients she had never heard of, like Indian meal or Indian suet. Fascinating! To think of two cultures, Amish and Native American, so entirely different from each other, colliding in those early years of Pennsylvania history. Maybe colliding wasn't the right way to think of it, if these recipes were any indication. Influencing each other might be a more apt description. *Interesting.*

She came across a recipe for Hard Sugar Gingerbread to be cut with a jagging iron. What in the world? She would have to research jagging irons. She spent far too long studying old recipes, curious about them. Most of the recipes, quite obviously, were designed to make use of any and all available food. A coffee cake required a full cup of leftover coffee. A cottage pudding used up stale bread. Mammi might like these recipes. She was always complaining that the Stoltzfus children wasted too much food. All but Molly.

It was fascinating, this chest, but not enlightening to the matter at hand: who was HOR mentioned in Freeman's family Bible? She closed the cookbook, set it aside to give to Mammi, and yawned. She was about to give up for the night when she noticed a torn, yellowed newspaper page lying on the bottom of the chest. She shone the spotlight on it and reached in to pick it up. It was stuck to the bottom of the chest, so she set the flashlight down and used two hands to slowly loosen it without tearing it. She lifted it up and shone the spotlight on it, reading it once, twice, a third time.

Abigail could barely breathe, hardly move. Here it was. The second piece of evidence.

⁓

After dropping the girls off at school, Abigail drove the buggy straight to the sisters at the Sisters' House. Sylvia opened the door and invited her in. "I found something," Abigail announced. "Something important."

"How nice," Sylvia said, as if Abigail had just delivered the day's weather forecast. "Come have a cup of tea and tell us all about it."

"No tea," Abigail said. "No time."

"Well, you'll have to make time. We can't do much thinking until we have our breakfast." She waved a hand toward the dining room. The other sisters sat at the table, eating breakfast, a rather slow process. They looked up with mild interest, then returned to their toast and tea and soft-boiled eggs. All but Ella. She sat at the far end of the table, her chin to her chest, there but not really there. The fog had settled over her.

"It's not a good day for Ella," Sylvia whispered. She pointed to a chair for Abigail and poured a cup of tea for her.

Reluctantly, Abigail slipped into the chair. "I was looking through the trunk and I found this." She took out a plastic baggie. In it was a tattered, yellowed newspaper page from the *Lancaster County Gazette*, dated May 15, 1881. She still couldn't believe that she had found it. She was *that* close to refilling the chest with the sisters' belongings and returning it to them. *That* close!

Fannie peered at Abigail over the brim of her teacup. "Tell us what you've found. We don't have our readers handy."

Carefully, Abigail lifted up the baggie with the paper in it. "Does the name Harry O'Reilly mean anything to you?"

The sisters looked at each other and shook their heads. "No idea."

"None."

"Never heard of him."

"Long before our time."

Ella stirred to life. "I remember," she started softly. She lifted her head and looked straight at Abigail, clearing her throat a few times before she spoke again. "Horsethief Harry."

"Yes!" Abigail said, clasping her hands together. "Yes, that's him."

"I remember a story Grossvatti told about Horsethief Harry."

All eyes turned to Ella, their faces a look of astonishment. "Do go on, dear," Sylvia said, hope in her voice. "We want to hear what you remember."

"It was right after the Civil War," Ella said, her voice gaining strength, her face gaining animation. "Boys returned from the battlefield without work or money, without knowing what to do or where to do it. Harry O'Reilly was one of those boys. He returned home to find that home was gone, burned to the ground. Even if he could get his farm back up and running, there was no market. The whole country was worn out from the war, low on funds, low on morale. Harry found the only market that was a sure thing. Horse dealing." She smiled. "Horse stealing."

She paused, closing her eyes, and Abigail panicked for a moment, worried Ella's memories might fade away as quickly as they resurfaced.

Ella coughed a few times to clear her throat, but then began again. "Everybody relied on their horses back then. Everyone, not just farmers. It was the only mode of transport."

"That's true," Lena said. "Other than the railroad."

"When did railroads go in?" Ada asked.

"Hush!" Fannie shushed them, and Abigail was glad. She'd seen too many conversations go off on bunny trails. "Ella, tell us what you remember about Harry."

Ella closed her eyes for a moment and Abigail worried she had fallen asleep. Then her eyes popped open. "Harry O'Reilly was well connected, and liked by all. He was tall and handsome, said to have a powerful frame. Mostly, though, he was shrewd, one of the smartest men in the whole of Pennsylvania. He had a way of stealing horses so that even the owner couldn't recognize his own horse."

"How?" Abigail said. "How did he manage that?"

"Quiet," Fannie said, pointing a thin finger at Abigail. "Don't interrupt her. When she's got something to tell us, we need to wait patiently for her to unpack all that's tucked away in her mind."

It was like waiting for the fog to lift, Abigail thought. Like waiting for the sun to warm the sky so the morning mist would dissipate. Painfully slow.

Fannie frowned at her, as if she could read her impatient thoughts. "Go on, Ella."

"Horses would be taken from the field or barn at night, and Harry would use tricks to change the appearance of the horse. He was so good at it that folks used to say even the colt's mother wouldn't know it."

"What would he do?" Ada asked.

She made a scrubbing motion in the air with her hand, back and forth. "He'd sandpaper a young horse's sides or shoulders so they looked like harness marks, just like an old seasoned workhorse. Or he'd paint markings on a horse with a brush, white socks on its legs, or a blaze down its nose. Harry was an artist, you see."

She stopped for a moment, took a sip of tea, swallowed. Her sisters didn't move a muscle; they leaned forward in their chairs, waiting for Ella's next chapter of the story to unfold. But Ella focused her eyes on the ceiling, not to be hurried.

"It wasn't long before he had a whole ring of horse thieves working for him, from Kentucky to Maine. He'd sell horses far away from where he stole them."

Lena tapped a finger on the table. "And they never caught him?"

Ella shook her head. "Harry supplied horses to every state in the union, every state! But no lawman could ever gather enough evidence to touch him. So in he came to Lancaster County, having heard about what fine horses this county had to offer, thinking he was safe from the long arm of the law. While he was here, he met a young woman."

Abigail tapped her heels. She could hardly keep herself contained, she was that excited. Although anecdotal, and although told by a woman whose memory sputtered like a candle flame, this legend verified other pieces of information. She waited and waited for Ella to continue, but couldn't hold herself back. "Elizabeth Glick!"

Ella looked over at Abigail as if she had just now noticed she was there. Her cloudy eyes crinkled at the edges in delight. "Yes. Elizabeth Glick. He and Elizabeth fell in love and wanted to marry, but they faced obstacles."

"Well, he wasn't Amish," Ada said.

"And he was a thief," Fannie said.

"Yes," Ella said in a thoughtful tone. "Yes, he was a thief, but he was known to be a thief with a heart of gold. He'd never steal a horse from someone who couldn't afford to lose one. And he wouldn't allow violence or cruelty among his men."

Ada clasped her hands to her heart. "Like Robin Hood."

"Oh yes!" Lena said. "And Jesse James. He was known to be a kind and generous thief."

"A generous thief would be considered an oxymoron," Abigail pointed out.

"Shhhhh," Fannie hissed.

Ella stopped then and took a sip of tea, one after another, while her sisters waited with bated breath. Abigail had to sit on her hands to stop fidgeting.

"Horsethief Harry loved Elizabeth, but he had promised his men one more raid. He was an honorable man, after all, good for his word."

"He was a thief!" Fannie said.

"But a good-hearted thief," Ada reminded her.

"Harry told Elizabeth it would be his last one, and then he would convert to the Amish and marry her. Unfortunately"—Ella's thin capstrings bounced on her shoulders as she shook her head—"he stole the wrong man's horses."

Now Sylvia chimed in. "What happened?"

"Yes, what next?" Abigail said.

Fannie frowned at them. "Let Ella finish the story."

"An English farmer, a proud man who raised the best horses in the county, the very best, had started the Lancaster Anti–Horse Thief Society." She shook her head. "It was too tempting to Harry. He had a greedy streak. If he was going to make one last raid, he thought it would be fitting to make off with

271

that proud farmer's fine horses. But he underestimated that farmer. He'd been expecting Harry. And so Harry walked himself right into a trap."

"Go on, Ella," Lena said. "Don't stop."

"The penalty for horse thieving was to be hanged without trial."

"No!" Ada said. "Oh no. Don't tell me that our Harry was hanged!"

Abigail's toes were dancing. "He was! Horsethief Harry was hanged for horse thieving. On the Hanging Tree!"

"Shush," Fannie said, her spectacled gaze grazing Abigail with a scowl. "Continue with your tale, Ella dear."

"Yes," Ella said. "That young girl is right. He was hanged on the Hanging Tree that very day."

"A man's life for a horse," Ada said sadly.

Abigail could wait no longer. "And then Elizabeth had Horsethief Harry's baby!"

An awkward silence fell over the table. The sisters exchanged looks, then they reached out for their teacups, all at once as if they'd rehearsed it. They sipped on their tea, eyes fixed on the brim of the cup.

What had Abigail just done? "But . . . isn't that the truth?" After all, wasn't that the point of discovery in the entire story of Horsethief Harry? She had broken through the brick wall. She had found the missing father.

"Well," Ella said, eyeing Abigail as if she was the one who was senile. Her mouth puckered into a tight purse and her chin doubled. "We don't like to talk about things like that."

Then, just like that, as vividly as if someone blew out a candle, the animation left Ella's face and the fog returned.

Late in the day on Saturday, David set out a Grocery Shower box by the cash register for Ida Burkholder, an elderly woman who had recently broken her hip in a fall. As customers checked out and noticed the box, they would often donate some extra food for Ida. As soon as the box was full, David would deliver it.

The sound of clopping hooves drew him to the window. Isaac Bender climbed out of his buggy and walked toward the store, beard tucked against his chest.

So. Here it comes. Isaac had made his decision. David knew it without being told.

He opened the door as Isaac reached the steps. The big man paused, gave David a nod, and strode past him into the store. He took off his hat, ruffled his hair, and gazed around the store, slightly taken aback. "Is it always like this?"

David looked down the long rectangular store and saw it with fresh eyes. The store was a mess. Boxes were everywhere, shelves were half stocked, half empty, a ladder blocked the only pathway to his storeroom. His mother's keen interest in reorganizing the store had sputtered out after Thanksgiving. He'd grown so accustomed to the disorder that he hadn't even noticed. Every day, he ducked under the ladder to get to his storeroom without a second thought.

Was this what it was like in the Sisters' House? The old sisters didn't even see their own clutter and chaos anymore. It had become normal.

"We're in the middle of a reorganization," David said. A very long middle. No end in sight.

Isaac turned to him. "Are we alone?"

"Yes. I was just closing up." He walked to the front door and flipped the OPEN sign over to read CLOSED. He pointed to the rocker by the woodstove—the only one left in place by his mother. Hank had insisted on it and David backed him up. Isaac sat in the rocker and David sat across from him on a box of dented green bean cans. As soon as his mother returned to Ohio, he promised himself, those rockers would be moved back in. The very day she left! "Would you like a cup of coffee? Or tea?"

"No, no." Isaac settled back into the chair. "You know why I'm here."

David nodded.

"We've met nearly everyone. I must say that Stoney Ridge has very loyal church members."

"Yes. There are wonderful people in this town. Some of the finest people I've ever known." Amos and Fern Lapp of Windmill Farm, Carrie and Abel Riehl, Sadie and Gideon Smucker, Rose and Galen King from the Inn at Eagle Hill, Bess and Billy Lapp at Rose Hill Farm, Thelma Beiler of Moss Hill, the sisters of the Sisters' House. And Hank Lapp, of course. One of Stoney Ridge's most loyal.

"I'll be candid with you, David." Isaac shifted one leg over the other. "The great majority of church members want to do nothing. Just sweep it all under the rug and move forward. Learn from past mistakes but don't dwell on them."

David took in every word, not at all sure where Isaac was heading.

"There are both good and bad reasons to do nothing," Isaac said.

Yes, David thought, *but more bad than good. The bad reason is that doing nothing is easier. Quieting an ordained leader* is *a drastic step.*

"In this situation," Isaac continued, "there might be some good reasons to do nothing. No one really has the heart for anything else. Freeman Glick has been a dedicated, conscientious minister. Everyone has known him for years. They want to help, not destroy the work he's done."

David swallowed. Indecision was a decision. *The* decision. *Well,* he told himself. *Well, well. You asked for outside help, to guide and direct this path. You have to accept what guidance is provided, even if it isn't the path you believe to be the right one. That's the burden and the blessing of community.* This was another form of listening well, listening attentively and respectfully. He couldn't hear only what he wanted to hear. Not from God, not from Scripture, not from his community.

"But in all my years of experience, I've learned that doing nothing means that problems are allowed to fester. Doing nothing, when one does something wrong for the greater good, means a long, slippery slope of decline." Isaac folded his big arms in front of him. "Therefore, on Sunday, the Quieting will begin."

21

The sun was beginning to burn off the chill from the morning. Icicles that hung from the house eaves began a steady dripping—*plink, plink, plink*—on the ground. David looked up, surprised by the sound, as the final hymn was sung for the morning service. It's strange how the natural world continues to move along unaffected, unconcerned, indifferent, while the human world is reeling from emotional storms and earthquakes.

Isaac excused all children and youth to go outside and wait, and asked the church members to remain for a meeting. It was a relief to have Jesse and Ruthie and the younger ones outside for this. The important thing now, David knew without any question, was to lead. This was no time for uncertainty. His heart hurt, but Isaac's decision felt right, and there was no doubt in his mind that the church was doing the right thing.

Isaac Bender stood in the center of the room, adjusting his glasses. "My brothers and sisters," he began, "today is a very significant day for the church of Stoney Ridge. After much prayer for discernment, it has been decided that Freeman

Glick and Levi Glick shall have their ordination revoked. In two weeks' time, your church will have another ordination to replace Freeman and Levi Glick. I ask you to pray for discernment over the next two weeks."

Freeman had been silent to this point, his heavy brow knitted, hands gripped behind him, tense and stiff. As Isaac's words settled around the room, Freeman rose to his feet. "This doesn't make any sense," he said. He looked around him frantically, like a man trying to stand upright in a rowboat. "This isn't right! I have done nothing but keep this church together. For generations, my people have been the backbone of Stoney Ridge. Why, my people were some of the first Amish to come to America, and we have preserved the faith for hundreds of years." He glanced at his brother. "Levi and I are 100 percent loyal"—he pounded a fist into his large palm as he made each point—"100 percent Amish, 100 percent German—"

"Actually," Gabby interrupted, "that's not true."

Dozens of white and black caps whipped in her direction.

Tentatively, Gabby rose, a large white envelope in her hands. "In yesterday's mail, I received the results of geno-graphing of the Glicks. It turns out that your people have a substantial percentage of non-Amish blood in your family lineage."

"You what?" Freeman said, incredulous.

Gabby opened up the envelope and pulled out the papers. "My research found an unknown father with the initials HOR in the family Bible, who was the father of Elizabeth Glick's only son, Mose. He was given her last name because she never married the father of her child. He was your great—" she paused to count back, eyes on the ceiling as if it was written there—"great-grandfather. A direct line to Freeman and Levi." She looked past Freeman to the back row of the men's side. "And to Dane. He would be the great-great-great-grandfather to Dane."

The back row of old men stared at her, slack-jawed. Dane, sitting on the edge, had a confused look on his face.

"Gabby," David said, "perhaps now is not the time—"

"I just want to be accurate, Uncle David. These circumstances in church today are so significant and unusual that it seems as if accuracy is important."

On that point, David couldn't argue with her. But she was treading in dangerous waters. Bloodline to Freeman was as cherished as . . . an old family Bible.

"You see, Dane Glick was mapping out his family tree and wrote to my father to ask for help. My father did all he could but, unfortunately, he stopped work on the project. I picked up where he left off and came to a brick wall. When I came to Stoney Ridge, I brought Dane's file along with me. We sent Dane's spit away to a company—"

"His what?" Freeman roared.

"His spit. His saliva. It's a valid and well-known procedure, though I don't deny that blood would always be a better choice for DNA analysis. Anyway, we sent Dane's saliva to a company that determines the percentage of a person's ancestry. It's called a Genographic Kit. Then, the sisters of the Sisters' House—they're Glicks, too, you know—they let me look through an old forgotten chest."

"I'm the one who found that chest," Jesse piped up. He'd been lurking at the window, cracked open for a little fresh air, taking in every word.

David reached over and shut the window with a thud, frowning at him. Jesse lifted his shoulders in a shrug.

"Yes," Gabby said, welcoming Jesse's input, even from outside the house. "My cousin Jesse found the chest in the sisters' carriage house. In the chest was a lot of memorabilia, nothing too enlightening, though I am curious about a pair of unused baby shoes."

"Gabby," David warned.

"Right." Gabby nodded at him. "Stay on task."

That wasn't at all what he meant.

"Anyway, underneath an old cookbook was a newspaper clipping. It described the hanging of Harry O'Reilly for the crime of horse thieving."

"Ella said he had a good heart," Fannie said in a loud voice. "A heart of gold, she said." All eyes turned to her. Sylvia nudged her with her elbow and a few people snickered, which annoyed Fannie. "Well, that's what Ella remembered and I believe her."

Ella smiled.

Freeman was not at all amused. He pointed at Gabby. "Girl, you don't know what you're talking about."

"She's not making any sense at all," Levi said.

"Actually, I have more evidence," Gabby said. "In the Glick family Bible, there's a notation for the father of Mose Glick, great-great-grandfather to Freeman and Levi Glick. His initials were HOR, and he was hung on May 15, 1881. Same day."

A buzz started around the room, mostly among the Glicks, but Gabby was oblivious to it.

"And it does seem logical too that your line of Glicks might have Irish blood in you. The newspaper article mentioned that the sheriff had to find a particularly tall tree limb to hang Horsethief Harry. I think that is where you Glicks get your height, from Harry O'Reilly. Ella said he was tall, with a powerful frame. You're tall, Freeman, and have a powerful frame. And consider your sister Birdy's height—"

David glanced at Birdy, who was staring at Gabby, wide-eyed and fascinated.

Freeman crossed the room and grabbed the envelope out of Gabby's hands. "Irish? *Irish?* You have no evidence of that!"

"But I do." She pointed to the papers. "And now you do. A full 16 percent of your ancestry. Pretty substantial, if you ask me."

Freeman tore the envelope into two halves and threw them on the ground.

"Gabby, sit down," Laura whispered.

"But . . . it's just part of the Glick family story."

Laura tugged on Gabby's sleeve until she sat down. "Freeman doesn't want that part of the story."

The room was utterly silent. A pin could have dropped.

Isaac cleared his throat. "Let me repeat, so that everyone is absolutely clear on this matter. The ordination of Freeman Glick and Levi Glick has been revoked."

David thought he glimpsed just a touch of something not totally clear, a fine mist coating Freeman's eyes, as all dwindling hope in him was extinguished. Slowly, like he was an old man though he wasn't at all old, he returned to his spot on the minister's bench and dropped his chin to his chest.

In the immense quiet, Gabby sneezed.

⌒

Dane Glick, Abigail observed, was wearing a lime-colored shirt today. She identified the color of the fabric but immediately corrected herself. This was a day of worship, a time of fellowship, and not a time to be thinking of limes. He stood by his buggy, hat off and held in both hands.

He lifted his head as she approached him. He looked extremely unhappy. "Abigail, what were you thinking?"

Abigail couldn't put a name to Dane's tone of speech and expression, but it was clearly negative. "Don't tell me that you think like Freeman thinks. That you feel tainted by knowing there's a horse thief in your lineage."

"Just the opposite. It's fascinating to know where I might have gotten my passion for horses." He took a long breath. "But you used me. You wanted my DNA to make a fool out of Freeman."

"No. I never intended to make a fool out of him. He did that himself."

Dane was now looking very upset. "The outcome was the same. You made a fool out of him, and I was part of it."

She was having trouble meeting his gaze. Finally, she made herself look over at him. "I thought I was solving all the problems at once. Cutting the Gordian knot."

"What?"

"The Gordian knot. It's a legend from the sixteenth century. A king named Gordius tied an intricate knot on an oxcart and declared that whoever could untie the knot would become the next king. Alexander the Great sliced the knot with his sword—" she made a slashing motion with her hand—"and became the next king. So a Gordian knot is meant to indicate a bold action that solves the problem. That's what I was trying to do. A bold action to solve the problem. Your family tree was completed and Freeman's assertion that he was beyond reproach was corrected."

He studied her over the next few moments of silence. His eyes saw more than she thought she was showing.

She felt a growing discomfort. "I was just trying to break through your family's brick wall. I thought it was important to you."

"It was, Abigail, it was. But you know, it's much more important who you are today, what you do with your life, than studying about people who lived long ago. We can't really know why they made the kinds of choices they made, or what circumstances they were in when they made them. We weren't in their shoes, so we can't judge. But who you are today, that's what God is asking."

"But the Bible is always telling us to remember. Even your mother kept those memory stones."

"To remember *God*. What he's done."

They drove back to Uncle David's house in silence.

She put her hand on the door handle. "I really should go," she said, even though she wanted to stay. She wanted things to be right between them. Comfortable and easy.

"Okay," he said so quickly that it hurt her feelings.

"I never meant to hurt you," she began.

He nodded, looking as conflicted as she felt. "Maybe not, but you did."

She saw his eyes barely well up, the tears men cry held back in check. He turned away from her, got out of the buggy, and came around the back of it to slide open her door. She stepped out and he closed the door behind her. He took two steps, then turned back to face her. "You never really cared about me, did you? I was just a means to an end." He swallowed hard, his gaze fixed somewhere miles beyond her. "I thought you were different, Abigail."

He climbed into his buggy and drove away before she knew what she wanted to say. Different? She'd been different her entire life. It never occurred to her that someone would want her because she *was* different, not in spite of it.

As Abigail walked toward the house, the awful reality hit her full force. Tears prickled her eyes, and she pressed a fist to her lips. What had she done? What had she done to Dane? The day had turned into a disaster.

22

At the Bent N' Dent, Hank Lapp heard someone say that Freeman was going to cut down the Hanging Tree, so he stopped by Jesse's buggy shop to persuade him to go watch. "Come on with me," Hank said. "It's a 'Big Hat, No Cattle' kind of day."

That was Hank's description of the day's bleak weather—leaden gray skies but no snow. Jesse looked around the buggy shop. Why not? Seeing the Hanging Tree get cut down might be a pretty exciting thing to watch, far more of a thrill than sitting in a buggy shop. He whistled for C.P. and started toward Amos Lapp's cornfield to make a shortcut to the Glick property. "SLOW DOWN, slow down," Hank yelled from behind him. "En Baam fallt net uff der erscht Hack." *A tree falls not at the first stroke.*

Jesse stopped, clapped for C.P. to return to him, and waited for Hank to catch up. When they came to the base of the hill of the big old oak tree, Jesse saw that a small crowd had gathered. Under the oak tree were Freeman and Levi, with winches and ropes and a chainsaw. Their sons stood around them, running and playing tag.

"I don't think I want the children so close," Freeman's wife said as she gathered her children around her like a hen pulls in her chicks.

Dane made his way around them to reach Jesse. "I can't believe it. I just can't believe it." He stood watching for a long moment. Jesse could see something swell up in Dane, until it overflowed.

Dane stomped up the hill a few paces and yelled, "Freeman, what do you think you're doing?"

Freeman turned to locate the voice. "What does it look like? I'm cutting down a dead tree."

"Why now? Why today? It's been dead for years."

"Then it's high time."

"It's your way of getting back at everybody. It's your silent revenge."

Freeman ignored him and reached down to pick up the chainsaw.

Jesse turned to Hank. "What did Dane mean by that? What's silent revenge?"

"That tree." Hank's one good eye was fixed on it. "It's the very tree their illustrious ancestor was hung on."

"Pardon?"

"The infamous horse thief. That's the Hanging Tree."

Oh.

"Freeman!" Dane yelled. "I asked you a question and I want an answer. What are you doing? When are you going to stop trying to make everybody in this town pay for your hurt pride? Nothing is going to change when you take this tree down. It's not going to erase the parts of the story you don't like. Cutting this tree down is your version of lot switching. You can't keep trying to cover things up. You can't pick and choose your history. And guess what? Nobody cares! Nobody cares whether our great-grandfather was illegitimate. Nobody cares that we have a horse thief in our family tree. Nobody cares whether we're 100 percent Amish or 84 percent Amish."

Freeman's jaw clenched and unclenched rhythmically. "Stand back, boy."

But Dane wouldn't stand back. He didn't budge. "All anybody cares about is who you are now. That's what David Stoltzfus has been trying to get through your thick skull. You're not who you should be. I'm ashamed to be related to you and it has nothing to do with a horse thief. It's because of *you*. Your stubborn pride, your selfishness, your hardheartedness. You're always preaching about humility, but you've got more pride than anyone else on God's green earth."

Freeman faced him squarely, his beard bristling. "I told you to stand back." He spoke the words in staccato, angry and pointed.

Dane threw his hands into the air. "What's it going to take, Freeman? What's *ever* going to get through to you?!"

Freeman braced himself, then pulled the chain to start the engine. Crows scattered out of the nearby trees. He set the blade against the tree trunk to start a hinge. He worked for a while, then stopped to take a break and turned off the chainsaw. Levi swept away the sawdust from the hinge.

Dane walked back to join Jesse and Hank, an angry, disgusted look on his face. "He's not even cutting the tree down the right way," Dane said. "He should be taking down more limbs before he starts the hinge. He's doing it wrong."

"RIGHT YOU ARE," Hank boomed. "There's a reason loose branches are called widow-makers."

"So tell him," Jesse said.

Dane folded his arms against his chest and glanced at Jesse. "Haven't you noticed? You don't tell Freeman anything."

"But if it's not safe . . ."

Hank took off his hat and scratched his wild white hair. "I guess he figures there's nothing to hurt out here when the tree drops."

True. But Jesse took a few steps back.

Freeman had his hand on the pull cord when a shout came from down the hill.

"No, Freeman, no! There's a great blue heron nest in that tree!" Everyone turned to see Birdy running up the hill. "You can't chop it down." She ran right up to him and put her hands on the chainsaw.

Freeman jerked it from her. "The tree is dead. The branches are brittle. Keeping it is a danger."

"To whom? No one ever comes out here."

"If I leave it, it will only get rotten and then I can't sell the wood. And I need the wood."

"But not that tree!" She nearly choked over the words. "There are other trees!"

He glared at her. "This tree will provide an abundance of high-quality firewood."

"You have a shed full of stacked firewood." She pointed toward the house. "You could at least wait until the heron moves on."

"Next year? Or the year after?" He shook his beard like a billy goat. "No reason to wait. Levi knows of a man in town who wants white oak lumber to build a sailboat."

"I do," Levi said. "Fellow wants to build a sailboat."

Freeman pulled the cord to start the engine. "Stand back,

Birdy," he shouted over the sound of the engine. "I can't be responsible for you."

Birdy turned to Dane for help.

"Don't bother, Birdy," Dane said, his lips twisting in revulsion. "He won't listen to you. He won't listen to anybody." He walked over to Birdy and pulled her by the arm to stand farther away from where Freeman was working.

Freeman continued to cut through the tree when, over the sound of the engine, a splitting sound filled the air. The vibration of the cutting caused a large branch to snap off, and as it came down, it brought several more with it. The tree started to sway, but in the opposite direction of the hinge made by Freeman. He looked up at the treetop in horror, then turned off the chainsaw and threw it to the ground as he yelled, "Run! Everyone run!"

He took off down the hill behind Levi. Jesse and Dane and Hank bolted a few dozen feet away, then stopped to turn and watch the tree fall. Jesse gasped as he saw Birdy near the tree. Instead of running, Birdy couldn't seem to move. She froze.

Jesse could do nothing except hold his breath, paralyzed by his own helplessness. He could see the whole thing unfold like a bad dream.

As the tree came crashing down on Birdy, the quiet that followed was immediate and complete.

⁓

Birdy was knocked out cold, with a large gash on her head and an arm broken in two places. The doctor set her arm and stitched her cut, but made her stay overnight in the hospital because of her concussion. She slept for fourteen hours, her temperature raised and pulse erratic. David didn't leave her side. This was where he belonged, here with this unadorned woman, whose wholesomeness and kindness made anyone pale in comparison to her. He sat in a chair in a darkened room, just being here. Near her. Praying and thinking.

He heard the door open and saw a doctor walk in. It took a moment for his eyes to adjust and realize that he recognized this doctor, wearing blue scrubs. This doctor was his sister Ruth.

"Hi, David," she whispered. She stood at the end of Birdy's bed. "I just heard about the accident when I started my shift. Sounds like she was lucky. It could have been much, much worse."

"Yes," he said. "She was hit by a branch, but the trunk of the tree missed her by mere inches."

"She's important to you, isn't she? I mean, more than just a church member. Or maybe you do this for all the church members."

"Yes, I would do this for anyone in my church." That was true. "And yes, she is important to me." David looked at Birdy, sleeping peacefully, with a white bandage wrapped around her head.

"The nurses say that whenever you walk into hospital rooms, patients' heart rates go down."

A light smile touched his lips. "Hopefully not too far down."

She grinned. "Is there anything I can do for you, David? You should eat something. I could get you something from the cafeteria. Even a piece of toast would be good for your ulcer. For your stomach. Don't let it get empty."

"I'm fine." It still seemed incredulous to David that his sister would be working at this hospital, of all places in the world. When he had sensed God's call to come to Stoney Ridge, this encounter with Ruth must have been one of the reasons why. How could he have ever doubted the wisdom of God in sending him here, as difficult as it had been? "Yes, you can do something for me. Come to the house for Christmas. Meet your nieces and nephew."

Ruth hesitated. "Mom will be there."

"Yes."

She picked up Birdy's chart and glanced through it.

In his mind's eye, David saw the girl she used to be, the wonderfully feisty sister who was never satisfied with the way things were, who was always challenging, always exasperating their mother.

Ruth turned back to David. "Soon, perhaps. I'm not quite ready. I've just started work here. My house needs unpacking. I'm still living out of boxes."

"Ruth, why did you come here? What made you leave Ohio?"

She kept her eyes on Birdy. "Same reason as you, most likely. Opportunity called."

"The reason I came here was because I felt God's call to come."

"As did I. There are many ways to serve God, David. The Amish don't have the corner on that. They just they think they do." She went to the door. "You can have me paged if you need anything." She put her hand on the door handle, then hesitated and turned back when he spoke her name.

"You'll come for Christmas? There's one person, in particular, who's eager to meet you. My fourteen-year-old daughter, Ruthie."

A few seconds of silence, then, "Is she as stubborn as me?"

"Yes. Very possibly, even more so."

She grinned and it lit her face. How he loved her smile! He'd forgotten how much he'd missed his sister. "I'll give some thought to Christmas. No promises."

"Okay," he said, returning her smile. "Consider yourself invited. And wanted."

She looked over at Birdy. "Your friend was lucky. She'll be fine before too long. The sleep is good for her. It's how the brain heals."

Not lucky, David thought. There was no such thing as luck. Birdy's life had been spared because she was blessed. He was blessed just knowing her. The thought of life without her was impossible.

A few hours later, Birdy started to stir. She slowly opened her eyes, blinked down at the cast on her arm, looked around the room in a daze, and asked what had happened. David explained that a branch from the Hanging Tree had fallen on her, the trunk narrowly missing her.

She nodded weakly and closed her eyes. "Poor Freeman," she said, her eyelids shut and quivering. "He must be beside himself."

Was he? David hadn't seen Freeman or Levi at the hospital when he arrived last night. He put his hand to her cheek and then let it fall. "Birdy," he began, slowly and firmly. "Can you forgive me?"

She opened her eyes. "You've had so much to deal with lately."

He ran a hand through his hair. "Yes," he went on almost sheepishly, "it's true that the last few weeks have been . . . distracting. But . . ."

Her voice softened. "David, you musn't worry so. I understand."

Their gazes met momentarily. That was the thing. She did understand. She didn't judge him for his weakness. Or meekness. Or cowardliness. She accepted him the way he was, flaws and all. He searched for a way to express the fullness in his heart, but couldn't seem to find the right words. There was no simple way to express what she meant to him.

"Everybody needs you, David."

"Yes, sometimes it seems like everybody does need me. But Birdy—" his voice broke—"I need you."

Birdy reached out for his hand. "I like hearing that."

He clasped her hand and lifted it to his lips. "Are you sure you're ready, Birdy?" Ready to be a minister's wife? Ready to become a stepmother to six children of assorted ages? And soon, a step-grandmother to Katrina's baby? Ready to be a daughter-in-law to Tillie Yoder Stoltzfus? All these thoughts ran through his mind. Could anyone ever be ready for this role? Was it even fair to ask? Perhaps not.

Birdy squeezed his hand and locked eyes with him. "Oh David, don't you know? I've been ready from the moment I first saw you."

They smiled at each other, and a moment of mutual appreciation fluttered between them.

"Come closer," she whispered.

He sat gingerly on the edge of the mattress, and she had to reach out and pull him toward her. He stretched forward to embrace her, awkwardly and carefully, so that he wouldn't bump her broken arm or jostle her sore head, though she didn't seem to mind at all.

He turned his face against her ear. "Birdy Glick, I love you."

～

Nothing much was happening in the buggy shop today and Jesse lay in bed, pondering the marketability of metal foot warmers for buggies. He had read an article in *Buggy News* about the use of bottles filled with hot water and thought he might be able to sell them at the Bent N' Dent. His musings were interrupted by a persistent rapping from below on the buggy shop door. He knew that kind of rapping did not bode well. He jumped out of bed, threw on his pants, and tucked his shirttails in his pants as he hurried down the stairs to open the door.

Eli Smucker glared down at him. "My wife was right. She said you have a tendency to be unreliable."

This was an unfortunate way to greet the day. "Good morning, Eli. Is something wrong?"

"You'd better believe something is wrong. It broke down! On my first trip in the snow, the ski sled attachment came right off my buggy!"

Jesse was afraid of something like that. Old bolts were old bolts. And Eli's ski sled attachments were handmade and primitive. Sooner or later, one had to face reality with an old buggy and accept that it had come to the end of its life. He understood the attachment that people developed to a buggy, but sentiment had to be kept in its place. Buggies couldn't last forever. Why not throw away old buggies once they had had their day?

He stretched to his tiptoes to peer behind Eli into the driveway. "Where is the buggy now?"

"On the road to town. Not far from your father's house."

"Abandoned? You left the horse and buggy there?"

"I took my horse home."

"Give me a minute to get dressed and we can go get your buggy."

Eli shook his head. "I have work to do. You figure out a way to get that buggy back to the shop and fixed. For good, this time!"

As Jesse made his way down the hill to see what needed to be done to retrieve Eli's buggy, he wondered what work it was that Eli had to do. Mostly, Eli sat at the Bent N' Dent and played checkers and drank coffee. He hopped over a fence and walked around a small herd of dairy cows who watched him with accusing eyes, as if they knew, they *knew*, he had tried to repair Eli's buggy with brittle old bolts.

Why did he listen to Hank Lapp? It always ended up getting him into trouble.

He came to the edge of the field, hopped the fence, and trudged through the snow to where he thought Eli had said he had abandoned the broken-down buggy. He looked up and down the road, but there was no buggy. He was sure that Eli said it happened very close to the turnoff to his father's house.

He walked up the road, thinking it must have happened farther than Eli had thought, but there was still no sign of the buggy. He walked back again to the turnoff. "Very strange." He doubled back and then a shocking thought dawned on him.

It had been stolen. Eli's old broken-down but dearly beloved buggy had been stolen.

23

When his sister returned to check on Birdy's condition, David went to the waiting room. He put a few coins in the vending machine to get a cup of coffee. He shouldn't be having coffee, knew that he might pay for it with a churning stomach, but he had been up all night and was exhausted. Just a few sips, he thought, just to stay awake.

"How is she?"

David spun around to face Freeman. "She'll be fine, the doctor said. In time, she'll be fine."

Freeman sat down in a chair. David bought another cup of coffee and handed it to Freeman, then sat down beside him. "She's worried about you. That you're feeling guilty for the accident."

"I do. The hinge I started to make was compromised by rotting wood."

David took a sip of coffee. It was terrible, like sipping mud.

"I put everyone in jeopardy."

"Yes, Freeman. Yes, you did." They weren't talking about the Hanging Tree.

Freeman lifted his eyes. "I wish I could reverse time. I would do things . . . differently."

"How so?" David asked. "I guess what I'm really asking is how could this all have happened?"

"I don't know," he said faintly. Words seemed to elude Freeman. "I don't know where to start."

"Start at the beginning."

Freeman leaned back in his chair, taking time to gather his words. "When I was thirty years old, I became a minister. I was full of anticipation, energized by the challenge of working. I was learning on the job, but I felt honored to be entrusted with the task."

David well understood those feelings, though he would add an unholy anxiety. Becoming a minister was wonderful and terrifying and he wasn't always sure which was which. He took another sip of the bitter-tasting coffee and watched nurses walking up and down the hallway, continuing past them as if nothing unusual was happening. And yet, it couldn't be further from the truth. Something wonderful was occurring.

"At first," Freeman continued, "I found the work deeply satisfying, despite the grueling hours. I was good at it. People came to me with intensely painful conditions, and I fixed them. With my skill and experience, I knew better than most what needed to be done. I never said no. Middle of the night, during dinner, anytime someone needed me. I was far busier than Elmo, than the other minister, and that fact became, in my mind, a key measure of my worth. Even though my family didn't see much of me, they gave me a nickname: The Fixer." He gave a half smile. "Those were the best years of my life. I reveled in the job.

"I used to enjoy this work, fixing people. Then, things

changed. I felt as if I had dived into the deep end of the pool and was just splashing around, not getting anywhere. Everything seemed wrong these last few years. No matter what I did to keep up, unforeseen difficulties arose. Young people left for greener pastures. Money was part of the problem. I anesthetized the anxiety with work, long hours of it. I worked out of fear of failing. I worked when there was no work to do, worked even harder when there was no work to do. Spinning my wheels. Grinding my gears. I wondered how I had gotten off on the wrong foot so badly. Various people warned me, with increasing sharpness, that I could be getting myself into serious trouble. But I ignored them all." He took a sip of the coffee. "You. I ignored you, David." He tossed the coffee in the garbage pail. "Do you think I'm a bad person?"

"No," David said. "I think you're a man with a problem." He saw the door open and Birdy being wheeled out, a big grin on her face. "And problems can be solved."

In their surfeit of spare time, Hank Lapp liked to take Jesse out to hunt. They rarely shot any game, as they had no rifle and relied on borrowing Amos Lapp's for that, but Hank was adept at following animal spoor and had taught Jesse how to do it too. He had shown him the prints made by the different animals—deer and rabbits, mostly—and ways to tell how long ago an animal had passed by. "It's like reading a book," Hank often said as he pointed out the bending of the grass made by a buck, or signs of scat. After fresh snow, it was particularly easy to track game.

Buggies too.

Jesse looked down at the ground and began his examination.

He saw several boot prints, three different sizes, ones that had walked round and round in a circle, as if contemplating the abandoned buggy. He bent down and looked at the confusion of spoor: boots, one sled blade mark from the buggy itself, one larger flat track, and then, quite unmistakably, the hoofprints of a large workhorse. Hooves as big as a dinner plate. Yes! thought Jesse. And then, yes! again.

He stood and stretched. It was uncomfortable bending down like that, but it was the only thing to do when one was tracking. He followed the hoofprints and tire tracks up the road a short way, and then turned off to the right, in the same direction as the path down which the pair of boots had walked. The horse had pulled its burden across undisturbed snow and the tracks were telltale. It was easy from there. Jesse followed the tracks across the snow for about half a mile before he came to a small turnoff to the back of the barn that belonged to the Inn at Eagle Hill. He paused and looked up, and as he did so, he saw the tracks roll right into an old shed, hidden in the shadows. He followed the tracks and pulled open the doors to the shed. Inside, mostly covered with a tarpaulin, was Eli Smucker's buggy.

The sight filled him with indignation. Luke Schrock was behind this. He had never been able to understand Luke. That boy was capable of kindness and cruelty, both. Jesse pulled the tarpaulin off the buggy. He saw how the buggy had been transported—one side was supported by a wooden toboggan.

The door opened and a word was uttered that Jesse couldn't repeat. "What are you doing here?"

Jesse whirled around to face Luke Schrock. Hiding behind him was his younger brother Sammy, his shadow and side-kick. "I've come to get my buggy."

Now Luke was in his face. "It's your buggy?"

Jesse was startled to realize Luke had grown taller than him in the last year, taller and bigger. He straightened to his full height, which wasn't much. But he wasn't about to let this hooligan set the tone. "No. It belongs to Eli Smucker. He'll be curious to learn that I found it at Eagle Hill."

Luke glanced away. Jesse watched him, and realized what he was thinking. It would be difficult for him to explain its presence, half hidden, in an old shed.

Jesse decided to be direct. "You've stolen the buggy. You had no right to take it."

"We didn't steal anything. We found it."

Up on the wall was a pegboard, with a Stanley hammer and a cat's claw nail puller, neatly hung. In exactly the same way that Jesse hung his tools. In fact . . . most *were* his tools. His screwdrivers. Wrenches. Tape measure. Pliers, even his favorite needle-nose pliers. All there. "Like you found those? You've made a big mistake, Luke." As had he. He'd been confident that Yardstick Yoder was the culprit.

"I told you. We found it. We brought it here for safekeeping."

"Do tell." Jesse listened, narrow-eyed. The sheer effrontery of this boy's explanation astonished him. Did Luke think that he was quite that gullible? That easily snowed? It was insulting. "And that's why it's hidden inside an old shed? Covered with a tarp?"

"Are you calling us liars?" But some of Luke's bluster was slipping away.

Yes, he was. "Liars and thieves." He looked through the open shed door toward the house. "Your mother might have something else to call you."

"I'm telling the truth," Luke whined, losing steam. "We

were just trying to look after that buggy, to get it off the road so it wouldn't get hit by a truck."

Jesse pointed to the pegboard. "And why are you stealing my tools?" Other people's tools too. There were all kinds of stolen items in this shed.

"I wasn't stealing them. I was just borrowing them. I like . . . fixing things."

That sounded fishy. Luke was known around town for un-fixing things. Like, blowing up mailboxes. Jesse narrowed his eyes. "Why didn't you just ask Galen to borrow his tools?"

"He won't let me. He thinks I'm irresponsible."

Jesse didn't doubt it.

"Believe us, Jesse," Luke said. "We aren't thieves."

Jesse knew that was not in the slightest bit true, but now he changed tack. "I'm prepared to forget all about this if you return the buggy to Windmill Farm." He found a gunnysack and started to collect his tools too.

Luke's face was the image of astonishment. "All the way to Windmill Farm? That will take all day!"

"I'm sure the two of you have a surfeit of spare time," Jesse said. "That is, unless you want to spend some of that time on the sinner's bench."

A pause fell over them. Now he was talking a language that Luke understood. He glanced a few times at Jesse to make sure he was serious. He turned round and called out to Sammy, who'd been watching from afar with wide eyes. "Get the horse," he shouted. "The rickety old buggy has to go."

Jesse smiled, for the first time. "Hold on. I have a few more conditions. You've got some mailboxes to replace around town."

There was fear in Luke's eyes, naked fear. He gave a short nod, and his voice came out in a raspy whisper. "Fine."

"And there's one more thing. Keep away from my sister Ruthie. Don't talk to her. Don't walk with her. Don't come by in the night to visit her." He took a step toward Luke and stared him down. "And never forget that I know everything that goes on in this town." He pressed a finger against Luke's chest, which had shrunk before Jesse's eyes. "I have interactions with everyone. Every. One." He smiled smugly. "That's what it means to be a buggy man. Eyes and ears everywhere."

The buggy was harnessed to Galen King's favorite Belgian workhorse, supported on one side with a long wooden toboggan, and the journey began. Jesse began to walk alongside, but thought better of it and decided to make the rest of the journey in the buggy. It tilted rather severely, but if Jesse stayed on the lower side, it was comfortable there, resting behind the wheel, watching the blue sky through the windshield and thinking with some satisfaction of the pleasure Eli Smucker would experience when he told him that his favorite buggy was safe at the buggy shop and would soon be in working condition—after Jesse located some square bolts, of course.

❧

It was still dark but for the yellow glow of a kerosene lamp hanging in the middle of the ceiling and another one sitting on the table. David watched his mother move across the kitchen. It was such a familiar sight to him; she was always in motion, rarely at rest. His eyes were drawn to those hands, such nimble hands, always absorbed in a task.

She glanced up and smiled when she saw him. "I haven't seen much of you lately," she said. "I've been wanting to talk to you."

"I've been wanting to talk to you too." He pulled a chair out and sat down. "You go first."

"Ora Nisley has an unmarried sister, about your age. She has digestive troubles, just like you do. So I've taken the liberty to invite her to dinner on Sunday. I thought I'd make a sweet potato hash. You're not supposed to have uncooked vegetables. They can irritate your stomach lining."

For a long moment he made no move, no sound. He could feel his own pulse hammering. "No."

His mother stopped wiping the counter. "No?" She put the rag down that she'd been using on the counter. "Well, then, I'll look for another recipe for delicate constitutions."

"The sweet potato hash sounds fine. I'm saying no to Ora Nisley's sister who has digestive ailments."

Ten seconds of silence. "You can say no after you meet her. Not before."

"Sit down, Mom." He pushed out a chair next to him and patted it. She sat down, eyeing him carefully. He studied her, finding it hard to know how to start. These things, they'd got to be said. "I thought—" He stopped.

She seemed impatient with him. "Go on then, say it."

He started again. "I know you've come to Stoney Ridge to help—"

"And have I not been helpful?" She sat with a stiff back, as if she was eager to return to her spot at the counter.

"In many ways, yes. But in many ways no."

Her shoulders stiffened and a wary look filled her eyes.

"Your intentions are good, Mom. I know that. But problems seem to occur when you decide what is helpful without taking into consideration whether I think it might be helpful."

"This is about Birdy Glick, isn't it?"

"Partly." He nodded. "Birdy is the woman I've chosen."

His mother shook a finger beneath his nose, as if he were a child. "You can do so much better! You mustn't settle for just anyone. I'll help you find someone ideally suited to you."

David lifted a hand to cut her off. How could he make her understand? Birdy treated his children like every child deserved to be treated. Always, she made his children feel important. And David too. She treated him better than he deserved. "What matters is that I love her." And he did. He loved her. "Next thing. The store. You've done enough."

"But I've hardly begun!"

"You've given us a good start. We will follow through on your suggestions. But where I need your help is here, at home. Not at the store."

"You don't want me at the store." She clapped her hands on her kneecaps, and David felt that familiar knot of meekness lodge in his throat. "All the years I've spent running a store, and you don't want me in the store," she repeated flatly. "And why not?"

He braced both hands on his knees, trying to steel himself. "You have a way of frightening off the customers." He leaned in. "I do need your help, but in another way. With Molly. Mom, she's so eager to learn how to cook and bake, but you've kept her out of the kitchen. If you want to help, you've got to slow down and teach her." He grabbed her hands. "You've got so much to give, Mom. But it's got to be where we need the help. Not where *you* think we need the help."

Her voice became sharper. "Why didn't you say something?"

"It's not that easy to tell you . . . no."

She yanked her hands out of his. "A grown man should have more of a backbone!" she retorted.

He nodded silently. True. So true. But then again, his mother had never allowed her children to speak their mind. It felt strange, saying the things he wanted to say to his mother. His glance lifted. "Another thing."

She wrapped her hands together in a tight knot.

"I've left messages at the hospital to try to reach Ruth. I'm going to do my best to convince her to spend Christmas with us."

His mother lifted her eyes to the window beyond David. He could tell that the sun would rise soon. "She won't come. She's still got her stubborn streak. It's bone-deep." She dropped her head, and David thought he saw a glistening of tears in her eyes. "She won't come."

Pictures of his sister as a girl danced across his mind, smiling, laughing, teasing . . . then later, when she reached her teen years, moody, sullen, argumentative.

His mother rose and walked to the window. A deep compassion came over David. He joined her at the window and stood behind her. "Maybe not. But I'm going to keep trying."

His mother kept her eyes on the horizon. "Those two. Your sister Ruth, your brother Simon. They're the stories I don't want to remember. A daughter who left the Amish, a son who won't get out of bed."

It was a rare moment of complete transparency for his mother, but he knew what fueled her coldness toward Ruth and Simon. They were a daughter and a son whom, for different reasons, she couldn't control.

He gently squeezed his mother's shoulders. "If you had never tasted the bitter, you would never know what is sweet." Softly he added, "Mom, it's just like Dane told Freeman on Sunday, a person can't pick and choose their stories. If you try to erase those hard stories, you might miss out on a miracle or two."

Abigail entered the kitchen to find Mammi sitting at the kitchen table, polishing her eyeglasses, staring up at the ceiling as she did so. This was always a sign that she was thinking, and Abigail wondered what she was thinking about. She glanced over at Ruthie, who was stirring some kind of batter in a big bowl on the kitchen counter.

Perhaps Mammi was considering the *People* magazine she had found under Ruthie's bed. Or perhaps it was concern over Lydie and Emily, who had amused themselves by crossing their eyes at each other during the sermon at church. Or perhaps she was worried about Jesse, who seemed to be in a funk over the girl next door, the Inn at Eagle Hill, who had jilted him for the tall and quiet bespectacled teacher.

Mostly, she hoped Mammi wasn't thinking about her.

Mammi slipped her glasses on and knotted her hands together on the tabletop. "Gabby."

"Abigail." She tucked a stray lock of hair behind her ears. "I've always preferred to be called Abigail." Always, always, always. Few people ever bothered to respect her wishes. Dane did, she just now realized, but very few others.

Mammi took a long look at her. "I just want to take this opportunity to say I've been heartened by the changes I've seen in you lately." An actual, honest-to-goodness smile curved her lips. "You struck a blow for truth-telling and accuracy by what you said in church on Sunday."

Struck a blow for truth-telling? And accuracy? Such goals might have appealed to Abigail a few days ago, but now she felt quite confused. She had hurt Dane by what she had said in church. She had struck a blow at Dane, that's what she had done. And it didn't feel good. It felt terrible. That's because, Laura told her, she was caught in a moral dilemma.

Laura said that Abigail felt such remorse because she was finally starting to see the gray in life, that everything wasn't sharply defined black and white. "Very few moral dilemmas come in black and white," she said. Abigail had pondered that troubling thought all night long.

"I don't get the chance to say this very often, Gabby, but I truly feel you've started to turn a corner. Keep it up. That's all I wanted to say." Mammi took a sip of tea, then quickly put the cup down and lifted a finger in the air. "One more thing. Ora Nisley is coming by this afternoon. I want you to be here."

"About that, Mammi. I should tell you that I am not at all interested in Ora Nisley."

"Nonsense. You haven't even given him a chance! And he certainly seems smitten with you. He drops by nearly every day for a cup of tea."

Every day? Abigail had no idea. This was a very uncomfortable piece of news.

"Oh, for pity's sake!" Ruthie slammed the spoon back into the bowl so hard the batter splattered. She marched over to the table, her hands on her hips, resembling Mammi in an eerie way. "Is it completely impossible for the two of you to see what's right under your nose?" She stared at both Abigail and Mammi, who stared back at her, then she lifted her hands in the air. "Mammi—Ora Nisley doesn't care a whit about Gabby. He's coming by to see you. You!"

Mammi's brows flew up into her forehead. "Goodness." One hand stole up to pat the hair on her neck.

"And Gabby . . . if you let Dane Glick go, then you're a fool. He's the best thing that's ever happened to you."

"I know." Abigail knew he was. She knew. "It's just that . . . I should get back to Ohio to help my father—"

"No, Gabby," Mammi interrupted. "Your father is the one who sent you here. He's the one who asked me to come to Stoney Ridge and help you find someone."

"No, no," Abigail said faintly. She drew her sweater tight at her throat. "It was my mother. And you."

Mammi shook her head. "Mind you, your father may or may not get well, but he does not want you to miss your chance at living. He sent you here. He asked me to come too. It was all his doing. Not your mother's. In fact, it took some persuading to get her to let you come."

Abigail swallowed past the lump in her throat. "My father, he needs me."

Mammi sighed and rubbed her temples as if a headache were coming on. "I'm not sure what your father needs to get well, Gabby, but it's not as simple as finishing a family tree. You're going to have to leave him in God's hands."

It baffled Abigail to hear those words of relinquishment out of her grandmother's mouth. Mammi, of all people, believed she was on a one-woman mission to fix everyone and everything. Most troubling of all was the notion that her father might not get well. No, that wasn't the most troubling thing. The worst thought was that Abigail couldn't do anything more to help him. She'd done all she could. Maybe her grandmother was right. Maybe all she could do was to leave him in God's hands. A strange swirling of peace started in Abigail's center and extended from head to toe. It was a new feeling for her, a new way of seeing. Maybe, this was the answer she'd been looking for all along. To give up. Not just to give up, but to give over.

Ruthie had been watching her. She plucked Abigail's bonnet off the wall peg and wrapped her black cape around her shoulders. "Go," she ordered. "Go now. Go tell Dane."

"But what do I tell him?"

Ruthie opened the door and gave her a gentle push through the threshold. "Tell him that you don't want to miss another opportunity."

24

As Abigail hurried Thistle down the road, she passed Ora Nisley and waved out the buggy window. He waved back cheerfully and continued on toward Uncle David's house.

How odd. Mammi was way too old to be thinking about romance. Ridiculous!

But . . . Abigail had other matters filling her mind.

She found Dane in the horse paddock, working with Bella, his new horse. He stopped to watch her hitch Thistle's reins to the post, then he went back to working the horse.

Suddenly Abigail was visited by doubts. For a few moments, she was unsure what to say, and even considered running away, like a child who was caught doing something wrong. Better judgment prevailed and she took a deep breath. She bit back her misgivings and walked up to the paddock. "Christmas is coming."

"Yes."

"My sister Laura will be heading home for it."

He flicked Bella's lead to get her loping.

"I'd like to invite you to my uncle's home for Christmas dinner."

A short silence ensued before Dane spoke. "I thought you said you were leaving for Ohio."

"Not me. Just Laura. She's leaving tomorrow. She's distressed about the sudden lack of interest from her boyfriend. I thought I'd be heading home by now, but I've changed my mind."

He let Bella slow to a walk, then he unclipped the lead and ran a hand down her flank. He walked over to the fence where Abigail stood. He had all the time in the world, Dane did.

"I'm staying here in Stoney Ridge. I've been thinking it over. I thought that, well, maybe I could work for the sisters in the Sisters' House. They said they needed someone to finish what Bethany Schrock had started. I think I could help them . . . get organized."

"I'm sure you could." He gave her a long look, curious and dubious.

He wasn't going to help her out, that was apparent. She gathered every ounce of courage she had and wished she had changed into her blue dress. "So what do you say? About coming for Christmas dinner?"

Dane rubbed the top of the fence post, thinking it over. "Will your grandmother be there?"

"Yes, I think so." When Laura had announced she was leaving, Abigail felt certain that Mammi would insist on returning with her. After all, the church crisis had passed, and her granddaughters were quite resistant to her matchmaking. The Thanksgiving Dinner Incident was the final straw. Andy Miller buckled under Mammi's steady grilling and admitted he would marry Katrina in the blink of an eye. Mortified and embarrassed, Katrina told Mammi to stop meddling in people's lives. Right in the middle of Thanksgiving dinner! Uncle David had gone off on some kind of an errand, and Abigail wondered if Katrina would be so bold had her father been seated at the table. Maybe so. Katrina had evolved into a woman who spoke her mind.

And Mammi was shocked by those spoken thoughts. You'd never seen a more surprised look on anyone's face. "Me? Meddle? Why, I never." Everyone burst out laughing and Mammi seemed thoroughly offended.

This morning, though, after seeing the way Mammi's cheeks grew bright pink over Ora Nisley, Abigail felt fairly confident that her grandmother would be staying in Stoney Ridge for the time being. "Yes, I'm sure Mammi will be there."

"Wouldn't your grandmother object to sharing Christmas dinner with a Glick?"

"It doesn't matter what she thinks."

Dane stared at her for a long moment, ten, maybe twenty seconds. "What does matter to you, Abigail?"

She took a deep, deep breath. "You. You matter."

"Are you kidding?"

"No. I never kid. I have no sense of humor."

Slowly, a smile spread over Dane's face. He chuckled and ran a hand down the back of his head. "Well, that sounds more like the Abigail I came to know in those letters."

The last word stopped her cold. In *those* letters? Those letters? The ones she had written to him on her father's behalf? Her mind raced as she took in the reality of what he had said.

It was several seconds before he spoke. "I've known it was you who wrote those letters for a long time."

"But . . . how?" Abigail had been so careful. *Extremely* careful.

"You have distinctive penmanship. Slanted far to the left. The way a left-handed person writes."

"But you've never seen me write anything." She made certain of that.

"I didn't have to. The Bent N' Dent notepad that was stuffed into Freeman's Bible. I saw the handwriting. I recognized it. Then I noticed after we met that you were left-handed. It all came together."

"You never said anything. Why?"

He shrugged. "I guess I figured that if I had, I would've scared you off. There's something about you that seems as skittish as a colt on thin ice. It's the same way with horses— better to let them learn to trust me than to come on too strong and frighten them away. Sheep too. Trust and love just comes slowly for certain types."

Love? Did he just say love? "Dane," she whispered, "why are you so sure about me?"

He slipped in between the fence's railing, until he was just a foot or so away from her. "Because I believe God brought you here. For me. I prayed for a wife, I prayed for a friend, and he brought me both. In you. Two for one."

A wife. He had prayed for a wife, and for a friend. And God answered his prayer with her. *Her!* Brimming with feelings she couldn't express, she felt the bridge of her nose start to tickle and her eyes start to water. The pressure built and built, until she squeezed her eyes and covered her nose, sure she was about to explode in sneezes. But just when it reached its peak, the pressure stopped. Slowly, cautiously, she opened one eye, then the other.

Dane was smiling at her with that big, ear-to-ear grin he had, the one that always made Abigail smile in return. He reached out for her, and she fell into his arms, fitting into his embrace like a glove, as if it was the most natural thing in the world.

Things were looking much more positive.

As Jesse loped up the long driveway to Windmill Farm, he caught sight of a bonneted figure standing outside his buggy shop. His footsteps faltered when he saw the woman raise a hand and wave. He heard his own heart drumming in his ears. Mim Schrock was waiting for him. Waiting for him, Jesse Stoltzfus. Even from a distance, he noted two spots of color in her cheeks. She used to always blush around him, but she hadn't blushed in months. A burst of elation rippled through his body as he smiled and stretched his stride.

As he approached her, she kept her eyes downcast. "I came to thank you," she said.

He felt his Adam's apple bob up and down, and his voice came out an octave higher than he had expected it to. "For what?"

She took a step closer, but still she wouldn't look at him. "For not telling anyone about the awful, horrible things my brother has done. To you, in particular."

Jesse was charmed. "How did you find out?"

"Sammy broke down under my interrogation and confessed everything. He could never keep a secret." She held out a pie tin, covered in foil. "Chocolate chip walnut cookies. For you."

His favorite! She hadn't forgotten. That was a stellar

indicator of her affections for him, despite her best efforts
to deny them. He took the tin from her and lifted a corner
of foil. The cookie was soft, still warm, the greatest gift
he'd ever received. His eyes closed as he chewed his first
bite. "Delicious."

"Why didn't you blow the whistle on Luke? You had every
right to. You could've told your dad and let him deal with
Luke."

Jesse lifted a shoulder in a half shrug. "I guess because
I've done one or two awful things in my day." Plenty of awful
with a side helping of stupid. It seemed to be part of a boy's
bumpy passage to manhood.

"Jesse, I was hoping . . ." Those two spots on her cheeks
turned suspiciously brighter.

Hoping? She was hoping? Jesse felt a stirring within him.
He had hopes too. Hoping that she and Danny Riehl would
go their separate ways. Hoping that she and Jesse could have
a second chance.

A quick exchanged glance, two nervous smiles, then silence
again. "I was hoping . . . you might be willing to take Luke
on as an apprentice. After school."

Jesse practically choked on the bite of cookie. "What?"
It came out in a squeak.

"You'd be a wonderful influence on him. He'll be done
with school in May and . . . what then? He doesn't like farming or horses or inn keeping. It's a topic of endless discussion
over at Eagle Hill. My mother and grandmother are beside
themselves with worry. Think of it. My brother Luke, with
too much time on his hands." She shuddered, then took a
step closer. "There's some talk of . . . sending him away."

More talk that Jesse had missed out on? How could that

be? A buggy man should know everything. It was part of the job. "Where to?" Juvenile Hall, perhaps?

"To my brother and his wife, Tobe and Naomi. They live in Kentucky."

"Maybe that's not such a bad idea. You know, a fresh start for Luke." Another town to vandalize and scandalize.

Mim let out a sad sigh. "Tobe doesn't want him."

Ah.

"The thing is, Jesse, Luke does like to try and fix things. To tinker around. That's why I thought of you, and how good you are at this buggy repair work. Everyone says so."

"Everyone?" He watched her as she spoke, watched her eyes remain downcast nearly the whole time.

Her eyes flickered up. "Nearly."

Jesse's shoulders straightened. "I . . . suppose I could try it."

Her appreciative eyes sought Jesse's and he felt his heart warm. "Oh, Jesse, thank you!" She covered her mouth with her mittened hands and blinked hard. "Thank you."

As Jesse watched her walk back down the hill, he felt two distinct emotions battle inside him. One, he was positive, absolutely convinced, that Mim Schrock still cared for him. She had said he would be a wonderful influence on Luke, did she not? Clearly, she held him in high regard. Quite possibly, she loved him as he loved her, though that might be stretching things a bit. Still, that awareness filled him with optimism.

The second emotion, dread, filled him with utter pessimism. It had just become his task to reform Luke Schrock, the town's ruffian.

And then a third emotion emerged. Alarm. He smacked his forehead, remembering Yardstick Yoder. He had already agreed, albeit under duress, to apprentice Yardstick in his buggy repair shop. Luke and Yardstick were archenemies. Both sweet on his sister Ruthie, though he had no idea why. Both too clever for their own good.

What had he just gotten himself into?

He walked into the quiet, peaceful buggy shop, his special place, a corner of the earth that had been all his, at least for the last month. The door closed behind him, and what a final sound that thump was.

⌒

The sun was barely skimming the ridge when David woke to sweet smells wafting up from the kitchen. His mother and Molly were baking pies to sell in the store—a "line extension" suggested by Jesse and Hank. The kitchen was brimming with scents of cinnamon, vanilla, ginger, and molasses. David helped himself to a cup of coffee and stood by the door for a moment, watching the two of them work together. His mother sifted the flour and stirred in salt, then cut Crisco into it. She worked the mixture into a ball of dough so Molly could roll out the piecrust.

His mother was particular about all things in the kitchen, but rolling out a proper piecrust topped her list. David cringed as Molly did nothing to his mother's satisfaction. She didn't flour the rolling pin, which caused the piecrust to stick to it. His mother continually reminded Molly to roll the dough from the center out, and not side to side. She whipped out a ruler and scolded Molly in a voice of forced patience as she measured the dough. "No, no! Not a half-inch thick. Not a quarter-inch thick. It must be exactly an eighth of an inch thick." Or she insisted that Molly start over.

This might be a terrible idea. His mother was no teacher. Memories of a similar scenario came to the forefront: a winter when his mother tried to teach his sister Ruth how to cook. His mother's perfectionist streak wore Ruth to a frazzle, until she gave up trying to please and did all she could to frazzle his mother right back. It wasn't long before Ruth was banished from the kitchen. That was probably Ruth's plan all along, but he knew it wasn't Molly's. She desperately wanted to please, and to learn from his mother.

He saw Molly lift her head to look at her grandmother, and David was just about to step in, to tell his mother that she was being too hard on his daughter, expecting too much. But he noticed something in Molly's eyes that made him stop himself, just in time. Molly looked to her grandmother without an ounce of self-pity in her eyes. "Again?" she asked.

"Again," his mother answered. "Still thinner."

So Molly folded the piecrust up and rolled it out again. Two more times after that, until his mother was finally satisfied. David watched the entire process, mesmerized. Molly took every single suggestion his mother made and tried again. She never wavered from the goal, never took his mother's criticism personally, never objected to the nitpicking and faultfinding.

What an example his Molly was to him. She failed. She tried again. She failed. And she tried again.

David smiled to himself. Wouldn't Anna be proud of their Molly? The daughter he worried most about, the one who was most like him in all the wrong ways—his meekness, for one. His lack of confidence, for another. Even with those weaknesses, he felt a deep-down assurance that Molly was going to be fine, just fine.

An hour later, he left the house to head to the store a little earlier than usual. He wanted to stop by Moss Hill and see the work progress with the pumps. The wind kept turning on him, a true winter wind. He climbed Moss Hill on the road created by the work trucks, listening to the creaking sounds of the pumps, groaning thuds, metal moaning against itself.

Andy spotted him and walked halfway down the hill to meet him, a big smile on his face. "Work is going quicker than anticipated," he said. "There's fluid at the top of the pipes, and they're only at 3,500 feet."

"Fluid? As in, oil?"

Andy nodded. "That's a really good sign."

"They'll still go down to 4,000 feet?"

"Yes—but it looks like it's a shallow well." Andy was beaming. "David, this could be a significant oil trap. It's amazing it hasn't been discovered before now. Pennsylvania is all about oil. The very first oil well was dug in northwestern Pennsylvania."

"Why do you think it hadn't been discovered?"

Andy shrugged. "For some reason, this rocky hillside was passed over in the 1950s. That's when the oil companies were sending out scouts to find oil in this area."

A worry nettled David. If these wells were a significant oil trap, would that bring other scouts to the area? If other oil traps were discovered, what might that mean for the little church of Stoney Ridge? Prosperity, he believed, could be every bit as dangerous as hardship.

He turned to ask Andy when he thought construction for the wells would wrap up, but Andy was looking beyond him. His face had grown soft and a crooked smile had begun. He looked to see what had distracted Andy. Ah! Not a *what* but a who. Katrina was walking up the hill to join them. It cheered David's heart to see the look on Andy's face, the look of a man in love. He hoped Katrina felt the same way. He couldn't read his daughter; she kept herself carefully guarded.

"Hi, Dad," she said as she reached them. "Aren't you supposed to be at the store by now?"

"I should be. Hard to pull myself away. It's fascinating to watch." But she was right; he should get to the store. He said his goodbyes and started down the hill.

David looked up and his steps faltered. There, waiting on the road, was a horse and buggy, and halfway up the hill was Freeman Glick, watching the oil pumps with his son Leroy, the one who teased his Molly.

David would have liked to talk to Freeman privately, but not with his son present. "You're welcome to go see the work up close."

"This is close enough," Freeman said. His son's face fell with disappointment.

"If Leroy stays by Andy, it would be safe for him to go up and see the work."

His son looked up at him, silently pleading. Freeman gave a quick nod and the boy bolted up the hill.

"So, how does it feel to be bishop?"

"Daunting. Overwhelming. Humbling." The church had a members' meeting last Sunday. David had drawn the lot for bishop, other choices had been made for ministers and deacon. A fresh team of leadership. A fresh start.

They stood there, caught in an awkward silence, unsure of what to say next, both momentarily yanked out of their accustomed roles.

"Isaac Bender sent me to a counselor," Freeman said, his

voice low and surprisingly soft. "I've gone twice now. It's not quite as awful as I thought it would be. I feel . . . as if I can breathe again. My life isn't over. I failed as bishop." His gaze shifted to the hill, to Leroy running to the top. "I don't want to be a failure with my family, as well."

"I'm glad for you, Freeman." He was glad, truly glad, and he even empathized with him. Failure was something he was very well acquainted with. Lately, though, it had occurred to him that the Lord God might love his children most when they fail and try again. When their hearts were softened by failure and its resulting humility.

"Have they found oil?"

"Looks promising, Andy said."

"What then?"

"Then? I guess the pumpjacks will pump oil."

"They could bring in a fortune."

"If that is true, I feel confident that Thelma and Katrina will make wise decisions."

For a moment, the spark of the old Freeman showed up, first in his eyes, then in his need to have the last word with David. "Anyone can carry an empty cup. It's the cup that's full that is hard to carry." He whistled to his son, waited for him to run back down the hill, then the two headed down the road. It was the first time David had ever found himself sharing an opinion with Freeman Glick.

Then Freeman did an about-face and walked back to David, extending his hand for a one-pump handshake. He turned and walked down the road.

David watched Freeman as he strolled away. Was he more than this man was now? More reliable? More conscientious? As aware and careful about his own limitations? He wanted to think so—and perhaps he had to think so to do what he did day to day. But he could not know so. And neither could anyone else.

"David!" Andy shouted down the hill to him, waving frantically. "David! Oil! We've hit oil! Come see!"

David lifted his hands to God, asking for wisdom and discernment to lead the little church. Then he strode up the hill to see the mystery of the earth unfold. "Anyone can carry an empty cup. It's the cup that's full that is hard to carry."

Lord, he prayed from the depth of his heart, *help us carry this full cup.*

Coming Fall 2016 from

SUZANNE
WOODS FISHER

The Devoted

The Bishop's Family, Book 3

1

The bad thing about Ruthie Stoltzfus's job was that it barely paid minimum wage and she had no job security. She was only employed when someone from the Schrock family, who owned the Inn of Eagle Hill, was busy or unavailable, like now.

The good thing about her job was that it was across the road from her home. She liked to think of the now-and-then job as a hotel concierge-in-training, minus the hotel. The Schrocks referred to the position as a filler.

But as for what happened last evening . . . nothing ever—ever!—could have trained her for that. She was still shaky from the shock. Just as she was locking up the cottage at the inn after she had worked all day long to clean it up (the guests who had checked out yesterday had trashed the place, completely *trashed* it!), she saw a man stagger over to her.

"Is this a motel?"

"Not really," Ruthie said. "It's a bed-and-breakfast." And then she noticed the man had a cut on his forehead. "You're bleeding."

He lifted a hand to his head as if startled by the thought. "It's nothing. Look, I need a room for the night."

She looked back at the main house. The lights were out. It was late and they'd gone to bed. But the guest cottage was empty, and she knew Rose would appreciate the income. Still, this man seemed odd. Not in a dangerous way, but he seemed dazed, a little confused. Drunk, maybe? She should send him on his way. But then again, what would he do if she turned him away? He was miles from town. "You'll have to pay cash, up front."

He reached behind him, then patted his pants, his shirt front, alarmed. "I don't seem to have my wallet." He reached into his pockets. "I'm good for the money. If you could just trust me. Just for tonight. In the morning, I'll take care of everything. I promise." His eyes pleaded with her.

In the end, Ruthie ignored her usual overriding caution and let him stay. She walked him over to the guest cottage, showed him how to use the kerosene lights, and left him there. As she closed the cottage door behind her, she felt a hitch in her heart. Had she done the right thing? Or the wrong thing? Birdy, her father's wife, often said that the Bible warned they might entertain angels as strangers in need. Nothing about this man seemed particularly angelic, but he definitely was a stranger in need.

Ruthie crossed the road and turned around, walking backward, as she climbed the steep driveway to her family's home. The light in the little cottage was already snuffed out. The man was probably in bed. She'd made her decision. She had to trust it was the right one, even if the stranger-in-need didn't end up paying for the stay.

She slept fitfully, tossing and turning. In the morning, she woke and dressed in a flash. She left a note for Birdy and her dad on the kitchen table, that she had to get to work early and would miss breakfast. She grabbed her shawl from the wall peg and rushed down the driveway. The cottage still looked as quiet as it did last night, though she wasn't sure what she had expected to find. Burned down? Exploded? *Don't be ridiculous, Ruthie,* she told herself. *You're letting your imagination run away with you.*

Rose was already in the kitchen at the main house of Eagle Hill as Ruthie walked right in. She looked up at Ruthie in surprise. "You're here early."

"There's a guest in the cottage," she said. "Late last night, as I was heading home—a man came and asked for a place to stay."

Rose straightened up. She looked out in the driveway. "Where's his car?"

"He didn't have one."

Rose got that look on her face, the one that seemed as if she knew this story wasn't going to end well.

"I might have made a mistake, Rose. He seemed to be in some kind of trouble."

"Did he threaten you?"

"No. Nothing like that. He was very polite." She told Rose the whole story.

Rose went to the window to peer at the cottage. "It's early. Let's wait another hour or so, then I'll take him some coffee."

"Are you mad at me?"

Rose swiveled around. "No. Not at all. Please don't worry, even if the man doesn't pay for the night. You were put in a tough spot and made a decision that felt right to you." She turned back to peer out the window, looking at the cottage, crossing her arms against her chest. "But maybe I'll have Galen take him the coffee."

An hour later, that's just what she did. Galen King, Rose's husband, a no-nonsense kind of man, took a pot of coffee over to the man in the cottage. Not two minutes later, he returned with the untouched coffee tray.

"Is he all right?" Ruthie asked. "Should I call for a doctor?"

Galen set the tray down and slumped into a chair at the kitchen table. "Not a doctor. He definitely doesn't need a doctor." He swallowed. "He needs . . . the county coroner."

And that's why Ruthie couldn't stop shaking. The coroner arrived, and after he saw the cut on the man's forehead, his bleeding knuckles, and discovered there was no identification to be found, he called for the Stoney Ridge Police Department. They dispatched their only two cars, sirens blaring, which alerted all kinds of townspeople to come out and see what on earth had happened at the Inn of Eagle Hill. A reporter from the *Stoney Ridge Times* said this was the biggest story to hit the town in two years, since someone had blown up Amish farmers' mailboxes with cherry bombs.

"Perhaps there's a link," the reporter said, sniffing for any clue he could find to flesh out his story. Hard news in Stoney Ridge was as scarce as hens' teeth.

"No link at all," Luke Schrock said with certainty. Rose's son, Luke, was Ruthie's on-again, off-again boyfriend, depending on how much patience she had for him. Lately, it was off-again. Luke seemed almost amused by the activity that was quickly filling up the front yard of his family's property. Ruthie found Luke's attitude to be callous and would have told him so, but the reporter kept pestering her with questions. When the reporter overheard one policeman tell the other that Ruthie was the only one who had seen and spoken to the man, he cornered her.

"What kind of weapon was used to murder him?"

"Murder? Who said anything about a murder?" How awful. What horrible chain of events had Ruthie set into motion last night?

"It's obvious," the reporter said. "The bedroom window was open. The man was found on the floor. It's a cut-and-dry case, elementary crime solving. Someone came in through the open window, killed him, and left through the front door. And now," the reporter muttered to himself, taking down notes, "we've got ourselves a John Doe, right here in sleepy Stoney Ridge."

The policemen were unrolling yellow crime scene caution tape over the front door of the guest cottage. Ruthie knew one of the officers, Matt Lehman. He told Rose to call tonight's inn guests to explain that their reservation had to be canceled due to unforeseen circumstances. He also reminded Ruthie, twice, that she wasn't to talk to anyone about what she'd seen or done until she'd been questioned.

"Right," Ruthie said. "So don't say anything about the blood."

Suddenly the *Stoney Ridge Times* reporter was by her side. "What blood?"

"The man's forehead was bloody."

Matt Lehman scowled at the reporter, led Ruthie to the backseat of his police car, and told her to sit there, say nothing, do nothing.

Luke Schrock watched Matt lead Ruthie to the car. "Don't say anything without a lawyer present, Ruthie! You have rights!"

Matt turned to Luke with a sigh. He was well acquainted with him. "She's not being arrested."

"Oh," Luke said. He waved a hand in the air. "Well, then, carry on."

Ruthie sat in the police car, arms tightly folded against her chest. *Murder.* She had let an injured man into the cottage, a criminal, probably, only to have him brutally killed in his sleep.

What did I do? she thought miserably.

A little later, Matt Lehman and the other policeman walked over to the police car to question Ruthie about everything she could remember from last night. It was surprising how many details her mind had taken in and filed away, without realizing it. The stranger was surprised when she pointed out that there was blood dripping down his forehead. He had seemed dazed and confused. Even still, he was very polite, very appreciative.

"Why didn't you ask for the man's name?" Matt said. "Why didn't you ask him for any information?"

For that, she had no answer. It was a set of circumstances that had flustered her, made her feel as if she just wanted to get the man settled in so she could go home. The main house was dark, she was alone, the man seemed like he needed to rest. Looking back, she realized how many mistakes she had made. But the stranger hadn't seemed dangerous.

"Who might have broken into the cottage to murder him?" she asked Matt and he looked at her strangely.

"What makes you think he had been killed?"

"The reporter said so. He called it a homicide."

"Aw, no," Matt said, turning to the other officer. "He's gonna get everyone twitchy."

The officer frowned. "They'll all be hearing things go thump in the night."

"But . . . *was* the man murdered?"

The two police officers exchanged a look. "We aren't sure of anything," Matt said. "Not until we get the coroner's report."

"What about the open window?"

"The innkeeper said there'd been a group in there the other night who trashed the place."

"That was true, but I was the one who cleaned up the cottage yesterday and I didn't notice an open window."

"Ruthie," Matt said. "Are you positive? Absolutely positive?"

"No. I guess not." She wasn't positive of anything anymore.

"Can you think of anything else? Anything at all?"

She squeezed her eyes shut, trying to make herself remember. Her cousin Gabby should have been the one here last night but had moved to Kentucky with her new husband Dane. With Gabby's unique attention for detail, she could've given the policemen a blow-by-blow detailed report.

Her eyes popped open. "He had no wallet." Something else tickled her memory. "When he reached for his wallet, he pulled out a ticket stub. It was to a Lancaster Barnstormer baseball game." She recognized the logo because her brother Jesse often slipped off to go to home games. She was rather pleased with herself. Such recall!

The officers were not as pleased. In fact, they seemed rather disappointed. They closed their notepads and rose to their feet. Matt handed her a card. "If anything else comes to mind, give me a call." A stain of pink started up the sides of his cheeks. "Or you could have your aunt track me down."

"My aunt?" Her aunts lived in Ohio.

His cheeks went redder still. "The doctor."

Oh! *That* aunt. "You know Doc? How?"

"I've bumped into her a few times at the hospital." His face was now streaked with red blotches.

Oh. *Oh!* Matt Lehman was *sweet* on her aunt! How curious.

As soon as the policemen finished with their questions, Ruthie walked over to the porch of the farmhouse, where Rose King stood waiting for her.

"Are you all right?" Rose asked.

"I suppose so." Ruthie looked at the cottage, at the ribbons of yellow caution tape covering the door. "I'm so sorry. I should never have let that man stay here last night."

Rose put an arm around her shoulders. "You did what you thought was best. Inn keeping is all about dealing with strangers. I'm not sure what I would've done if I'd been in your shoes."

"But look at what it's turned Eagle Hill into. A human zoo."

Rose's gaze swept over the driveway to the cottage. A police car, a handful of horse and buggies, dozens of scooters, clumps of Amish men and women standing together, all curious onlookers. "Well, no doubt it'll all blow over soon."

Ruthie hoped so, but something deep inside her felt this was just the beginning.

Discussion Questions

1. Every person in the Stoltzfus family shared qualities in common with each other, though they didn't want to acknowledge them. Ruthie was opinionated like Mammi, Jesse was single-minded like Abigail, Molly was meek, like David, and tried to avoid conflicts. What similar traits, good or bad, do you see in your children that you also see in yourself?

2. Do you think those traits are hereditary? Or modeled through lifelong examples? Why is it that the things we most dislike in ourselves are hardest to tolerate in others?

3. Ruthie said that studying genealogy made it seem like life was fixed. No choices. And she wanted choices! How would you respond to Ruthie?

4. One theme in this story is about the art of listening. In one scene, David was listening to his daughter Ruthie, but in truth, his thoughts had wandered off and left the

room. He caught himself. Here is his inner monologue from that scene: "This was not the way to listen to his daughter. Respectful listening was a learned skill, a key component to all harmonious relationships, and especially critical in our relationship with God. No wonder James, the brother of the Lord Jesus, challenged his readers to be quick to listen, slow to speak. It was always better to listen than to speak. Always."

Think of someone in your life who listens well, attentively and respectfully. How does that kind of listening make you feel? Why? How can this motivate you to be a better listener?

5. Another theme in this novel is that nothing happens by chance. David said it when he ended up in the hospital with an ulcer and happened upon his long-lost sister in the emergency room. He also said it when he held snowflakes in his hand and observed, with awe, the complexity and the simplicity of God's creation. What are your thoughts about David's belief?

6. In one scene, Dane challenged Abigail's thinking about the importance she placed on gathering family history. "But the Bible is always telling us to remember," Abigail said. "Even your mother kept those memory stones." Dane's reply: "To remember *God*. What he's done." How does Dane's point shift your thinking about the past?

7. One of the main reasons that Abigail wanted to complete the Glick family history was because she believed telling the complete story was essential. "You can't just pick and choose the parts you want to," she told her

grandmother. And she's right! Our complete story—highs and lows and everything in between—creates our identity. What are some parts of your family story you wish you could erase?

8. How have you seen God's work of redemption in those difficult parts of your family story?

9. Freeman Glick failed as a church leader, and tried again. Molly Stoltzfus failed at rolling out a piecrust, and tried again. We all fail, we all try again. David Stoltzfus said that he wondered if the Lord loved us best when we fail and try again. Why would God love us best in those circumstances?

There's much to learn from examining our history, why we are the way we are, why we've made the choices we've made. "But who you are today," Dane said, "that's what God is asking." Whatever your past might include, it doesn't mean you can't end your story well.

Mammi the Meddler's Beef and Cheese Noodle Casserole

———— ⁓⁓⁓⁓ ————

1	8-ounce package wide egg noodles
1 pound	ground beef
¼ teaspoon	salt
1	clove garlic, minced
2	8-ounce cans tomato sauce
1 cup	sour cream
1	8-ounce package cream cheese
1 cup	cottage cheese
1	yellow onion, diced
½	green pepper, diced
½ cup	cheddar cheese, grated

Cook and drain noodles. Set aside. Brown ground beef, stir in salt and minced garlic. Add tomato sauce and simmer for a few minutes. In another bowl, mix together cream cheese, sour cream, and cottage cheese. Add onions and green pepper. In casserole, alternate layers of noodles, meat sauce, and cheeses. Top with grated cheddar cheese and bake at 350° for one hour. Serves 4–6.

Acknowledgments

I wrote this story during a particularly challenging season in my life, where I often felt a great sorrow for some circumstances I couldn't change. A sweet benefit came out of this stretching season, something I would never have expected and yet would never trade. I've gained a deeper dependency on God in all things, and a wider trust in his relentless, patient work of redemption.

Within *The Quieting* is a story about Abigail, a young woman who clings to the past to find answers to life. There's nothing wrong with sifting through the past; at times, it's critically important to fully understand a situation. But God is far more interested in how we are going to respond to life today. And tomorrow!

> Forget the former things;
>   do not dwell on the past.
> See, I am doing a new thing!
>   Now it springs up; do you not perceive it?
>   Isaiah 43:18–19 NIV

This was what Abigail had to realize: God was doing a new thing! But she couldn't perceive it. She was too snared by the past to see what was right in front of her.

And don't we all have a little Abigail in us? I certainly do. But God and I, we're working on it.

Many thanks to my entire A-plus team at Revell, including Andrea Doering, Michele Misiak, Barb Barnes, Twila Bennett, Karen Steele, Cheryl Van Andel. You all help make my stories the best they can be. My gratitude to Joyce Hart, my wonderful agent to whom I owe so much.

A shout-out to my first readers, Lindsey Ciraulo, Meredith Muñoz, and Tad Fisher, who have a special way of pointing out flaws in a novel without tossing in discouragement, only opportunities to improve. A warm hug to Nyna Dolby, a hobby genealogist, who helped me with loads of family tree–tracing information, and to Luanne Devere, a skilled nurse, who helped me work out credible details of David's ulcer. And a big thank-you to my family for being patient and understanding about my writing obligations. I love the chaos around here, most of it happy, none of it dull.

Deborah Simmering, a reader, emailed me about a memory from her childhood. With her permission, I wove the memory into a situation with Molly in *The Quieting*. You readers, you're the best! I value your input and feedback. I'm listening!

Above all, my gratitude goes to the sovereign Lord, who is continually at work in all of our lives. Yours and mine. Thank heavens he doesn't leave us alone!

Suzanne Woods Fisher is the bestselling author of *The Letters*, *The Calling*, the LANCASTER COUNTY SECRETS series, and the STONEY RIDGE SEASONS series, as well as nonfiction books about the Amish, including *Amish Peace*. She is also the coauthor of an Amish children's series, THE ADVENTURES OF LILY LAPP. Suzanne is a Carol Award winner for *The Search*, a Carol Award finalist for *The Choice*, and a Christy Award finalist for *The Waiting*. She is also a columnist for *Christian Post* and *Cooking & Such* magazines. She lives in California. Learn more at www.suzannewoodsfisher.com and connect with Suzanne on Twitter @suzannewfisher.

Return to Stoney Ridge and the Stoltzfus family
in book 1 of The Bishop's Family series

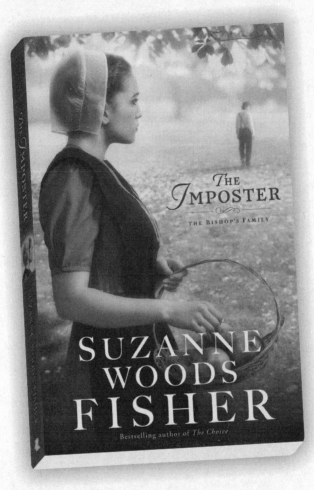

"Suzanne is an authority on the Plain folks. . . .
She always delivers a fantastic story
with interesting characters, all in a tightly woven plot."

—BETH WISEMAN, bestselling author
of the Daughters of the Promise and the Land of Canaan series

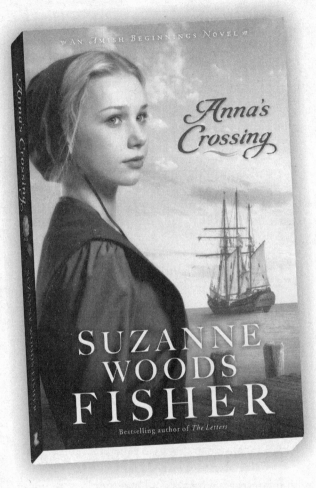

Don't miss the
Stoney Ridge Seasons series!

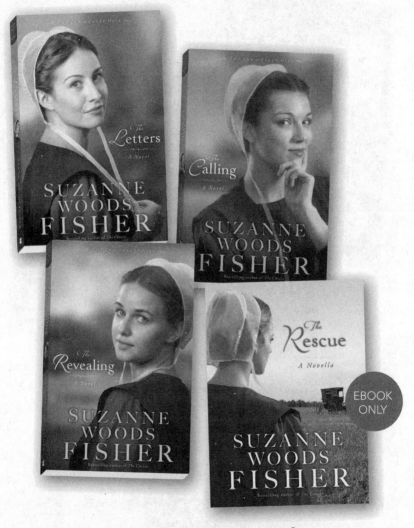

Don't miss the
Lancaster County *Secrets* series!

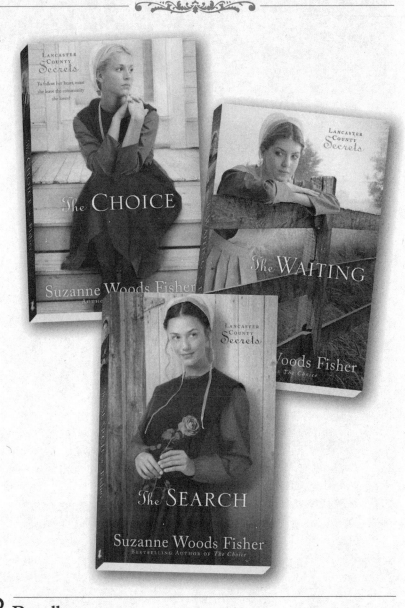

"Powerful. Life-changing insights shared simply.
The Heart of the Amish can change your life for the better!"

—Elizabeth B. Brown,
author of *Living Successfully with Screwed-Up People*

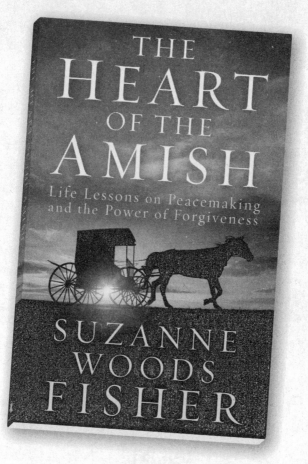

Through moving stories from the Amish, the bestselling author of
Amish Peace shows readers how to handle conflicts, offer authentic
forgiveness, and live in peace with others.

Meet Suzanne online at

www.SuzanneWoodsFisher.com

Download the
Free Amish Wisdom App